The Death of July

Waylon Joshua

First paperback edition February 2020

Cover by Beetiful Book Covers
Map by Natasha Mariani

Published by Widow White Publishing

ISBN: 9780578571690 (paperback)
ISBN: 9780578613468 (ebook)

To the parents, you know who you are

"Small towns are minimum-security insane asylums."

—Jack Mariani

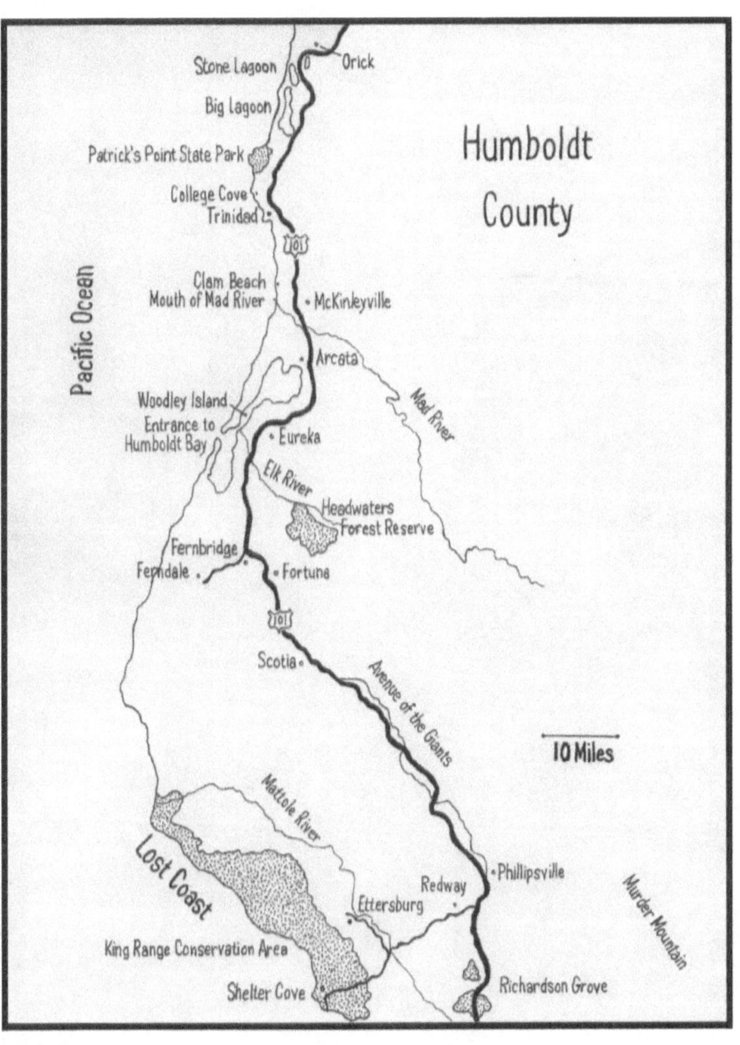

Humboldt County
Pacific Ocean
Stone Lagoon
Orick
Big Lagoon
Patrick's Point State Park
College Cove
Trinidad
Clam Beach
Mouth of Mad River
McKinleyville
Arcata
Mad River
Woodley Island
Entrance to
Humboldt Bay
Eureka
Elk River
Headwaters
Forest Reserve
Fernbridge
Ferndale
Fortuna
Scotia
Avenue of the Giants
Mattole River
Lost Coast
Phillipsville
Redway
Ettersburg
Murder Mountain
King Range Conservation Area
Shelter Cove
Richardson Grove
10 Miles

Prologue

HE DROVE BY HER car a second time. She had been parked in the turnout for over five minutes and now she was on her phone. His heartbeat quickened. They were twenty miles from the nearest town, on a winding mountain road. On his third pass, he pulled his truck behind her, cut the headlights, and hopped out. The sun had been down for an hour, and the air smelled like mist on hot gravel. There were no driveways or streetlamps in this part of the King Range, only trees, black against the starry sky. He had not seen another car for twenty minutes.

She opened her door, stepped out, and looked at him. "What are you doing out here?" she said, scowling. She had large blue eyes, straight black hair, and a long, slender neck.

As he walked toward her, he could smell her perfume. Her eyes were alert. She looked beautiful. He grabbed her neck with both hands and pressed his thumbs into her throat. She lurched back and fell against the car. Wheezing, she kicked his shins and stomped his feet. She scratched his hands and arms and punched at his face and head. He felt a sharp blow land above his ear, and he threw her to the ground, stabbed his hand into the waist of her jeans, and dragged her behind the car. Her sweatshirt slid up her torso, exposing her stomach. She screamed.

He jumped on top of her, felt the blood in his veins rushing through his face, head, and hands. He felt a lightness in his limbs and body—exhilaration—as her legs bucked and her hands fluttered around his chest and face. She showed her teeth to him and flashed the whites of her eyes as he took her neck in his hands once more.

He was surprised by how thin it was, how easily his hands wrapped around it.

She arched her back and squirmed onto one side, nearly throwing him, but he held on and leaned an elbow into her shoulder until she was on her back again. The tension in her muscles eased, and she reached a curled hand out to one side, slid her arm back and forth through the gravel like she was making a snow-angel with one wing. Then she stopped. Her eyes lost focus. But he kept squeezing. Even through the adrenaline, he could feel his hands burning, cramping. When it became almost unbearable, he let go, and he placed an ear to her chest, then her lips. She was dead. He crouched beside her, slid his arms under her body, and lifted as he stood. He carried her around her car and heaved her into the bed of his truck—head, then legs—and he drove west up the mountain.

1

Old Town

THE EVENING FOG AMASSED over Humboldt Bay, seeped into the streets and alleys of Old Town Eureka, and settled around the Victorian shops, apartments, and mansions the long-dead timber barons had built. Transients huddled in archways or led their dogs on rope leashes to the shelter on Second Street, while couples, families, and groups of friends strolled down the pebbled sidewalks to and from restaurants, bars, art galleries, and boutiques. Three long-haired, older men set up amps and drums on the sidewalk across the street from me, in front of a clothing store—one of a half dozen on the waterfront, selling high-end hippy garb to well-off, middle-aged women who liked to dress like Jimi Hendrix.

It was the first Saturday of the month: Arts Alive. Most of the businesses in Old Town were open late, hosting exhibits for local artists.

I stood outside Mudflats Bar and Grill. The lights were off inside, and the sign on the door read "CLOSED." Taped to the glass next to the sign was a xeroxed photo of a smiling, young woman. She was missing, and there was a five-thousand-dollar reward for information leading to her whereabouts.

Driving up from San Francisco the night before, I had stopped for gas just over the county line and seen three similar posters—three more vibrant, young women, gone. With nearly one and a half million acres of dense forest to hide in, and outlaws growing dope on every hill, it seemed Humboldt County had become the land of missing women. And I was about to go looking for one.

I had been waiting on the sidewalk twenty minutes when I saw April turn the corner and march toward me.

"I'm sorry I'm late," she said, breathing heavy, the bag with the pair of shoes we had discussed earlier bouncing against her knee as she walked. She looked more like her sister than I remembered—the same blue eyes and straight black hair, and the same smile. When she smiled, her whole face puckered, like she had just eaten a lemon and was really happy about it. For a moment, I was seeing the woman I had planned on marrying sixteen years ago, when I was eighteen. For a moment, I was seeing a ghost.

I felt a knife of anxiety in my gut, instantly followed by a surge of chaotic and frenzied energy that rushed throughout my body. Since my mental breakdown and the subsequent collapse of my life over a year ago, I had become intimate with these little attacks. They were always there, waiting just under the surface, ready to flare up and take over if I let them. My nerves were still frayed and frazzled, still recovering from the abuse I had put them through. Not sleeping well the night before, my first night back in my parent's house, didn't help either. I consciously forced my stomach to relax, breathed in slowly through my nose, breathed out, in, hoping April wouldn't notice.

She and I had been emailing back and forth for the last few days, but I hadn't seen her since I went off to college in 2004. She was eleven then, which made her twenty-three now. Despite the seven-year age gap, she and her sister had always been close. When July went missing five years ago, April would have been eighteen, an especially bad time of life to lose a sister, or at least it seemed to me, since I lost mine when I was fifteen. I remembered April as a little girl who liked to draw, who would sulk if no one took her to the movies. Now she was meeting me at a bar.

"I tried to call you," I said.

"You did?"

"This place is closed. What kind of bar and grill is closed on Arts Alive?"

"The drug-front kind. They're everywhere you look these days. They open and close whenever they feel like it." She slapped me on the shoulder. "Welcome back to Humboldt County."

"Thanks," I said. "You look different than the last time I saw you."

In the tone you would use to praise a child: "What an astute observation."

I smiled. "I just call it like it is."

"Well, I'm glad you're here, then. You can tell me if it starts to rain."

I laughed, and she touched her hair. The ruby ring that had belonged to her late mother was missing, the one she had shared with her sister. When July and I were together, she and April would trade off weeks wearing it. Eleven-year-old April would wear it on her thumb because her fingers were too small. The ring was one of the only things they had left of their mother's, and they had always shared it with each other. I knew how important it had been to both of them. I knew if it was gone . . . .

"What?" April said, catching me staring at her hand.

"The ring, did it . . . ?"

"It disappeared with my sister."

"I'm sorry."

We walked to the shore, then along the boardwalk, past seagulls and homeless men sleeping on benches or drinking from bottles in brown paper bags. Above the fog and across the bay, I could see the smokestack of the abandoned pulp mill on the North Spit and the tops of the trees on Indian Island. Closer to me, across a narrow channel, men were stacking crab pots as high and wide as they could on the decks of the fishing boats docked at Woodley Island. As a kid, I had seen men like these—maybe some of the same ones—on the opening day of the season, sitting on top of their mountainous stacks of pots in their yellow slicks, swaying from side to side as their boats embarked for the mouth of the bay and the Pacific Ocean beyond.

We turned off the boardwalk and walked down F Street and stopped at a purple, two-story Victorian that had been converted into a clothing store called Moonflower. A bell rang as we entered. Blouses, slacks, sweaters, dresses, and coats hung on racks or were folded and stacked on tables. One wall was dedicated to shoes. Dolphin-themed wallpaper covered the walls. The air smelled of incense. A half dozen people shuffled around the room, holding glasses of wine and peering at black and white nature photographs with price tags below them.

A woman near forty, wearing blue slacks and a gray cardigan, sat on a high stool next to the cash register. A beaded necklace hung from her neck, and bead bracelets dangled from her wrists. She smiled serenely at us as we approached. On the wall behind her was a large painting of three women on a beach looking up at the moon, dolphins leaping in the background.

April took the shoe box out of the bag and set it on the counter between the register and three ceramic dolphins leaping from ceramic water

"Are you the owner, Heidi Gerhardt?" I said.

The woman looked at the box, frowning, then at me. "Yes. Why?"

"Look inside the box, please." I nodded at the box.

"Why?"

"You'll understand when you open it. Please. It was bought at your store."

Ms. Gerhardt picked up the box and shot me a confused look before opening it. I watched her eyes find the Post-it note I knew was on the inside of the box. I watched her eyes grow as she read, then turn to slits as she threw the box back on the counter as if it were full of spiders.

The message on the Post-it note was, "These are the last shoes I will ever sell you. If I see you in my store again, I will have you arrested for trespassing."

Ms. Gerhardt stood from her stool and looked me in the eyes. "Who are you? What is this about?"

"I'm Tim Kitchens. This is April Morrison. Her sister is July Morrison. Do you recognize that name?"

Ms. Gerhardt shook her head. "No."

"July disappeared five years ago. They never found her body, but her sister thinks she was murdered. I'm starting to think so, too. The day before she was last seen, she bought this pair of shoes at this store. We know because the purchase was verified on her credit card statement at the time. But the shoes and the note were only discovered recently. Did you write that note?"

Ms. Gerhardt frowned and pressed her chin into her neck. "No. This is ridiculous."

I leaned against the counter. "You know, my mom has been coming to this store for years, so I know you give out handwritten Christmas cards to all your best customers. What do you think a handwriting expert would say if I asked him to compare that hostile note in the box with one of your delightful Christmas cards?"

Ms. Gerhardt crossed her arms and glared at me. "I am an upstanding member of this community. I sell boots to longshoremen."

"Please, Ms. Gerhardt. What do longshoremen have to do with this? Let's just be honest with each other, okay? I'm not an expert in handwriting, but even I can tell you wrote that note." I held out my hands in an appeasing manner. "You're not in trouble. July's family just wants to understand the circumstances surrounding her disappearance. Why did you threaten to have her arrested the day before she was murdered?"

"You know what?" Ms. Gerhardt said, pointing at me. "I recognize your last name. I know your mom. Tell her she's no longer welcome in my store."

"Are you kidding me?" My stomach dropped. My mom was going to be insanely angry with me when she found out I'd somehow got her banned from her favorite shoe store. I pleaded with Ms. Gerhardt: "Don't do that. Come on. Let's be reasonable. You're not acting like an innocent woman right now, you realize that?"

She put one hand on her hip and pointed to the door with the other. "You need to leave. You need to leave my store, or I'm calling the police."

Maybe I had conducted the interview poorly, but I hadn't expected her to be such an obstructionist, or to eighty-six my mom. I felt the chaos creeping in again, the anger, the flaring nerves. This time I couldn't push it down. I grabbed one of the ceramic dolphins off the counter and held it up. "I grew up around here. I've known people like you my whole life. You're so god damn groovy on the surface, but underneath, you're hiding something. Is this a drug front, like Mudflats down the street?"

"Put that dolphin down right now," Ms. Gerhardt said.

"Oh, this thing is perfect. Did you know dolphins have a secret too? They like to rape each other. Look it up. It's true—"

"Excuse me!"

I raised my voice—"Yeah!"—and gave her a dismissive waive with the back of my free hand. "Everyone thinks they're so playful, so sweet, but that's all on the surface, like you, with your beads and incense and all your other nonsense. Everyone thinks you're harmless, but then you buy a business and look what happens: two-faced dolphins raping the community. Just when no one's expecting it. All these quaint little shops around here." I gestured towards the street. "All these restaurants that close on Saturdays. They're all drug fronts as far as I can tell, dolphin-raping everyone. This whole county's full of dolphin rape."

"Put my dolphin down right now!" Ms. Gerhardt shouted. "I'm calling the police." She held up her phone and began dialing.

Everyone in the shop, everyone holding wine and cheese, had stopped sipping, chewing, and shuffling, to stare at us.

April grabbed my arm. "Come on, Tim. Let's go. Put the dolphin down and let's just go."

I set the ceramic dolphin back on the counter, but only after holding it above my head for a second, which I am not proud of, and I turned and walked out. April grabbed the shoes and followed. The air outside was cold on my cheeks, and I could see my breath.

"Wow, you have a bad temper," April said. "I've never seen anyone get kicked out of a boutique before."

"How about a drink?" I said.

April took a beat to respond. "Sure. I know a place."

We passed up two bars with loud, live music for a third without a band or a huge crowd. It was brightly lit inside, with beautiful watercolors of a redwood forest on the walls. Behind the bar, they had hard cider and kombucha on tap. Customers had spilled out packs of crayons onto the tables and bar top and were using them on elaborate black-and-white drawings that had been torn from adult coloring books. When they weren't concentrating deeply, they spoke to each other in hushed tones and took small sips from their glasses.

"What is this place?" I said.

"It's a brew and craft bar," April said. "You never been to one of these?"

"No, this is new to me."

"We can talk here."

We bellied up to the bar next to a man wearing Carhartt pants and a dirty T-shirt. He could have been a roofer or a millionaire dope grower. It was hard to tell in Humboldt.

I ordered gin on the rocks, April ordered a bottle of India Pale Ale, and we took our drinks to a corner table.

"Was that how it was in the courtroom when you got disbarred?" April said. "Do you just go around having these episodes all the time?"

"I didn't get disbarred. Disbarment isn't an instantaneous, on-the-spot kind of thing," I said, and took a long swallow of gin. "Did you bring your little case file?"

Flat stare from April. "No, I left my *little* case file at home. Why?"

"Tell me more about the baby-daddy."

"He's a grower, been to jail a few times for assault."

"What's his name again?"

April ran her fingernail along a crack in the table. "Jared Tidwell."

"Sounds familiar."

"I'm not surprised. He's from Orick, originally, so you probably heard his name a few times growing up. He's pretty infamous for being violent."

"Sounds like half the people I grew up with. Did the police question him at the time?"

April scoffed. "They questioned all her old boyfriends, but nothing came of it."

"How many boyfriends we talking about?"

"Three. Well, three main ones. Jared, Lou Da Rocha, and Ryan Lowell."

"I remember Lou," I said. "But who's Ryan?"

"He was July's professor at College of the Redwoods. She was living with him at the time. They were going to move to Paris together. He was part of some faculty exchange program. She was excited to go. but . . ." April trailed off with a slow sigh. "Jared took July to court to get sole custody of Sage. He didn't want her taking him to Paris with some other dude. July said he was acting crazy. Around then, she started finding threatening notes scratched in her car. She thought it was him. Hard to match handwriting to scratches in paint, though."

"What did the notes say?" I said.

"Things like, *Die dumb whore*, and *Fuck you slut*. Also, pizzas that she never ordered kept getting delivered to her apartment. And on her last birthday, just two months before she"—April made air quotes—"*went missing*, her tires were slashed."

I followed April's eyes down to my hands, and I realized I had been loudly unclasping and clasping my wristwatch. I stopped and placed my palms on the table. "So where can I find this guy. Jared?"

"That's not a good idea," April said. "He's a violent man. Unpredictable."

"What are we talking here, bull shark, tiger shark, leopard seal, what?"

April squinted at me. "Huh?"

"In terms of aggressiveness."

She shot me an amused but skeptical smile. "Well, whatever sea creature is the most aggressive, that's Jared."

"The tiger shark."

"Sure," April said, giving me the shake-head/role-eyes/shrug combo.

"I just want to ask him some questions, April. You asked me for help. Well. I'm here. I conduct interviews. I gather evidence. That's how I help."

April sighed. "Okay. Jared and his dad, Don, have two places, a trailer park by Stone Lagoon, and some land out by Ettersburg, where they grow their pot. Don't go there. You'll get shot for sure." She scowled at me, silent for a beat.

"Okay," I said.

"You think I'm joking, but I'm serious. If you have to talk to them, go to Stone Lagoon on a Sunday or Monday. They won't do anything crazy with witnesses around. Just don't let them bait you into doing something stupid."

"I won't. Don't worry. I'll talk with Jared, nice and easy, then I'll talk with July's old friends. Anyone, in particular, you would suggest?"

"Yeah. Krista." April barked the words. "You remember her." She took a swig of ale. "The cops found bottles of whiskey, vermouth, and bitters in July's abandoned car. Those are the ingredients for a Manhattan, which she never drank." Then, with a sing-songy voice and a bitchy smile: "But her friend Krista does. I told the cops that. Nothing came of it."

"Where can I find Krista?"

"Who knows with her. She's around, though. I see her now and then, but she pretends not to see me."

One of the bartenders walked up, set down two coloring pages and a box of crayons on our table, and said, "Enjoy." My picture was of an exotic bird, April's was an underwater scene, with hermit crabs, jellyfish, kelp, sharks . . . .

"I think this one's better for you," she said, switching our pictures. She took out a yellow crayon and began coloring.

"I need to get a copy of the case file you made as soon as you can," I said. "Anything else you can think of before then?"

"July got a call from a Shelter Cove or a Whitethorn number about a week before she went missing, belonged to someone named Dave Massey. The police followed up on it and determined the guy had just called the wrong number. But it's suspicious to me. The night she disappeared, she told me she was going on a date night with Ryan and wanted me to watch Sage overnight. I found out later, from Ryan, she told him she was having a girl's night with me. She lied to both of us."

"You think she was having an affair with this Dave Massey?"

April shrugged. "If she was, why didn't she tell me? She always told me those things. I don't know. It's suspicious." I couldn't get the name Sage out of my mind. It seemed out of character for the July I had known to give her kid such a hippy name. "I can't believe she named her kid Sage."

"Hey, that's my nephew."

I put my hands up. "It's a good name. Just surprising, that's all. He's twelve, right? How's he doing?"

April looked down at her drink, adjusted her coaster. "That's a long story, but . . . not good. I think . . ." Her eyes became shiny and wet, and she had a pained expression. Her voice broke. "I can't talk about it right now."

2

McKinleyville

HUMBOLDT COUNTY WAS AN isolated place, pinned against the Pacific Ocean by a phalanx of wild mountains. When I was a kid, during winter storms, mudslides often took out the roads connecting us to the outside world. The densely-forested mountains were a natural barrier, a divider some people called "the Redwood Curtain," a thing we lived behind, a thing not easily penetrated. It described not only our geography but a state of mind, an attitude: We lived on "the Lost Coast," behind "the Redwood Curtain," in the fog, in the smoke, independent, separate, hidden.

Trends and fashions were slow to arrive, if they arrived at all, and commerce could be a little limited. When I was a kid, there were hardly any new cars on the road. I couldn't find the latest toys on the shelves. My dad always complained about some part or another not being available at the auto and hardware stores. I have baby pictures of my sister from '77 that looked like they were taken in the '50s. Family members wore horn-rimmed glasses. The men had buzz cuts and pompadours, and my grandma still had a beehive.

Over the years, better roads and the Internet made the Lost Coast a little less lost, but even now, forty years after Charlie's Angels, some women, of a certain age, still had the Farrah Fawcett haircut.

After April left the bar, I found a homeless man and contracted him to buy a pair of shoes from Moonflower in my mom's size. Then I drove twenty minutes north on Highway 101, around Humboldt Bay, to McKinleyville, my hometown, pulled into the driveway of my childhood home, and snuck into bed without my parents noticing, almost like I had practice at it.

Locals called McKinleyville Oklahoma by the Sea, because of all the Okies that had settled here after fleeing the Dust Bowl. When I was little, the town was mostly cow fields, and there was a wooden sign on the north end that read, "Welcome to McKinleyville, Where Horses Have the Right of Way." As I grew up, most of the cow fields were being replaced by subdivisions and shopping centers. There were construction sites everywhere. My friends and I played King of the Mountain and dirt-clod wars on the mounds of earth displaced by the heavy equipment used on construction job sites. We played hide-and-seek and camped out in the skeletons of new houses, and we stole lumber and nails and built forts on the banks of Widow White Creek.

Town landmarks included the world's tallest totem pole—if the lightning rod was included in the measurement—and Bigfoot Gas Station on Central Avenue, which had a controversial mural of Bigfoot carrying a large log extending out from his crotch.

I woke up the next morning in my childhood bed to my dad playing The Rolling Stones on YouTube. He had turned my old room into his office and an extension of his garage, with two desks, one for his computer and paperwork, the other for his fishing supplies. He rolled back and forth between the desks in his leather office chair, organizing tackle and clicking on music videos. He had a storage freezer against the wall under the window full of salmon and rock fish, and one of his homemade crab rings hung from the ceiling with a half-woven net. My sister's piano still sat in the corner, but my bed was gone. I was sleeping on a futon, and all of my childhood possessions had been crammed into the closet.

"Come on," he said. "It's time to get up. It's the first day of crab season."

"What time is it?" I said.

"It's late. If we don't leave soon we'll lose the tide."

"Leave him alone," my mom shouted from the other room. "If he doesn't want to go, he doesn't have to. He gets seasick."

"I'm not talking to you," my dad barked back. "I'm talking to my son. I want to go fishing with my son. Is that so terrible? You act like I'm a monster. Pretty soon he'll move back to San Francisco, and we'll never see him again, or I'll die. I could die tomorrow. You would deny me one last day of fishing with my son?"

"It's okay, Mom," I said. "I want to go." Turning to my dad, "What's the swell?"

"Eight feet at ten seconds. But we'll just be in the harbor, maybe as far as Pilot Rock. And it's not like we'll be out there five hours. We're just setting the pots and picking them up."

I groaned. "Eight feet?"

"I know, life sucks then you die. Come on. Get up."

That was my parents' favorite expression when I was growing up:

Why do I have to eat my peas?
Because life sucks then you die.

As I ate breakfast, I told my mom the story of what had happened at Moonflower, and how I had gotten her eighty-sixed. When I was done, she responded with, "I can't believe you did that. I thought I raised a sensitive man. I love that store. What is wrong with you? And don't say another word about dolphin rape being a metaphor. I know you. All that poor woman saw was an aggressive man repeating the word rape over and over again."

"You're right," I said. "I'm sorry."

"I can't believe you."

"Think of it as an opportunity to shop somewhere else. It's time you stopped dressing like Jimi Hendrix anyway."

"Stop saying that. I don't dress like Jimi Hendrix."

I laughed, then reached down and grabbed a shopping bag from behind the couch and set it next to my mom. "I know this doesn't make up for it, but I got you a pair of Heidi's shoes. That should hold you over until I get a chance to apologize to her."

My mom glared at me, but one side of her mouth curled into a smile.

After breakfast, while my dad finished loading his fourteen-foot aluminum boat and hitched it to his old Chevy LUV, I called Dave Massey, the man April thought July might have been having an affair with, and I left a message on the answering machine.

Then we drove north on Highway 101. The cab of the truck smelled like ocean, fish, and exhaust. I was getting seasick already. Whenever the highway followed the bluffs, and the fur trees didn't block the view, I scanned the coastline. The surf looked rough. After a ten-minute drive, my dad took the exit to Trinidad, a fishing and tourist town with million-dollar homes on the bluffs overlooking the Pacific Ocean. The cove had a pier, a bait shop, a boat launch, and a restaurant, all sheltered from the northern winds and swell by a rocky promontory called Trinidad Head, which was covered in wind-beaten trees and huckleberry bushes.

My dad and I launched his boat just south of the pier, on a beach packed with trucks and trailers. Groups of men stood around fires drinking beer while they waited for the pots they had set earlier to fill with crab. They would be drunk by the time they went out to collect them in the afternoon. A few of them helped us turn the boat around in the surf, and they complimented my dad on his trailer, which put him in a good mood.

We taxied slowly through the harbor, over kelp forests and past the commercial boats scattered around the pier, bobbing beside their moorings. The swell had grown since sunrise. As we left the cove and the shelter of Trinidad Head, motoring toward Pilot Rock, the waves crashed around the aluminum bow. My dad steered the outboard and I sat near the bow, scanning the water for the pots he had set the day before. His buoys were yellow and green. I spotted one while we were on the crest of a wave, and I pointed and yelled over the wind and engine. When we got close to the buoy, my dad slowed alongside it while I snagged the rope with a long gaff. I pulled the pot up hand over hand, as the boat dipped toward the weight of it.

In the troughs of the waves, walls of water surrounded us on either side, tall enough to block out the view of land.

As the pot breached the churning brown water, my

phone rang. Holding the rope with one hand, I bit off the glove of the other and checked the screen: Dave Massey's number.

"What are you doing?" my dad yelled.

I answered. A woman's voice was on the other end: "Is this Tim . . . Kitchens? Did you call me?"

"Yes, I was calling for Dave Massey. Is he around?"

"No, dear, he's been dead some time. May I ask why you're calling?"

The boat rocked against the waves as my dad grabbed the rope, bumped me to the side, and hauled the pot into the boat.

I said, "I'm sorry to hear that. Was he your husband?"

"Yes. I'm Evelyn Massey."

"I was calling about a phone call Dave made to July Morrison about two weeks before she went missing. This was about five years ago."

I heard a heavy sigh. "I'm sorry, I don't know a July Morrison."

"Do you live in the Whitethorn area?"

"Shelter Cove."

Shaking his head, my dad grabbed the crabs by their butts, avoiding the claws, and threw them into an empty bucket like they were hot potatoes. Their shells clacked against each other as they scrambled and fought for position in the bucket.

With my free hand, I unhooked the fish head used for bait and tossed it to the screeching seagulls bobbing beside us. I had to shout over them: "Her car was found on the road between Whitethorn and Shelter Cove? I believe there are still missing posters of her on the telephone poles lining that road. Her dad maintains them."

"Ohhh, her. Of course I remember that. That was in the news a lot. But Dave didn't know that poor girl. You're saying he made a phone call to her?"

"Yes, on October 10, 2011, and she went missing on the eighteenth."

"That must have been a wrong number, dear."

"Do you know where your husband was on the eighteenth?"

Pause, then, "Are you with the police?"

"No. I'm a lawyer investigating for the family."

My dad resumed his position at the outboard and hit the throttle. I put a finger over my free ear and faintly heard, ". . . in an urn by that time, dear, since he died of a heart attack on the fourteenth. Now I'm sorry, but my grandchildren just arrived, and I'm sure they're hungry."

"One more question, please. What did your husband like to drink?"

"Oh, he drank beer now and then. A few cocktails at parties. But I don't see why you want to know."

"Did he ever drink Manhattans?"

"No. Never. Now, my grandchildren are visiting and my time with them is precious. Why don't you call back after Thanksgiving? Or better yet, why don't you come by for coffee? I'll tell you everything you want to know about my husband. He was a very handsome man in his time."

After a polite goodbye, with my dad glaring at me, I shoved my phone in my pocket and picked up the gaff as my dad swung the boat alongside the next buoy.

We picked up five more pots, and because we caught more than our legal limit of ten each, we threw most of the smaller females back.

On shore, we backed the crabs alive, which meant

wrapping their legs and claws up in each hand and splitting them in half against the bed of the truck.

We fed the guts to the seagulls.

"Most people like to boil them whole," My dad said. "They say it tastes better. They call the guts crab butter. But it's not worth it. The kitchen trashcan just gets full of guts that stink up the whole house, and for what? I can't tell the difference."

A man holding a beer walked by moments later and said, "You're throwing away the best part."

At home, my dad unloaded the boat while I filled a five-gallon pot with water and put it on the burner to boil. I threw four halved lemons and some seasoning into the water and started coffee.

My mom sat at the kitchen table shredding Brussels sprouts she had picked from her garden for a salad.

My dad spent his retirement harvesting the sea, while she spent hers growing heirloom fruits and vegetables.

While I waited for the water to boil, I opened the drawer in the china cabinet where my mom kept her marijuana.

"What are you doing?" she said.

"Nothing," I said.

I rolled a joint and smoked it on the porch while the cat rubbed against my side and the neighbor's dog barked at nothing in particular. With my phone, I looked up the Facebook accounts of July's old boyfriends, Lou Da Rocha, Jared Tidwell, and Ryan Lowell, and I sent them friend requests.

When the water came to a boil, I stuffed the pot to the brim with crab and set a timer for fifteen minutes. The house filled with the smell of coffee, lemon, and crab. When the timer went off, I melted some butter with garlic powder and paprika, and I called my dad inside, and he and my mom and I drank coffee and cracked crab at the table.

I was exhausted and hungry after spending the morning in the cold surf and wind. My fingers were just starting to tingle with feeling.

"Where else are you going to get a meal like this?" my dad said.

The dog next door took a ten-second break from barking, then started up again. It barked off and on all day. The neighbors never let it out of its kennel. My parents asked the animal shelter about it, but they said it was legal as long as the dog had food, water, and shelter.

"That poor dog," my mom said, then put down her nutcracker and looked me in the eyes. "So are you thinking of moving back here for good?"

"What?" I said. "No. I told you I wasn't."

"I know, but I was just wondering. Maybe you changed your mind. But I guess you still hate your parents."

"Jesus Christ. The guilt trip?"

"You move five hours away and you never visit. Your cousin visits more than you and she lives back east." She pointed at me. "Why don't you play piano for money, get a job at the Carson Mansion. They would love you there. You could play Jazz."

I rolled my eyes. "You're the only parents in the world who would rather have a musician for a son than a lawyer."

"When was the last time you played piano?" my mom said. "It breaks my heart that you're letting your talent go to waste."

"I'm not going to play piano at the Carson

Mansion, Mom. We talked about this. Heather was the one who taught me piano. She was the talented one."

"You can be a lawyer and play piano on the side. I don't see why you can't get a job here."

"Not enough money."

"You can run for DA."

My dad broke in: "Satisfaction is more important than comfort. But what do I know?"

"I know you have some hard memories here," my mom said. "And I know our family was never the same after your sister died, but we're still your family, and we love you."

"I know, Mom, and I love you too, but this isn't about Heather. And she didn't die by the way. She was murdered. This is about money. I can't make money here."

"When was the last time you played piano?"

"I don't know. You want me to play right now? Would that make you happy?"

"Yes."

I grabbed a bottle of wine from the cabinet and a glass, went to my room, and sat at the piano my sister had given me before she left for college. I filled my glass, drank half of it, and started to play a sloweddown version of "Ophelia" by The Band. I played until my wrists got tired, then went into the living room to grab another bottle of wine.

My mom and dad were on the couch. The dog next door was barking again.

"That was beautiful, honey," my mom said. Her eyes were red and swollen. She had a tissue in her hand. "Your sister used to play that song."

3

Clam Beach Inn

I WAS TIRED, BUT I had to get out of there. If memories are like ghosts, then going home is like dying. I saw on Facebook that one of my oldest friends was playing a gig nearby. Levi Rafferty. I needed to see him anyway, so I put on my coat and went to the Clam Beach Inn—or the Digger to locals—a bar on the north end of town a few hundred yards from Clam Beach.

The parking lot was full when I pulled up, and I had to park down the road and walk in the rain. On a good low tide during clam season, cars lined this road from The Digger to the beach, and crowds walked the shoreline with their shovels, pounding the wet sand, searching for razor clams.

I heard Levi singing and playing guitar over the PA as I walked up. A few people were smoking cigarettes and pot under the awning. I opened a heavy oak door and went inside. There was a pool table to my left and a shuffleboard table to my right. A horseshoe-shaped bar separated them. A crowd of people stood or danced in the backroom, where Levi was playing. I wedged into an open spot at the bar and tried to get the bartender's attention, but she was busy serving a few old men sitting at opposite ends of the bar. She had a deep voice and strutted back and forth, chest out, chin in, bellowing things like, "I need that like I need another knee problem," and, "I hate the smell of Eucalyptus."

While I waited for my drink, Levi sang a folk song with long verses and a chorus in which he wailed about "De Soto the conquistador." He had always had the best voice out of all of us.

In our senior year of high school, he and I, and our friends Ron and Keith, started a band. Ron played the drums, Keith and Levi played guitar, and I played keyboard. The only gigs we could get were at coffee shops, university events, and battle-of-the-bands, because none of us were twenty-one, although that never stopped us from getting blind drunk. At every show, before the first chorus of the first song, someone would always turn up their amp—though everyone promised before they wouldn't—then the others would follow, until the drums were completely drowned out by the guitars. The audience usually dispersed after the first song, leaving only the girlfriends, which was good, because halfway through the set Ron would be so drunk he'd come out from behind the drums, snatch the mic and insult anyone in the audience he didn't recognize.

Levi was the only one of us who'd continued to play after I left town. We'd kept in touch over the years. He'd stay at my place when he played gigs in San Francisco, and we'd always get together on the holidays between family obligations.

In a quiet moment during one of his songs, I yelled, "Play Smoke on the Water."

I thought I was funny. No one else did. His fans turned and looked at me like I had just slaughtered a pig in front of their children. They knew, as I did, that Levi hated requests, and rarely played covers.

I decided not to heckle anymore.

After Levi's set, I waited for him to finish packing up and talking to his fans before I found him in front of the shuffleboard table holding a beer. I put my arm around him. "Look at this polyester suit," I said. "This is serious. You're not fucking around anymore."

He smirked and rolled his eyes. "I'm the real deal, man."

"Even artists have to wear a uniform."

He glared at me.

I laughed and slapped my thigh. "What a look. Where do you find all these vintage clothes, anyway?

"I don't know if you're aware of this, but there are these things called secondhand stores where dead people's clothes are given a second life."

"That should be your next song: 'The Blazer Has Two Lives.'"

Deadpan stare. "Do me a favor and never try to give me song ideas again."

"That's a little defensive. Really, I should be charging you for my ideas."

He shook his head, then pointed at mine. "What about you? Since when do you have a mullet?"

"What are you talking about? This is an adult man's haircut."

He nodded. "I'm pretty sure it's a mullet, man. Maybe a little more business than Camaro, but still a mullet."

"What do you want me to have, a fade? I had a fade when I was sixteen."

He took a sip of beer. "Did you hear my conquistador song?"

"Was that the folk song?"

"I wrote that about you." He pointed at my head again. "You have the conquistador's mentality, but on a smaller scale. You're like a petty conquistador. Instead of conquering countries, you go around conquering small things, like arguments, and insulting people on their clothes."

I laughed. "Maybe you got something there."

We sat at the bar. The jukebox was playing Hank Williams' "I Saw the Light." I ordered a gin and tonic and Levi ordered well whiskey straight. His face was gaunt, and his eyes had dark circles under them.

"Gin and tonic?" he said. "That's what I used to drink when I had my shit together."

I laughed. "Well, I'm far from having my shit together. I'm pretty much broke. That's part of the reason I came to see you. I was hoping to get a job with your uncle. Do you know if he needs any help?"

"I thought you got disbarred for dumping a pile of dead fish on a judge," he said.

"No, I got contempt of court for that. And I didn't get disbarred. Jesus. Why does everyone keep saying that? My license was suspended for eighteen months. That was it."

"Well, if the fish got you contempt, what'd you do to get suspended?"

"That's a long story," I said. "And we'd need a lot more drinks than this."

"Everyone's been asking me what happened to you, saying shit like, 'You can take the man out of McKinleyville, but you can't take the McKinleyville out of the man.'"

I shrugged. "That's funny."

"But it's not, though, is it?" Levi stared into my eyes, smile gone.

I knew the history of substance abuse and mental illness in his family. I could tell that he was trying to get into it with me, that he was sincerely worried. I appreciated that, but I didn't want to get into it, so I slammed the rest of my gin and changed the subject. "You stop playing and everybody leaves," I said. "You're like a local celebrity now."

Most of the crowd had left. The few people that remained stumbled around a pool table in the corner.

He smiled. "I know. It's weird. People ask for my autograph. I'm thinking of going to Nashville again and giving it another shot."

"Good. You should."

"I've been saving money."

"You still got that job putting up satellite dishes with Ron?"

"Hell no. I don't need money that bad."

I ordered another gin for me and a whiskey for Levi. "Have you seen Krista lately?" I said. "I need to get a hold of her."

Levi slowly crinkled his face and looked at me with one eye. "What's this? First thing you do when you come to town is start looking up my exes?"

"This is McKinleyville. If everyone stopped sleeping with each other's exes, no one would get laid."

He nodded, stared into the middle-distance, and said, in that somber tone that sometimes ambushes drunk people, "That's true. That's true."

I laughed, slapped him on the back, told him I was just kidding, and explained that I wanted to talk to Krista because she was one of July's oldest friends, and I had come back home, in part, to investigate July's disappearance.

"I was wrong," he said after a long pause. "You're

trying to look up *your* old ex. This is crazy. Why are you doing this, man? It's been five years. I'm sorry, but I just have to say the obvious: This sounds like you're chasing your sister. This sounds like obsession, maybe. It's not healthy. I read what you said in that courtroom. I know what that is. Are you getting help? Are you seeing someone?"

If it were anyone else, that comment about my sister would have set me off. But Levi was family. He was there for me when she was murdered. We were there for each other. He had always been her favorite friend of mine. She'd always teased him like he was her second brother.

"I saw a guy for a while," I said. "He helped a lot. And yeah, he'd say this was all about my sister, too. And you're probably right. But so what? It's about other shit too. I loved July, and I know I broke her heart. It kills me to think someone murdered her and got away with it, always has. Working at the DA's office, seeing scummy fucks go free all the time, always tortured me more than it did my colleagues. I couldn't sleep. So yeah, I had a mental breakdown. Now I'm in a hole. I lost my wife, my job, my way of making a living, and I had to move back in with my parents. My parents! And I'm trying to scratch my way out any way I can. This is going to sound corny, but I just need one win, one time where I can look at something and say, 'Yeah, that was right. That was right what happened.'"

Levi threw an arm around my shoulders in that sloppy and rough way that drunk people have. He put his face close to mine, and I smelled the whiskey on his breath. "I love you man," he said. "You know I'm here for you. I'd take a bullet for you."

I threw my arm around him—two drunk guys

hugging at the bar. "Yeah, but would you tell me where Krista is?

"What's Krista got to do with it?"

"Krista's favorite drink was a Manhattan. I remember July always teasing her for liking an old man's drink."

"So?"

"They found the ingredients for Manhattans in July's abandoned car. I figure she was on her way to party with Krista, but Krista told the cops she hadn't seen July for months and wasn't planning on seeing her that night, or any other night."

Levi smiled, shook his head, and said, "Sounds like she's lying, but that's on-brand with her. I don't know how to get a hold of her anymore. I don't even have her new number. She was seeing this guy named Ted Nadler for a while. I guess he's some big shot accountant who launders money for growers." He laughed. "Then I heard she left him for one of his clients. She's probably out on the hill somewhere now, on some farm. Turns out, growers make much better sugar daddies than struggling musicians."

4

Founders Hall

THE NEXT DAY, SLIGHTLY hungover, I went to Eureka to run a few errands for my parents, earn my rent. Also, I wanted to stop by some law offices to introduce myself and offer my services as a paralegal. I wore a suit for the occasion—felt good to put one on again, like I was doing something. It had been well over a year since I had last worked as an attorney, and over three months since I had last picked up some paralegal-type contract work.

Just before noon, while I took a coffee break on the waterfront, I got a notification on my phone. Ryan Lowell, July's boyfriend at the time of her disappearance, had accepted my friend request on Facebook.

His profile picture was of him on the beach in a wetsuit holding a surfboard under his arm. His hair was short, black, and combed to one side. He had a long thin face, a flat chin, and a slightly protruding brow. Humboldt State University was listed as his place of work—a move up from the community college where he had met July. His last status update was two hours ago: "Do any theater majors out there have an 8mm camera I could borrow?"

As I scrolled through his feed, a cold rain began to fall. I didn't have an umbrella, so I ran the few blocks to my car.

While I waited for the defrost to clear the fog from my windshield, I pulled up the website for Humboldt State University on my phone and found the page for the English Department. Ryan Lowell was on the list of professors. I clicked on his name and his picture came up, along with his email, phone number, degrees, and office hours. His photo, taken outside, had captured him on a flight of concrete steps, looking at something off-frame to his right. His Friday office hours were between twelve and two.

I took Highway 101 to Arcata, which was about fifteen minutes north around the bay. I couldn't find parking on campus and ended up in a spot over the highway about a mile from where I wanted to be. A young woman with an umbrella walked by me while I opened the car door. I caught up with her.

"You have another umbrella, by chance?" I said.

She sized me up and decided I wasn't a creep—maybe it was the suit. "We can share."

I made some small talk about rain and her preparedness for it, then asked her if she knew Professor Lowell.

"I had him last semester."

"I was thinking about taking his class next semester."

"Definitely do it. It was the best class I've taken in college. He's really smart and funny. I really learned a lot in that class. He makes it easy, you know? He's passionate."

I nodded. "Good. "That decides it."

The campus was sprawled over a fairly steep hill. I climbed four long flights of steps before reaching the quad. Students ran between eaves and overhangs to escape the rain, their backpacks bouncing and jangling. A group of shoeless young men wearing loose, cotton, earth-tones were gathered around a rope strung between two round metal columns holding up an exterior corridor. They took turns walking on the rope, and they laughed and clapped when someone fell. Their laughter was slow and quiet. While I walked by, a young woman in similar clothes stopped and watched, smiling.

When the nice young woman with the umbrella left me, I had three more flights of stairs to go before I reached Founders Hall, where the English Department had their offices. The rain had let up by the time I reached the top, and I could see most of Arcata from there. The clouds had dissipated over the northern end of Humboldt Bay, and the sun shined on the water.

Founders Hall was built in the Spanish Colonial style: white stucco walls, red tile roof, a wide tower in front, and a tall arch over the entrance. It did not match any of the other buildings on campus, or the county in general, since the Spanish had never colonized this far north.

I walked through the halls and around the courtyard to the offices in the back wing. There was a line of four young women outside of Ryan's office. There were no students waiting outside the other offices. The women in line ahead of me talked about how they had done on their midterms and where they were going for Thanksgiving break. I listened to them for nearly forty-five minutes before it was my turn to go in.

Ryan sat behind his desk, wearing a white V-neck T-shirt and a gray blazer. Jazz played from an iPhone dock next to his landline. I could see a picture of Miles Davis on the screen of his phone.

He spread out his arms and looked me in the eyes as I entered. He said, "Ahh, the face of Evil. Come in. Come in. How can I help you?" He smiled. "Sit down."

I sat down. "I didn't realize I was the face of Evil."

"William S. Burroughs: *The face of Evil is always the face of total need.* You obviously need something, which makes you evil. Lucky for you, I am a vanquisher of evil. And yes, *vanquisher* is a word." He smiled. "Beautiful suit, by the way."

"Thank you. I'm Tim Kitchens." I stuck my hand out over the desk.

Ryan looked confused as he shook it. He wasn't used to shaking hands with the students who came to his office.

I said, "I'm a friend of April Morrison."

He smiled. "Oh? How is April? I went to one of her plays last year. She's so wonderfully competent. There are aspirations for the urbane in her work that are almost unconsciously self-deprecating and quite charming."

I raised my eyebrows. "Unconsciously self-deprecating?"

"She's quite charming."

"That seems to be the consensus."

Hanging on the wall behind Ryan were twelve framed swatches of carpet arranged in three lines of four. Under each frame of carpet was a plaque with the name of a different animal: tiger, coyote, elephant, and so on. The swatches of carpet came in different types and colors. In the center of each swatch was a dark stain.

I pointed to the display and said, "What's with the carpet on the wall?"

He smiled. "That's my art."

"So the orange shag symbolizes a caribou?"

"It's art. You can interpret it however you want. But that piece is called caribou because of the caribou semen stain in the center." He smiled, unabashedly enjoying the shocked look on my face.

"That's what that dark spot is? Is there semen in all the carpet up there?" I read the animal names again. "How did you get your hands on sloth semen?"

"I travel a lot."

"That's pretty provocative art for a professor."

"There's nothing wrong with being provocative."

I resisted the urge to talk further on the subject. He seemed a little testy.

"What can I do for you?" he said.

"I was hoping to ask you a few questions about July," I said. "I'm investigating her disappearance."

Ryan snorted. "You mean her disappearance to Mexico?"

"Do you have proof that she's in Mexico?"

"No, but I wouldn't be surprised if she was."

"Did you ever have any unpleasant encounters with Jared Tidwell?"

Ryan leaned over the desk. "Every encounter with that guy is unpleasant. He's one of those people with unsettling eyes, you know. When I lived with July, he and his dad used to come by the apartment to pick up Sage." He leaned back. "So what's going on? Are there criminal charges or something? Are you working for the DA?"

"No, this is on my own time. April told me July was looking forward to going to France with you. Why would she then go to Mexico and leave her son behind?"

"Who knows with her. She was a wild one. I'm sorry, are you a private investigator?"

I shrugged. "Something like that. You know, forty percent of the time a woman is murdered, the boyfriend or husband is the one who did it."

Ryan leaned his head back and opened a palm to the ceiling. "Who's being provocative now? What the hell is that supposed to mean?"

"I'm just saying it must have been tough for you at the time. I'm guessing the police were all over you. April says your alibi was pretty solid, though. You were with another girl, another student of yours, the one you ended up taking to France in July's place. Are you still with her?"

"Are you questioning me?" he said.

I smiled. "Sorry. I used to cross-examine people for a living. It gets the best of me sometimes. I'm just trying to help out April, you know. She wants to know what happened to her sister. She feels the police never followed through and justice was never done."

"I totally understand that," he said. "Here's what I know: July was cheating on me first. She went away sometimes, and I know it wasn't to her sister's."

"Where did she go?"

"I don't know. No one does."

"Was there anything about the night she disappeared that was unusual? Did she say anything that struck you?"

"No," he said. "She was normal. Nothing seemed out of the ordinary to me."

"When did you realize something was wrong, that maybe she wasn't coming back?"

"I guess when Pete called."

"Pete?" I said.

"Pete Holloway. Her stepfather, or ex-stepfather, I guess."

"The County Supervisor?"

"Yeah."

"What did he say?"

"He was looking for her. He said he was supposed to meet her that night, which threw me off because she told me she'd be hanging out with her sister. That's when I called April, and she told me July said she'd be with me. And that was it. I called July, but she didn't answer. Everyone called her, but she was gone." Ryan sat up straight. "Look. I'm running a little late here . . ."

Remembering his post from earlier in the day about needing a camera, I pointed a thumb over my shoulder, and said, "Oh I forgot to tell you. When I was waiting in the hall a professor asked me to tell you she had an 8mm camera for you in her office."

Ryan's eyes got big. "No kidding. What was her name?"

"I forget."

"Vanessa?"

"That was it. She said she's going home at two if you want to pick it up."

Ryan checked his watch. "I have to catch her." He stood up. "Do you mind?"

"I don't mind. I can wait."

"Uhh. Okay."

When he was gone, I reached over his desk, grabbed his cell phone from the dock, and pulled up the recent calls. I didn't need a password since the phone had already been unlocked to play Miles Davis. There were mostly female names in his recent calls: Tammy, Vanessa, Kristen, Becky. I was looking through two-day-old calls when I found Ted Nadler. Took me a moment, but I remembered that was the crooked accountant Levi had told me about, who had dated Krista.

After docking the phone back into the stereo and turning Miles Davis back on, I got up and waited for the professor outside his open door.

He walked toward me, smiling, shaking his head. "She doesn't have a camera."

"Oh, sorry. I must have got the name wrong," I said. "You mind if I ask you one more thing before I take off?"

"Sure."

"April said you had a suitcase and a large portfolio that had some of July's things in it. She was hoping she could get that back."

The professor wrinkled his nose. "Oh shit. I think I left all that stuff at my parent's place in Sonoma County. Sorry."

"Why didn't you give them to April after July disappeared?"

"Sentimental I guess," he said.

"April's sentimental too. That portfolio has some of their old grammar school projects."

Nodding, Ryan raised his eyebrows and looked over my shoulder. "Fair point. I'll grab it when I go home for Thanksgiving. Tell her not to worry."

"I'll do that." Although I wasn't so sure I could tell her that with confidence. April's macaroni art could be covered in buffalo semen by now, hanging on some rich couple's wall in Sonoma County.

I stuck out my hand. "I'm going to take off. Thanks for talking to me. I appreciate it."

He stuck out his lower lip. "Not a problem. Any time."

"I might take you up on that."

5

Stone Lagoon

ON SUNDAYS THE MOOSE Lodge in McKinleyville was open for breakfast to everyone, as long as they were chaperoned by a lodge member. My chaperone was Levi, who had been playing gigs there for two years. The lodge consisted of a dining hall, a kitchen, and a bar room. Levi and I sat in the dining hall at a table under a stuffed moose head. We were served eggs, sausages, biscuits, and Bloody Marys.

"My uncle says he has work for you," Levi said, after taking a bite of the pickled asparagus that had come in his drink. "He wants you to go in on Monday."

"That's great," I said. "Thanks, buddy."

"I am a river to my people."

"Okay River, maybe you can do me another favor. What do you think about taking a ride with me after this?"

"Where?"

"To Stone Lagoon."

"You want to go fishing?"

"No, I want to go to an RV park out there."

"Why?"

I told him that April thought Don and Jared Tidwell were most likely responsible for July's disappearance, and I wanted to talk to them.

"And you want some backup," Levi said.

"Yeah, basically. I guess these guys are a little nuts."

"I am a river to my people."

After Levi and I finished our meals, the waitress gathered our plates, while chiding Levi for how drunk he was at his last show and how he owed her a Waylon Jennings' song. She was around fifty, with feathered bangs and a raspy, smoker's voice. Levi told her she was the only one he'd play Waylon Jennings for. Then she looked at me and said, "How was everything?"

"Great," I said. "Give my compliments to the chef."

She turned toward the kitchen and yelled across the dining hall full of people, "Hey Frank! This guy says to give his compliments to the chef."

I heard Frank laugh through the order window, over the sound of sizzling bacon. Then the waitress turned to Levi, rolled her eyes, and nodded sideways to me, like a horse shaking off a fly.

"Don't ask me," Levi said.

In the parking lot, after settling the bill, Levi insisted we take his truck to Stone Lagoon instead of my BMW 328i. "No one would talk to us if we pulled up in something like that," he said. A slight drizzle had started, and I wasn't going to argue as long as he let me drive, which he did.

There were three lagoons about thirty minutes north of McKinleyville along Highway 101: Big Lagoon, Stone Lagoon, and Freshwater Lagoon.

We drove along the coast and dropped down a hill into Big Lagoon first. The sun had come out in patches.

Three ridgelines were stacked against the north-eastern horizon, their treetops tearing the lifting fog.

Views of tree-covered bluffs, foothills, and mountains were inescapable in Humboldt County. When I was a kid, I would stare out the window of my parent's car as we drove one place or another and be awestruck by the scope of the forests. They were so vast and dense and wild and full of mystery.

Big Lagoon was fed mainly by Maple Creek and blocked to the sea by a three-mile spit, which, after heavy rains in the winter months, would break at the northern end, opening Maple Creek to the salmon and Steelhead trout waiting to spawn. Levi's dad once told me he and his buddies would sometimes get tired of waiting for the Steelhead, and they would dig a trench in the spit to make the lagoon break before it was ready.

After passing Big Lagoon, we drove through tunnels of maple, alder, and redwood. The bark of the maples and alders were carpeted in moss that sprouted ferns. The sun strained through the leaves so that the rain-soaked grass and sorrel glowed in the shade, and the road looked almost purple.

I drove the truck up another hill, catching glimpses of the beach occasionally, and then down until I saw an old-fashioned little red schoolhouse on the right, surrounded by a grassy field, picnic benches, and RVs. Stone Lagoon was left of the highway, along with a meadow, where a herd of Roosevelt elk grazed.

A few of these elk were on the highway now, holding up a line of cars. Tourists, parked in turnouts, took pictures of the bulls, standing at least ten feet tall with their antlers.

After the elk crossed, I turned right and parked at the little red schoolhouse. Levi pointed to a satellite dish on a pole near a tent and said, "I put that one in. I'm going to say hi."

He got out and walked toward the satellite dish, and I walked toward the schoolhouse. Abalone shells bordered the porch, and two little bears carved from redwood burl guarded the front door. A sign hanging on the outside read "Be back after lunch." It was just after 11 a.m. Apparently, lunches were long and open-ended here. I turned around to catch up with Levi.

A man with a protruding brow, an untrimmed black mustache, and an eagle tattooed on each forearm, came out of his RV and stared at me. His dirty black cap sat on the back of his head, revealing bangs stringy with sweat.

"How's it going?" I said.

He studied my face, trying to place me.

"I'm Tim," I said when I got closer.

The man said nothing. He was holding a bicycle tire wrapped in unwound clothes hangers.

"Have you seen Don or Jared around?"

"Who are you?" he said.

Levi called my name from about twenty yards away, near the satellite dish he'd pointed out earlier. The site was on the edge of a cluster of redwoods and had a large tent and a small travel trailer on it. A middle-aged man in khaki shorts and a faded blue polo shirt stood beside Levi.

Eagle-Tattoos was still staring at me. I pointed to the bike tire he was holding. "Good luck with your project," I said and walked toward Levi.

When I got close, Levi said, "This is Tom. I hooked up his dish."

Tom and I shook hands. "How do you like my living room?" Tom said, waving his arm at the redwood forest beside us. "You can't beat it," he said. "Like a sore dick, you can't beat it." He laughed hard.

"You should stay away from that guy," Tom said, nodding to the man with the bike tire. "No one likes him."

"Yeah, he didn't seem very friendly," I said.

"I used to give him rides into town but he never gave me gas money. I just ignore him when he asks now. I'm pretty sure he stole my remote too. His has a dirty spot where mine used to have a sticker." Tom held up the remote he was holding in his hand. "I had to get this one at the pawn shop in Eureka. Twelve bucks. Only now I can't figure out how to program it to the new flat screen I got."

"I can do that," Levi said. "I still have the codes memorized."

Tom's face lit up. "Well all right. Let's do this." He unzipped the tent door. Inside, three tow-headed kids and a woman in jean shorts lay on an air mattress watching TV. When the kids saw us, they jumped on all fours and started asking questions. While I answered them with, "My name is Tim. . . . Just visiting . . . He's fixing the TV," Tom showed Levi the thirty-two-inch flat screen on the opposite side of the tent, and Levi took the remote and pressed a few buttons. The TV turned on.

"Wow," Tom said. "That's awesome. I gotta give you something for this. You like meat?"

"Sure," Levi said.

Tom walked over to his travel trailer, went inside, and came out with a frozen, vacuum-sealed steak. "I converted the trailer into a big freezer," he said. "We go into Eureka once a month and fill up. The butcher at WinCo gives us a deal." Tom slapped his belly. "You guys want some beer?"

"Sure," I said.

He handed Levi the steak, then gave us both a beer out of a cooler. As we drank, I asked if he'd seen Don or Jared Tidwell, and he pointed to an RV in the grove and said Don had been helping the lady there with her water hookup the last he'd seen. He asked if we were friends of Don's, and I said no, we were insurance investigators. His eyes got big, and after telling him I couldn't give him any details of my investigation, I said, "Would you say Don was capable of violence?"

Tom laughed. "You're kidding, right? He's the craziest dude I ever met. I saw him beat a man with a tire iron once. I saw him hit his grandson with a stick just for playing with my daughters. What kind of man does that?"

"Are you talking about Sage?"

"Yeah. Sweet kid. Hit him with a stick right in front of me. Don makes him stay in his office now when he comes. Poor kid." Tom exhaled and furrowed his brow. "This is confidential, right?"

"Of course," I said. "Where's Don's office anyway?"

He pointed behind me. "The schoolhouse."

"How long have you lived here?"

Tom looked up at his eyebrows. Cartoon sound effects from the TV inside the tent filled the pauses in conversation. "Off and on for three years."

"You ever hear any rumors about Sage's mom?"

"The girl that went missing?"

"Yeah. July Morrison."

Tom leaned toward me and said in a hushed tone, "This is what I'm talking about. Craziest dude I ever met."

"What do you mean?"

"Daisy. She dated Don for a little bit around then." Tom leaned back and held up both hands. "I don't know. All I'm saying is that she saw fresh dirt on Don's property out in Ettersburg right after that girl went missing."

"Fresh dirt?"

Tom's eyes got big. "Like someone had just dug a hole."

"Like a grave?"

"You said it, not me."

"Where can I find Daisy?"

"She moved to Orick a couple of years ago, to the trailer park on the north end of town."

Levi and I thanked Tom for the meat, said goodbye, and walked back to the red schoolhouse. The door was still locked.

6

Orick

LEVI CLAIMED THE TOWN of Orick, located a few miles north of Stone Lagoon and Don's RV Park, was a metaphor for the whole county. Since its mill closed and the Bureau of Land Management and the national parks took away the logging, the people turned to carving redwood burl for tourists. There were twelve burl shops in all, in a town that consisted of a bar, a motel, a small store, a trailer park, and an abandoned movie theater. The stretch of highway through town was lined with burl statues of bears, sasquatches, eagles, gnomes, castles . . . all designed to siphon cash from the people who came to see the tallest trees in the world. But, according to a park ranger Levi knew, the tourists were too scared to get out of their car to buy anything.

"Obviously, that's ridiculous," Levi said. "They've seen *Deliverance* too many times. But it's hard to blame them. I knew a guy who grew up in Orick. When he was in sixth grade his teacher made the two fat kids in the class fight once a month while all the other kids watched and laughed. Can you believe that? A teacher."

We drove to the north end of Orick and pulled into

the trailer park, slowly, splashing through potholes full of muddy rainwater. Levi pointed to the satellite dishes on poles outside the trailers and said, "I put those in, too."

"Looks like solid craftsmanship."

"The kind America was built on, baby."

We parked and talked to a guy who could have been Eagle-Tattoos' brother. He took a break from building an awning for his trailer out of blue tarps and driftwood to point us to a silver RV parked on the end of the line, where Daisy lived. He stared as we walked away.

An older woman answered my knock, and the smell of urine and rancid bacon grease wafted through the open door.

I introduced myself as a private investigator working for the Morrison family, confirmed that she was Daisy, then asked her about the freshly dug grave she had seen five years ago on Don's property in Ettersburg.

She frowned. "What's this for?"

"I'm working for the family," I said. "They just want some answers."

"You're talking about Sage's mom?"

"Yes."

"You ever hear of Adam and Eve?"

I cocked my head. "Yeah."

"They ate fruit from the devil and then they wanted to wear clothes after that. Don thinks they should have never put on those clothes."

Levi and I looked at each other. I could tell he was trying not to smile. "Okay," I said, nodding. "Did Don or Jared ever threaten to kill July?"

"You think this is funny?"

"No."

"Fuck off." Daisy slammed the door shut. I knocked a few more times, and she yelled "fuck off" a few more times.

As we walked back to the truck, people stared at us through their trailer windows. "Why did you have to laugh?" I said to Levi.

"What do you mean? She's crazy."

We drove south, through Orick, past Freshwater Lagoon, up a hill, and around Stone Lagoon, back to the little red schoolhouse. Now the sign was gone, and the door was unlocked.

Inside, an older woman with short blond hair and a tight perm grinned at us and said, "Hi. You looking for anything in particular?" The sales floor was full of lacquered tables and chairs made from gnarled stumps and burl. There were even a few bed frames. The prices ranged from three hundred to two thousand dollars.

"Is Don around?" I said.

"Yeah, somewhere out there," she said. "Working on something, or chatting more likely."

"That sounds like him," I said. "Can I use your bathroom?"

"Sure. It's in the back, to the left."

Levi pointed to some carved furniture. "I like this. Is this mahogany?"

"Heaven's no. That's redwood. Where do you think you are?"

"It's beautiful. Is it a chair or a table?"

While Levi and the woman chatted, I found Don's office next to the bathroom. The door was open. I stared at it for a moment, then went in.

Papers, rusty carpenter tools, and fast food wrappers were scattered over a desk below a window on the far wall. A cabinet and a greasy red couch sat to the right. File boxes and abalone shells were stacked in the open closet to the left. It wasn't the best place for a kid to hang out.

I looked through the drawers in the desk and found four old abalone reports cards and a photo of Don standing with a woman, three girls, and a boy. From the clothes, I guessed the photo had been taken in the eighties, maybe early nineties. I took a picture of the photo with my phone.

In the next drawer, I found an ashtray holding a gold ring with a single red stone. The ring looked old. It reminded me of the ring July used to share custody of with April.

When we were seventeen, July made me drive her home from a camping trip at Patrick's Point. She had forgotten it was the day she and April were supposed to exchange their mother's ring. We didn't even pack up the tent or say goodbye to our friends. We just drove off, trying to get to April before midnight, like it was the most important thing in the world. And it was to July, and to me too at the time. I was high on mushrooms, and I was young and in love. The universe seemed to depend on making it back before the day ended.

I heard footsteps down the hall, and I shut the drawer just as the office door opened. The saleswoman started when she saw me. "What are you doing here?" she said with a hand on her chest.

"I'm looking for the bathroom," I said.

"That's the door before this one that's labeled bathroom."

"I must have missed it. Sorry. I had a big breakfast." I scooted past her through the door and walked down the hall back to the sales floor. I told Levi we were leaving, and he followed me out.

As we descended the porch steps, a man with gray and black shoulder-length hair and a white beard walked across the grass toward us. He wore a tan leather jacket and blue jeans.

"Are you the ones looking for me?" he said.

My instinct was to leave—just something in his tone maybe—but we had come all this way. I wanted to ask my questions, so I walked out to him. Levi had my back. "Are you Don Tidwell?" I said.

He nodded slowly.

Then I heard the bell on the showroom door ring, and the saleswoman shouted, "I caught him in your office, Don."

Don furrowed his brow and narrowed his eyes. "Call Evan and Chris," he shouted back. Then to me, "Who are you?"

"I didn't mean to go into your office," I said. "That was a misunderstanding. But I'm Tim Kitchens. I'm investigating July Morrison's disappearance."

He snorted. "That was a long time ago. What are you, a private investigator?"

"Just a concerned citizen," I said.

A female elk plodded into my periphery two yards away. Another followed, then another, until we were surrounded by the entire herd. Calves followed mothers, and young bulls sulked on the outskirts. They were giants. The calves and cows in the herd began calling to each other. The calls were loud and came from all directions. They reminded me of the moans and chirps in whale songs. Don ignored them and stared at me.

"Where were you on the night of July's disappearance?" I said.

He snorted. "You fucking the sister?"

A beat-up old black Ford pick-up pulled up by the herd and spooked the elk a little, but not enough for them to run. Two men in jeans and T-shirts got out holding baseball bats. Both had black curly mops of hair. I looked at Don, and he smiled.

"Those are the Crittenden brothers," Levi said. "Let's get out of here."

Several elk were between us and the brothers, who just stood there with their bats, staring at us, waiting for the herd to pass.

I remembered the Crittenden brothers from school. They had been two years ahead of me. Growing up, they had terrorized the younger kids, as well as their peers. But I had been lucky enough to stay out of their way. The rumor was they had taken too many psychedelic mushrooms in middle school.

"It was nice meeting you, Don," I said. Then I waved at the Crittenden brothers for some reason. I guess because I was scared and didn't really know what I was doing.

Levi was on his toes, rocking forward and back, waiting for a corridor to open up between the elk, so he could slip through and get to his truck, which was parked on the opposite side of the herd from the Crittendon brothers. Levi was supposed to be my backup, but I didn't blame him. Seeing those boogeymen from my childhood inspired me to run, too.

The elk were used to tourists, and it was illegal to hunt them for the most part, so they weren't scared of us at all, but that didn't stop me from being scared of them. They were giant, wild beasts, and if they thought in their tiny pea brains that I was threatening their young, they would trample me to death.

When a gap opened up, Levi and I stepped gingerly

through it, making no sudden moves, as if we were navigating a minefield.

Once on the other side, I turned and saw the brothers running around the herd to get to us. Thankfully, we weren't far from Levi's truck. He got there before me and jumped in the driver's seat. We backed out and took off as the brothers ran toward us, yipping like maniacs.

When we pulled onto the highway, my hands were shaking with unused adrenaline.

"No shame in running from that," Levi said, as if he could read my thoughts. "People like that are natural disasters. If you survive an encounter with them fairly unscathed, just count yourself lucky."

7

Arcata

I CALLED APRIL ON the way back and told her I had some things to discuss with her. She was busy but agreed to meet us in two hours at a hipster bar on the Arcata Plaza. We decided to arrive early.

Arcata was a small town seven miles south of McKinleyville on the northern edge of Humboldt Bay. Almost half its population was enrolled at Humboldt State University, which always appeared on lists of the greenest campuses in America. Their flagship programs were Botany and Forestry. The campus was a fifteen-minute walk from downtown. During the summer, when all the students went home, the town was quiet. But now, a few weeks before Thanksgiving break, the streets were full.

We parked on the Plaza and walked past the statue of President McKinley and toward the bars. Every year some college kid would spray-paint "Tyrant" or "Indian Killer" on McKinley's chest, and a city worker would have to wash it off the next day.

A transient stood outside the bar door playing Grateful Dead on an acoustic guitar. A few of his buddies sat at his feet, drinking from bottles in paper bags.

There were four other bars on this side of the Plaza catering to the students, but this one was the trendiest. Student art hung on the walls, and everyone inside wore the hipster uniform: skinny jeans, plaid shirts, zip-up hoodies. The men had trimmed beards and a few of the women wore glasses without lenses. I felt like I was back in San Francisco.

The bar was quiet for a Saturday, just three groups of friends.

After getting a beer, Levi parked in front of the jukebox.

"Play Whitesnake, *Here I Go Again*," I said without any shame. I would enjoy the song sincerely, without my tongue in my cheek. That was one of the perks of being thirty. I wasn't imprisoned by good taste anymore. I didn't have to engage in some kind of ironic pretense just so I could secretly enjoy something.

After an hour of listening to eighties music without any sense of irony, and drinking gin and tonics, pretending we had our shit together, Levi's girlfriend picked him up, and I pulled out my phone and started composing a text message to my ex-wife. I was at it twenty minutes before April arrived with a man.

"This is Bogdon," April said.

Bogdon was young, tall and thin, with shaggy dark hair. He seemed well-composed, self-assured for a college-aged kid, chin up, chest out, wearing a scarf and pointy dress shoes. I shook his hand.

"Nice to meet you," he said in what sounded like an Eastern-European accent, maybe Russian. "April says you're helping her with her sister. That's good."

I said, "Yeah, well. Things are happening."

"I just came to say hello," he said. "I have to wake up early." He turned to April and kissed her on the cheek. "I'll see you tomorrow."

April said goodbye, and he left. I waved. Something annoyed me about his easy self-confidence and social-media-ready presentation.

"Is that your boyfriend?" I said.

"He's an ex," she said, and leaned in close. "He wants me to marry him for citizenship."

I shook my head. "Don't do it."

"He said he'd give me ten thousand dollars."

"First of all, you can't trust that. And there's a huge fine for marriage fraud.

"You sound vaguely xenophobic. Super cute."

"That's not it. Just a little concerned for you. These matters are under scrutiny these days. They'll investigate you, interview your friends and family, your employer. Are you going to ask everyone to lie?"

"Relax," April said. "I wasn't taking it seriously."

The bartender came by and April ordered an IPA, then snatched a peanut from the bowl on the bar, smashed the shell between her fingers, and sorted through the wreckage for shards of peanut.

"What the hell are you doing?" I said.

"What?"

"You don't know how to open a peanut?"

"What are you talking about?" She smashed another. "How do you do it?"

"Not like a gorilla. Here." I grabbed a peanut. "You gently apply pressure at the seam." I popped off half the shell and showed her two whole peanuts inside. "That's how Homo sapiens do it."

"Such wisdom," She searched my eyes. "How deep do those waters run in there?"

I smiled, shook my head, finished my drink, ordered another, and ushered April to a quiet corner of the bar where I told her what had happened to me and Levi at Stone Lagoon.

When I was done, she almost whispered, "I had a feeling they were abusing Sage. Oh my God." She rubbed her face with her hands. "I'm calling Child Services first thing in the morning. Now it makes me wonder about so much else. He's got this thing now about wearing gloves all the time. I thought it was just something he did because he's almost a teenager and teenagers do weird things, but now I don't know. What if he's hiding something? What if he's cutting?"

We stopped talking for a while as the music and conversation around us continued. Then April said, "That ring you saw. You said it looked like my mom's. How sure are you?"

"I just saw it for a second. It looked the same, but the last time I saw it was probably fifteen years ago. And I'm sure there's lots of ruby rings like that."

April stood up. "My house isn't far. Come over and I'll give you the file I've been working on."

She put on her coat as I settled the tab, and we walked down the street in the dark. We didn't say much, maybe both thinking the same thing. Her house was eight blocks away, near Portuguese Hall. Most of the houses in the neighborhood were stucco and painted like Easter eggs. Under the streetlights, I could see the pastel pinks, yellows, oranges, and blues. The front lawns were either full of lava rocks or vegetable gardens.

The Arcata Bottoms was just west of us—wetlands converted into dairy farms and cow pastures. In the summer months, the wind off the bay carried the smell of fertilizer and cow waste into town.

April lived in a small Craftsman house with an old Dodge Dart rusting in the front yard, its flat tires surrounded by tall grass.

"What's with the old car?" I said as we walked inside.

"That's my parents' old car. I'm trying to get it fixed up, but it needs a lot of work. My neighbors hate it, but I can't get rid of it. My parents used to take July and me on vacations in that thing when we were little."

April's living room had a couch, a piano, two small trees in pots, and three tables—a coffee table, a kitchen table, and a fold-out table. There was a projector screen hanging from one of the walls next to a landscape painting, next to a dry-erase board with a to-do list written on it. One wall was dedicated to family photos: July and April as kids, their parents getting married . . . . The tops of each table were crowded with brushes, paint, make-up, nail polish, and small plastic vats. On the kitchen table, I found plaster molds of faces, hands, and ears, along with prosthetic noses, cheeks, brows, and even a double chin.

"What's going on here?" I said, holding up a nose.

"This is what I do," she said.

"I thought you were a reporter at the *Times-Standard*."

"I'm barely a reporter. Mostly I work on the graphics." She spread out her arms over the chaotic mess. "But this is what I do for fun."

"You run a shop of horrors for fun?"

She shook her head and smiled. "This isn't a shop of horrors. I help out the theater companies around here with their make-up. I'm getting my MA in Theater Arts." She snatched the fake nose from me. "These are old man noses for the musical they're putting on at the Playhouse. It's *A Christmas Carol* this year."

"I didn't know you were getting a Masters in Theater Arts."

"That's because you're self-involved," she said, adopting a deep, professorial, clearly facetious tone. "But you also have like zero self-awareness. It's a paradox."

"What do you mean zero self-awareness? Where did this attack come from? I was just joking about the shop of horrors thing. You have a lovely home."

She squared her shoulders to me, and the smile fell from her face. "Seriously, though, I'm a little concerned. I don't really know how to put this, but I have to ask . . . um, are you stable?"

My head jerked back. "Whoa, where did that come from?"

"I read the article they wrote about your little meltdown." She reached under a pile of papers, paint, and make-up, and pulled out a tablet, as if that was where it was always kept. Her fingers danced across the screen for a few moments. "I have the article right here. They quote you from the court transcripts that day: 'No, Your Honor, your white, middle-class, bleeding heart is out of order. You think you're the big fish around here, but you're not. You're a minnow leading sharks to a child's birthday party.'"

"That sounds insane when you say it monotone like that," I said, picking up a prosthetic ear and examining it.

"It sounds insane no matter what." April put down the tablet and grimaced. "Seriously. After these last few days, I'm starting to get a little concerned. And don't get offended by this, but I'm wondering if you're going to do more harm than good."

I put down the ear, nodding. "I understand why

you might think that. But what happened in San Francisco was a unique set of circumstances. I had just gotten a DUI and a divorce. I was about to lose my job for withholding documents from the defense, and the defendant was getting off for rape, mostly because of me. And everyone in court knew he was guilty. On top of that, I'd failed to convict that same defendant three years earlier for raping another woman. So that's two times he got off because of me. And now he's free. So I don't know why I said what I said, or why I brought dead fish to court. I was literally insane at that point. I hadn't slept for three days. I was on a few different drugs. I had to spend time in sempervirens after that. But I'm much better now."

April looked down and was silent a moment, then: "Are you sure working on this is healthy for you? Because originally I just asked for your advice, and you kind of just inserted yourself into this whole thing."

I wasn't going to continue without her blessing, but I was afraid if she knew how much finding July meant to me, she wouldn't give it. I elected not to spill my heart. I elected to be evasive, but I felt bad about it. I found her eyes. "I've been out of work a while. I'm just eager to do something. I want to help."

April was silent a moment, then, "Okay, as long as you promise to keep yourself under control."

"I promise."

She went to the kitchen, grabbed a beer from the fridge, handed it to me, then took a file from the bookshelf and opened it over a few paintbrushes and fake mustaches on the kitchen table. "This is as far as the police got in July's disappearance."

I cracked my beer, took a gulp.

"Why did she lie to me that night?" April looked at

me like I should have an answer for her, then said: "They found a receipt for the bottles of booze in the car. She bought them at the Courthouse Market in Eureka about fifteen minutes before the last time she called me. They also found a key to a PO Box in Eureka that she apparently never used. None of her bills, or any correspondence, used that PO box as an address."

April pulled out a magazine from the file and plopped it on the table. On the cover was a photo of a shirtless white man with a perfect smile. Over his head were the words *Men's Fitness*." This is all they found in the safe-deposit box that we shared. Figure that out. Why would she put a *Men's Fitness* magazine in a safe-deposit box? It's crazy."

"That is crazy. Or at least odd." I sat down at the kitchen table. "Is that what she normally kept in there?"

"Of course not. She kept bonds in there for when I turned eighteen. That's what she told me anyway, and I was almost eighteen then, but I never checked. And the bonds weren't there when the police opened it."

"A Men's Fitness magazine?"

"I know. And it wasn't like she was on drugs. She was keeping everything together. She loved Ryan, and she was crazy excited about going to France."

"And the cops never found anything else?"

"Not really. They found out about some sex parties she went to in Mexico when she was younger. So some of them figured she just went back. There's a little airport in Shelter Cove. They think someone gave her a ride from her car and she flew away on one of those Cessnas. It's ridiculous." April pulled a phone bill out of the file and pointed to a circled number with the name "Ted Nadler" written by it. "Ted Nadler's an accountant I heard the Tidwells use to launder their pot money. As you can see, my sister was calling him the week before she disappeared."

"I heard about this guy. Krista dated him."

"Really?" April made an "O" with her mouth.

"Did July ever date him?"

April shook her head. "The cops told me he was a friend, and he had an alibi. I circled him because he was another connection to the Tidwells."

I kept thinking of the ruby ring in Don's desk and the way Don had talked to me. I was beginning to think maybe April was right. Maybe the Tidwells had been involved in July's disappearance. I felt hatred blooming inside me. "Give me the file," I said. "Do you have any coffee?"

"Oh no," she said. "I mean, yes, I do, but you're not getting any. I have to go to sleep. I have work in the morning. I'm going to bed. You can sleep on the couch."

"That's okay. I don't want to leave my car on the Plaza."

"Your car will be fine." She pushed me with both hands, hard. I almost fell out of my chair. "Do you want another DUI?"

"Jesus! Okay. I'll sleep on your damn couch."

After she cleared the couch of clutter, I sat down and sank into one of the cushions.

She grabbed a folded blanket from the hall closet and laid it next to me. While she was bent over, our eyes met and lingered. But only for a moment, then she turned and walked to her bedroom. I could see the shape of her body through her loose, thin skirt as her hips lurched from side to side. "Good night," she said over her shoulder.

I did not sleep well. The couch sagged in the middle and was a foot too short. I woke up in the morning to the faint sound of a door closing, and I saw April tiptoeing to the bathroom in bare feet and short, red jogging shorts. When I heard the water come on for the shower, I grabbed the file and left out the front door. I sent her a text while I walked to my car thanking her for letting me stay the night.

8

The Law Offices Rafferty & Lewis

IN MY EXPERIENCE, CASUAL Fridays mean jeans and a collared shirt with no tie, maybe khakis, but at the Law Offices of Rafferty & Lewis, it meant Hawaiian shirt, shorts, and even sandals. There were two weeks until Thanksgiving and Levi's uncle, Bill Rafferty, insisted on sharing his hairy thighs with the entire office. He claimed not to be cold, but I could see the goose bumps.

I had to file a complaint at the courthouse sometime before lunch, so I was in a suit. I must have looked like a concierge in a Hawaiian hotel.

I had been doing paralegal work for Bill all week. He ran a modestly successful practice, making money where he could: criminal law, estate planning, personal injury, even some workers' comp. Bill was clear when I started: "This is no big city firm. We have to take what we can get. If they pay, we don't turn them away. Pursuant to ethics and conflict rules, of course."

He owned the Victorian where we worked and leased out the office in the back to another lawyer with his own practice, who shared our kitchen and bathroom. A Mexican family lived upstairs. The kids came home from school about two hours before quitting time each day. Sometimes they would play so loud—running, squealing, and bouncing on the bed— that Bill would go upstairs and talk to the mom in a mixture of Spanish nouns and English verbs.

I was one of two paralegals in the firm. The other was Melissa, a lanky woman in her fifties with short, spiky gray hair, who was always going to movies and new restaurants. There were two lawyers besides Bill: Pete, Bill's partner, who was around seventy and came by the office maybe twice a week to bullshit and review his in-box, and Gary, a young guy with a perpetual frown.

Melissa and I and the legal secretary, Jeanette, shared the front room, while each of the lawyers had their own office. Jeanette was the only friend I had made so far. My first day, I overheard her complaining about how the bakery down the street had stopped making her favorite sticky buns, so the next morning, I picked one up for her from the hipster bakery in Arcata, which named all their pastries after eighties action movies: sticky buns were Robocops, brownies were Die-Hards, and so on. After that, we began chatting here and there. Mostly, she told me stories about her husband, whose hobbies included gold prospecting in the Trinity Alps, smoking various meats, and glass blowing.

I was growing accustomed to a slower-paced work environment.

Bill walked out of his office, stopped at my desk, and held a file in front of me until I grabbed it. He had blue eyes, a tight, round belly, and a smooth cherub face that was red with too many lunches spent at The

Sea Grill bar. "Morning Big Shot," he said. "You put plaintiff instead of plaintiffs, plural, as in more than one, as in we have two plaintiffs. Do I need to get you your own office so you can focus? Would you do better if we brought in some dead fishes? I mean, I can do that if it will help. Just messing with you, man. I do need that fixed, though."

Around 10 AM, I walked to the courthouse, which was only a few blocks from the office, to file a personal injury complaint with the Superior Court.

The three-story Victorians of Old Town gave way to boxy hotels, banks, gas stations, and abandoned businesses. Men and women strung out on meth roamed the streets like survivors of the apocalypse.

At night, they wandered the residential neighborhoods, scavenging the unfenced yards and unlocked cars for anything they thought might be worth something: ladders, planter pots, CDs, sweaters . . . . In the morning, they hauled their loot to the pawn shops. My coworkers who lived in Eureka each had a few stories involving petty theft in the middle of the night.

There were rumors cities down south shipped their homeless north to Humboldt County on Greyhounds. For such a sparsely populated county, there were an incredible amount of transients and mentally ill. They made camps in the parks and the empty lots between the bay and the mall in Eureka. I saw a camp catch on fire once while I was leaving Sears. The smoke was dense and black. The homeless ran out of the bushes and into the parking lot, where they watched the fire with me and the rest of the Christmas shoppers.

The county courthouse was a sixties-style, five-story gray box on the north side of downtown, straddled by the north- and southbound lanes of Highway 101. The county jail, a pinkish concrete box, had been built next to the courthouse in the nineties. The jail was overfilled most of the time and regularly spilled its lesser offenders back onto the street. The courthouse and jail together covered an entire square block and made the largest building in town.

After filing the complaint inside, I walked across the street to the Courthouse Market to pick up something quick for lunch. I grabbed a bag of chips and a pre-made sandwich, got in line, and stared at the wall of liquor behind the register, thinking of July's last night on earth. She had been here.

When I reached the counter—I don't know why—I asked for a bottle of bitters, sweet vermouth, and whiskey.

As I walked outside, Coast Central Credit Union was on the corner to my right. The same Coast Central where July had kept a safety deposit box. She had checked her safety deposit box before buying her liquor the day she had disappeared. Her PO Box was at the post office three blocks around the corner.

She stopped by the bank so she could read a Men's Fitness magazine, then pick up some liquor?

April had told me that one idiot detective had thought she kept the magazine at the bank because she liked masturbating in public. While I ate my lunch, I called July's old stepfather, Pete Holloway, to ask him if Ryan was telling the truth about Pete having an appointment to meet July the night she disappeared, and if so, what was their meeting supposed to be about. He wasn't available at home or work, but I left messages with his wife and his staff explaining who I was and why I wanted to talk.

9

Lost Coast Brewery

NEAR THE END OF the workday, I called the number for Ted Nadler that April had circled on July's mobile-phone bill.

A woman answered: "Nadler and Associates. How can I help you?"

"When do you guys close today?" I asked.

"Five o'clock. But we're all booked up for the rest of the day. Would you like to make an appointment? The soonest available date I have . . . is next Friday, in the morning."

"Uhh, I'll have to check my schedule. Where are you guys located?"

"Eight-twenty-one Third Street. Eureka. Between I and J."

That was near the Courthouse Market.

I told Bill I was leaving early, smiled at the shit he gave me, then gathered my things. Nadler & Associates was only a few blocks away. I could see the top of the pink jail peeking over the Victorians as I walked.

I passed a muffler shop and a printing company before reaching a rundown Victorian with a wooden sign out front that read, in faded blue lettering: "Nadler & Associates, CPAs."

I climbed the steps, opened the front door, and entered a foyer with a reception window in front of me. A young woman between the ages of seventeen and twenty-one stood behind it. She had round cheeks, big brown eyes, broad, sloping shoulders, and a pageboy haircut.

The waiting room on my right had green carpet, square wooden chairs with brown vinyl cushions, and a coffee table with a mound of magazines. Two men and two women who looked to be in their twenties sat in the waiting room. The men had tattoos covering their forearms, and they wore T-shirts, pre-faded jeans, oversized baseball caps, and hoodies with wild designs printed on the front and back. The baseball caps had straight bills, one had a star stitched on the crown, the other had "NorCal." The clothes and hats were immaculate—no signs of natural wear. They looked like they had been purchased hours ago and would be thrown away after just one use.

The women next to them wore yoga pants, quilted puffy coats with fake fur trim around the hoods, and sheepskin boots with fleece on the inside. Both of them had bleach-blond hair.

I leaned over the reception window. "How's it going?" I said.

The young woman on the other side looked at me, then looked down at the clipboard on the shelf in front of her. "Pretty good," she said. "Until I remember the fact that old people are still walking among us, and no one is punching them in the face constantly for all eternity until their faces cave in and we use them as ashtrays. Other than that, I'm okay."

"Wow," I said. Her tone indicated she was joking.

A middle-aged woman sitting at a desk on the far wall turned and looked up at me. She had short, sandy blond hair, and fine wrinkles around her pale blue eyes. "Don't listen to Kristen," she said. "She's always like that. I don't know what's wrong with her."

I looked Kristen in the eyes. She shied away and pretended to organize the stapler and pens in front of her. Her movements were stiff and self-conscious.

She liked me. That was my conclusion anyway.

She said, "There's nothing wrong with me. Old people suck, that's all. They smell funny and they move like zombies. I just want to punch them all in the face."

The older woman let out a nervous laugh. "That's enough Kristen. She's usually not this bad."

"We all have our hang-ups," I said. "I was hoping I could see Ted Nadler today."

The woman said, "Sorry. There's no openings till next Friday. He's booked solid. Tax season's coming up."

"I just need some quick advice," I said. "Just a few minutes. You think I could see him between appointments?"

"No can do," Kristen chimed in. "And don't be a baby about it either, because I hate babies too. I will punch a baby in the face. Babies and old people are what's wrong with this country."

"I think Winston Churchill said that." That got her to laugh. "I'm serious," I said. "I have a book of Winston Churchill quotes at my house. He used to say crazy stuff like that all the time. He was a drunk."

Kristen curled her lip, furrowed her brow, and shook her head.

"I'm serious. You got a smart phone?"

"Am I an old person?"

"Google it. I bet you five dollars."

Kristen smiled and took her phone out of her pocket. "Ten dollars." Kristen's thumbs danced across the face of her phone. Thirty seconds passed, then she said, "Nothing. I mean nothing. Maybe something about getting old, but that's it. You owe me ten bucks. Ha ha." She flexed her traps and said in a deep voice, "I told you."

I held out my hand. "Let me try."

She thrust her phone through the open window. "Go for it."

I grabbed the phone, closed the browser, and pulled up her contacts. Ted Nadler's number was under, "Nadler Man." The number was different from the one on July's phone bill. I repeated the number in my mind a few times to memorize it, then pulled up the browser again and handed the phone back to Kristen, along with five dollars. "I guess I was wrong," I said.

"Hey. It was *ten* dollars," she said.

"That doesn't sound right." I turned and opened the front door. "Thanks for your guys' help. I'll come back next Friday."

As I walked out the door I heard: "You have to make an appointment."

I called the new number for Ted as I walked along the sidewalk.

He answered on the first ring. "Ted talking here."

"Hi, my name's Tim Kitchens. I was wondering if I could ask you a few questions about July Morrison."

"July? Wow, man. Where you from, left field?" He laughed. "How did you get this number?"

"I asked around."

"Okay? Seriously though bro', I can't talk right now.

I got clients out the door, and it's Friday. I'm trying to get out of here ASAP. You know what I mean?"

"Sure. Maybe when you're done with work I could buy you a beer or something."

"Are you a cop?" he said.

"No. I'm a lawyer. I've been working with July's family to settle some estate issues."

"What family? All there is is a sister and a drunk dad. I assume you're working for the sister."

"I'm working with the family," I said. "Some assets were recently found in July's name, and there may be some complications regarding how to pass them on to her heirs, since there is no proof of her death."

Ted huffed. "That's because she's not dead."

"I keep hearing that."

"I have to go."

"How about that beer?" I said.

"I'll tell you what. I usually go to happy hour at Lost Coast, and I usually don't turn down free beer."

"Okay, Ted. I'll see you there."

I turned and walked to the Lost Coast Brewery around the corner from Ted's office, entering through the back. The bar and staircase made a narrow hallway that opened onto the main dining area. Green tables were arranged in rows, and an oak floor reflected the light streaming through the wall of windows facing Fifth Street. T-shirts and hats hung on the wall, along with the blown-up labels of the brewery's most popular beers: Alleycat, Downtown Brown, Great White. The labels were Cubist-style paintings of a cat, a man, and a shark.

The crowd was mixed. There were some burnt-out hippies, some rich, yuppie hippies, a few plaid-shirted hipsters, a group of wide-assed good ol' boys, and the flat-brimmed-hat contingent, down from the hills to blow the money they made on their harvests. The bars and tribal casinos were filled with these guys this time of year.

I sat at the bar with seven other men. The bartender wore short, khaki shorts, and the men stared at her legs whenever she turned her back.

She walked over and stood in front of me. "What can I get for you?" Her voice was monotone, and she almost had to shout to be heard over the clinking glasses and plates and loud, alcohol-fueled conversations.

I smiled. "I'd like a burger and a gin on the rocks."

"We don't serve hard alcohol. This is a brewery."

So much for having my shit together tonight. "Okay, I'll take the Alleycat."

She rolled her eyes and walked away. She had the air of a woman who only laughed around potential mates, and I wasn't one.

While I waited for my burger, I looked up Ted's Facebook account again. He hadn't accepted my friend request yet, but I was able to view his profile picture. I wanted to make sure I could recognize him when he came into the bar. The picture was a close-up of his face. He had blue eyes, clean-shaven red cheeks, and perfect white teeth. His short blond hair was the same length on the sides of his head as it was on the top, like a buzz cut that had grown out and been trimmed around the ears. There was a hint of a double chin coming in.

By the time that face walked up to the bar, I was working on my third Alleycat and thinking about texting my ex-wife. My stomach was bloated and gurgling, but I had a decent buzz.

Ted wore a brown corduroy blazer and bulky white tennis shoes. His collared blue shirt was tucked into faded blue jeans. The top button of the shirt was unbuttoned. He threw an elbow onto the bar and said, "Now the party can get started."

The bartender brought him a glass of dark brown ale. The glass had "Teddy" etched into it.

"Ah, the good China," he said. "Thank you, Rayna, dear."

The bartender actually smiled. "Here comes trouble," she said.

"Put the kids to bed, Mama." He turned, leaned his back against the bar, and scanned the room while he took his first sip. Then he walked over to the table where the contractors were sitting and started slapping them on the back.

He took about ten minutes to finish his first beer. When he got back to the bar, Rayna refilled his pint glass.

"I'll get that one," I said, after she set the beer down in front of him. I stuck out my hand. "I'm Tim. We talked on the phone earlier. Mind if I ask you a few questions?"

Ted ignored my hand. "I don't put out for just one drink," he said.

The guy on the stool next to me laughed.

I smiled. "Well, let's start with one and see how it goes from there."

"That's what she said."

The guy on the stool laughed again. He had a pickled smile and half-closed eyes.

"It will just take a few minutes," I said.

"That's what he said."

Now Rayna was laughing.

"Funny," I said.

Ted laughed and put his arm around me. "I'm just fucking with you, man." He lifted the fresh beer to his mouth and downed it in about five seconds, then slammed the glass on the bar and wiped his mouth with his sleeve. "Step into my office." He pointed a thumb toward the back.

I paid for his beer and followed him outside. The sun had been down for a while. A few streetlights cast their yellow light over the parking lot, and an early evening mist was drifting in from the bay. The mist was cold and wet on my face. It settled on Ted's blazer and sparkled under the lights.

Ted walked up to a new Ford F-250, which beeped as he unlocked it. "Let's talk in here," he said. We climbed in. I smelled new leather and vanilla air freshener. Ted turned on the stereo. The blue digital words on its face lit up the dark cab. The words read, "Ja Rule." One of his rap songs blasted through the speakers. Ted turned it down.

"So you're a lawyer, huh?" he said.

"Yeah," I said.

"I thought about being a lawyer once."

"Oh yeah?"

"But then I thought, fuck it, I can't go to school that long. I almost took the GMAT and everything."

"You mean the LSAT," I said.

He laughed. "Yeah."

Ted reached into his pocket and pulled out a plastic bag the size of a quarter with white powder inside. He opened the bag, scooped up a small pile of the powder with one of his keys, and snorted it. Then he handed me the key and the bag, and I did the same. "That's what I'm talking about," he said, and he took another bump, rubbed some of the cocaine on his gums, and lit a cigarette." So you're looking for proof that July is dead or alive so you can give away her shit?"

"Essentially," I said.

"So how can I help you with that?"

"Do you know Ryan Lowell?"

"I don't think so."

"He's a professor at HSU. He was July's last known boyfriend."

"Oh yeah. I know that guy. He's a client."

"You do his taxes or something?" I said.

He shook his head. "Man, I can't tell you that. I never talk about my client's business to third parties. I have professional ethical duties."

"I'm just trying to get some facts to help some people. There's nothing illegal here. There's no such thing as an accountant-client privilege."

"Yeah. But I have ethical duties nonetheless. Professional and as a human being."

The cocaine had dripped from my nasal cavity into the back of my throat. It was bitter. I swallowed several times, but the drip just stayed there. I felt a rush of good feeling, and I clenched my jaw.

I said, "I was in your office earlier. If I had to guess, I'd say many of your clients are dope growers. How ethical is that?"

"I'm ethical as hell, dude. There's a lot of young up-and-comers in the community these days. It's an exciting time to be in Humboldt. There's a real entrepreneurial spirit. It's a fever and it's catching."

"Come on, Ted, they're dope growers. And it's your job to make them look like entrepreneurs, right? It's your job to clean their money. And I don't care either way. I'm not with the Feds. I'm just a lawyer trying to help a few people."

"Bro', I have all types of clients. Some people are local businesspeople, and others come from a broad cross-section of this community. It's the nature of being a small-town accountant. *Ergo*, I certainly can't help it if some of my clients are people that are involved in *local* business. But I've never been involved with a known drug dealer. And I have the utmost respect for my peers in this profession and have always kept my professional standing and license in pristine condition."

"Sounds like you should run for First District Supervisor," I said.

Ted laughed. "Now that being said. It's like a gold rush out here. Everyone's growing. I know grandmas that have ten plants in their garage. I know grocery clerks. Everyone wants a few extra G's here and there. But there's also the dark side that nobody likes to talk about, the home invasions, the thugs robbing grandma for her retirement medicine."

From the look in his eyes and the passion he had for this conversation, I figured the cocaine and beers were hitting Ted pretty hard. "What are you talking about?" I said. "Every time there's a home invasion it makes the paper."

"Yeah, but nobody knows what to do about them. It's the Wild West out here. These guys are the new cowboys. There's some real O.K. Corral shit going on in those hills, man. This county is booming. You know what I mean? It's The Green Rush." He pointed his key at the bag of cocaine in his hand. "This is good coke. And I can get this whenever I want. I *give* this shit away. I give it to you and I don't even know you, you know what I mean? I'll make it rain cocaine. I don't give a fuck."

He took another key hit and passed the bag to me. I snorted a small pile.

He said, "You should read the public notice section of the Time Standard. Check out the fictitious business name statements. It's hilarious, man. I read them every day. Crazy sounding fake businesses are starting every day. Every little grower has at least one. There's thousands of these things. I saw one last week named Dinsmore Global Communications. What the fuck does that mean? They don't even have cable in Dinsmore. They don't even have internet. Then this morning I saw one called Island Mountain Massage. You know where Island Mountain is? It's in the middle of nowhere. People call it Murder Mountain because shit gets real up there. No one. I mean no one is going out to Island Mountain to get a massage."

I laughed. My heart was racing. My stomach muscles would not relax. I was anxious to hear what Ted had to say and anxious to say what I wanted to say. The crappy old hip-hop playing through the speakers sounded fantastic.

I said, "April told me July used to run pot to Idaho for Jared Tidwell."

Ted raised his eyebrows. "Jared's not into that stuff. But July used to run in certain circles, so I wouldn't be surprised if she'd done that for someone."

"So you know Jared?" I said.

"Yeah, Jared's my boy."

"Is he a client?"

"That too."

"Was July a client?" I said.

"At one time."

"Was she your client when she called you a week before she disappeared?"

"No," he said.

"Why did she call you?"

"Because she wanted people to ask me a lot of questions about it later."

"Were you sleeping with her?"

Ted scoffed. "Hell no. She called because she wanted some advice. She wanted to know about gift taxes."

"Gift taxes?"

"Yeah. She wanted to know how much the government would take out of a gift of cash, and if there was any way around it."

"Was she giving someone cash or receiving it?"

"I don't know. I was on vacation. She was supposed to come to my office when I got back, but she was gone by that time, sitting on a beach somewhere in Mexico, drinking piña coladas."

"Was she running dope for Jared again?" I said.

"I told you Jared's not into that stuff. And even if he was, he wouldn't touch that crazy slut again."

"So you think she just left her kid and took off to Mexico?"

"I know she did. July is a crazy slut, man. She's a grow-ho. I guarantee she's down there fucking every Mexican taller than five-ten. Before Jared ever even got with her, we used to see her at these parties in San Pancho. Crazy sex parties, man, just brandy glasses full of Viagra on the counter and shit. Probably the purest molly you ever had. And freaks wearing masks. Dicks and tits hanging out all over the place. I swear I saw Sammy Hagar at one of those things. Well, probably wasn't Sammy. Probably some lawyer from Orange County. But makes it a better story for parties, right man?" He looked at me for confirmation, and I obliged with a half-smile and half-nod. He continued out of his laugh, "Bro', you know what I'm saying. And so what if July had a kid. She was a slut and sluts don't change. They get older, that's it. They get older and they get wrinkly tans and diamond rings and new SUVs, and kids, and they drink Chardonnay out of giant wine glasses. But they don't change, man. Sluts don't change."

"Sounds like we're not talking about July anymore," I said. "Who's the Chardonnay drinker, your ex-wife or your mom?"

"Fuck you, man, I'm talking about July," Ted said. "She cheated on Jared, and that's my boy right there. She screwed him all up."

"Maybe he shouldn't have taken her to those sex parties."

"He didn't. He just met her there."

"And I bet he didn't let her forget it, either," I said.

"What's your problem anyway?"

"Nothing. Just that the dead can't defend themselves."

"I told you, man, she's not dead. She's in San Pancho. Someone I know saw her there. She took a picture of July partying like a rock star."

"Who does?" I said.

"You don't know her."

"I'd like to talk to her. You have her number?"

Ted shrugged. "Sure."

He took his phone out of his pocket and started reading off numbers. I entered the numbers under a new contact in my phone.

"Her name's Becky," he said.

I looked up from my phone. "How about Krista's number? You got that too? I'd like to talk to her. You guys dated for a while, right?"

Ted jerked his head back. "Whoa, man, you been doing your research."

"Just doing my job."

"Well, I threw out Krista's number when she started dating my boy, Mike. Don't want to be tempted, you know what I mean? I even unfriended her on Facebook. But Becky can give you her number if she wants. They all live on the same road. Jared too. That's how we all met. Parties be poppin' out there, man."

"It's a small world," I said.

"That's Humboldt County, baby."

"One more thing." I pulled up the picture of Don Tidwell on my phone and showed it to Ted. "You recognize these people?"

"Yeah. That's Jared's family. Why do you have that?"

"Who are the women?"

"What does that have to do with July?" he said.

"I'm not sure. I'm just checking out everything I can."

"I recognize his dad, but that's it. Rayna might know the other ones."

"Who's Rayna?" I said.

"The bartender inside. She and Jared were together for a while."

I opened the passenger-side door. "Thanks for talking with me." I stuck my hand out, and Ted shook it.

"I wouldn't keep flashing that picture around," he said. "Jared's not someone you want to fuck with."

I gave Ted a wave and went back inside to talk to Rayna, but she was gone and a man had taken over behind the bar. She could have been on a break, or serving someone upstairs, but I didn't feel like waiting in there, so I walked back to my car. The cold air felt good on my face.

I found the bottles of whiskey, sweet vermouth, and bitters I had bought from the liquor store. In my water bottle, I mixed a giant Manhattan, then took it and an extra coat down to the waterfront, where I walked along the promenade. The bay had receded into its channels, and the exposed mud glistened in the moonlight.

I was seven the last time I had seen a low tide like that in the bay. My dad had taken me to collect mud worms before the sunrise. The rednecks said they were the best bait around. My dad gave me rubber boots for the occasion, but they didn't keep me dry. Slogging through the mud, I'd sink past my knees. Whichever foot was in front would sink deeper as I fought to free the back one. There was a constant, wet, sucking sound. The disturbed mud smelled like sulfur. When my dad thought we had ventured far enough from shore, we started digging. The creatures we found were out of my nightmares. They looked like living pieces of intestine, and they were longer than my arm. They had no eyes, only two sharp triangular teeth, which were too large for their small round mouths. My dad wanted me to collect them in the bucket, but I refused, and he just laughed. He gathered about eight of them, and we trudged back to shore. When we got home, my mom made us take off our shoes and clothes before coming into the house.

The mudflats looked like a wasteland, but there was life beneath the surface, strange and hideous life.

I took a sip of the Manhattan and walked along the promenade as far as D Street, where I could see Steve & Dave's Bar and hear the distant, drunken exhortations of its patrons. A few yards away, a man was getting ready to go to bed on a park bench. His nightcap was a tall can of malt liquor. He was old and not unfriendly.

"You can't beat your view," I said. "Like a sore dick, you can't beat it."

The man laughed hard. He was missing teeth, and he called himself Rainbow. We talked for ten minutes, mostly about the weather and what someone named Karl had stolen from him. After we finished the Manhattan, I gave him a twenty and walked back to my car.

I decided I had to see April, so I drove the back way into Arcata, taking the Samoa Bridge over the bay onto the north spit, then turned northeast on New Navy Base Road and passed through the small, beach town of Manilla and then the Bottoms.

The time was 10:30 p.m. when I pulled up to her house. There was still a light on inside, so I knocked. She opened the front door a minute later, wearing sweatpants, with her hair in a ponytail.

"Hello," I said.

"You're drunk," she said. "Did you drive here?"

"No."

"What is wrong with you? You could kill someone. You could kill a child."

"You're right. You're right. I'm making a vow right now to never drive drunk again."

"Are you making a joke?" she said.

"No. I'm serious."

"Why do you keep doing things like this? You're going to wind up in jail."

"It doesn't matter. I only have three years to live anyway. I should be drinking champagne."

"Stop shouting," she said. "What do you mean you only have three years to live?"

"That's when Brian Mallard has his first parole hearing. If they let him out, I'll have to kill him, and then I'll go to jail."

"Who's Brian Mallard?"

"He's the guy who raped and murdered my sister."

April touched her forehead with her thumb and forefinger. "You're really drunk, Tim. I'm calling your mom."

Bogdon came to the door. "Hello, Tim," he said.

I waved. "I'm leaving," I said. "Sorry to bother you guys. It's just that I talked to the accountant. But I can tell you about it later. He was wearing a blazer. That might be significant."

I started walking away.

"You can't drive," she said.

"I know," I said. "I'll run home. I can run like a deer. I'll pick my car up later. I'll tell you everything. I'm sorry."

Fueled by cocaine and Manhattans, I walked seven miles on the freeway to my parent's house. I called the number Ted gave me for Becky seven times to ask her about the picture she supposedly took of July in Mexico, but she didn't answer. Cars and trucks drove by going seventy. Wingtips were not the proper footwear for this undertaking. I had blisters and aching, burning heels by the time I made it through the front door.

"Tim?" my dad said from the top of the stairs.

"Yes. Sorry. Going to bed."

I went into my room and shut the door. The cocaine darkness had settled in. I sat at my sister's piano and slapped my palms onto the keys and let them lay there.

10

Patrick's Point

"HOW COULD YOU HEAR it over the dog barking?" I said. "I'm going over there."

"Don't cause a fuss," my dad said. "You're leaving in a few months, but we live here. I don't want to be stuck with a neighbor that doesn't like us. He'll start reporting me for burning the paper trash."

"So you don't want me to say anything to him because he looks the other way when you burn garbage? What's going on here? Where are we? You burn your garbage, the neighbor tortures his dog. We're trying to have a civilization here."

I grabbed my checkbook and walked out the front door, around the yard, and into the neighbor's driveway. I smelled pot as I mounted the steps to the front porch. Fluorescent light streamed through the cracks around the door of the garage. A manhole-sized fan had been installed in the wall and was running.

The neighbors were not overly concerned about hiding their operation.

A shirtless man in his twenties answered the door. He wore basketball shorts and had Chinese lettering tattooed on his chest.

I introduced myself and told him I wanted to buy his dog.

He laughed and said, "Are you kidding?"

"I need a dog," I said.

"That's my dog."

"I know it is. I want it to be my dog."

"No," he said. "Go to the pound, man."

"I'll give you twenty dollars."

He laughed. "No."

I kept making offers. When I got to three-fifty, he accepted. But then he refused my check, so I had to drive to the bank in town. In my mind, I went over everyone I still knew in McKinleyville who had dogs. I could think of three but was sure if I went on Facebook I could find more. I was fairly confident I could get someone to take the poor thing.

When I got back, the grower opened the door with a large brindle pit bull on a leash beside him. "Her name's Tuna," he said, taking the cash from my hand.

Tuna's whole backside wagged with her tail, and she jumped on me. She was heavy. The neighbor yelled at her to get down, but she didn't listen. I scratched her back for a second then pushed her down.

When I brought Tuna back to my parents' house, my dad's mouth fell open. I let Tuna go, and she jumped on my mom and licked her face.

"Are you kidding?" my dad said. "No. No."

"She can stay in my room," I said.

"And who's going to clean up her poop?"

"I will."

My mom hugged Tuna. "Who's a good girl?"

After going back into town to get some dog food, I got the call I'd been waiting for from Pete Holloway, the County Supervisor. The conversation only lasted five minutes, but he managed to tell me he was a busy man four times. And because of how busy he was, the only time I could meet with him was in forty-five minutes, at Patrick's Point, where he would be picking the rocks for abalone at low tide.

I had met Pete only once before when he had attended July's high school graduation ceremony sixteen years earlier. July had introduced me to him afterward. He had been April and July's stepfather for two years before their mom died of breast cancer, and before they moved back in with their biological dad, Rodney Morrison, when April was seven and July was fourteen.

In 2014, he had been reelected as Fifth District Supervisor, after eight years off the job. I remembered his campaign signs from when I visited my parents the summer before. They had been all over McKinleyville: "Pete Holloway for Fifth District Supervisor, A Call for Action."

As I loaded Tuna in my car, I heard another dog barking behind the neighbor's fence. I looked up at the sky and said, "Shit."

I drove fourteen miles north of McKinleyville, took the exit for Patrick's Point State Park, paid the ranger at the front-gate kiosk seven dollars for day-use, and wound through the campgrounds to Palmer's Beach, passing a re-creation of a traditional Yurok village along the way.

In high school, July and I had camped at Patrick's Point with friends. We had sneaked off together during the night with the plan of having sex on Agate Beach and maybe finding an agate to commemorate the moment. But the trail down was too steep and long, and we were drunk and high on mushrooms and couldn't wait any longer, so we found a secluded spot in the bushes. The moon was bright, and we could see and hear the surf below. Her calf brushed against some stinging nettle, but she laughed it off . . . .

Memories.

I parked and let Tuna out. The trail to the beach curled a quarter mile down a bluff, through wind-battered huckleberry bushes and Spruce trees. When we reached the bottom, Tuna took off after some sandpipers. The overcast sky spread the light equally over the rocks and driftwood so that there were no shadows. The air smelled of decomposing seaweed. The surf was almost two hundred yards away, past a field of boulders, craggy rocks, and tide pools.

Halfway between me and the surf, I saw two men wearing wetsuits, taking slow, deliberate steps, and stooping now and then. Assuming one was Pete, I set out toward them, hopping from rock to rock. I could hear seagulls squawking and sea lions barking over the crashing waves. Colonies of black muscles and aggregates of green sea anemones covered the rocks, along with seaweed and some kind of living red enamel that was as slippery as ice. Crabs scuttled into crevices as I passed, and little sculpin swam into holes as I disturbed their pools.

As I came closer to the two men, I recognized Pete. He was the bigger of the two, and clean-shaven. His short hair was parted and slicked to one side. Though he was graying at the temples and had bloated cheeks and rough, porous skin, his face maintained a boyish quality.

I stuck out my hand. "How you doing? I'm Tim Kitchens."

Pete showed me his teeth and gave my hand a firm three shakes. "Pete Holloway." He was wearing gloves.

"I met you once at July's high school graduation. I was her boyfriend at the time."

"No kidding. I'm sorry but I don't remember meeting you."

"You gave her five thousand dollars as a graduation gift. We went to Hawaii on that money."

"Oh," he said, "you're the one she took with her. I remember that. Lucky son of a gun. I was happy to give that to her. She deserved it."

"She did. And we had a blast. Thank you."

"That's good." Pete sloshed through the water, sticking his arm in the crevices between rocks, and sometimes crouching until his shoulders were underwater. A cormorant stood on a rock nearby with its wings spread out to dry, oblivious to us. Twenty yards beyond the surf, a little raft the size of a coffee table bobbed up and down. A head wearing goggles popped up next to it. He or she was diving for abalone. Pete and his partner were picking, which was much less dangerous. Divers were known to drown in kelp forests or be bit in half by Great Whites.

Pete said, "If you don't mind me saying, it seems odd to me that you would start investigating July's disappearance so many years after it happened. Why now?"

"Because I have time now, and experience," I said. "It's selfish, really. I would feel guilty if I didn't try to find out what happened to her. I cared about her deeply."

"Experience?" he said, grunting as he moved to the next rock." What type of experience?"

"I was a prosecutor for the San Francisco District Attorney's Office."

"Oh, you're the fish guy. I've heard about you. Oh, this is rich."

While Pete laughed to himself, I heard a splash behind me and turned around to see Tuna bounding through the tide pools towards us. I called her name, but she went straight to Pete and jumped on his chest. Though her nub of a tail was wagging and her tongue was hanging out, Pete had a look of undressed terror on his face. I jumped off the rocks I had been balancing on, waded through the shin-deep, frigid water, grabbed Tuna by the collar, and dragged her away.

"Sorry about that," I said. "She's an excitable girl."

"That dog needs training," Pete said, indignant. "As a pit bull owner, you have a responsibility to the community."

"You're right. I actually just got her today, so I haven't had a chance—"

"My ex-wife has a school. Sitting Pretty Dog Training. You should look her up."

"I will," I said, guiding Tuna to a large flat dry rock nearby. "Thanks."

"Now you're all wet."

"This is true."

Pete turned and went back to searching for abalone. "Well go ahead and ask your questions," he said, "before you get hypothermia."

I sat down next to Tuna and let her rest her front paws in my lap, while I scratched her wet, stinking back. The cold offshore wind was numbing my ears. "First, I'd like to know where you were the night July disappeared."

Pete scoffed. "I was at my cabin in Ruth Lake with my old assistant, Winona Stapely, and her youngest, Jennifer."

"Stapely? Are they related to Krista Stapely by chance?"

"Yes. Winona's Krista's mother."

"Do you know where I could find Krista?"

Pete's head stopped moving, and he stared at a rock. "No. I've lost touch with that family."

"Were you at the cabin all night?"

"Yes."

"July's old boyfriend told me you called him that night looking for July. Is that true?"

"It is, yes."

"Why?"

"I was just checking in. As I'm sure you already know, July was more than just an ex-stepdaughter to me. I treated her like she was my own. We were very close. Just like me and her sister."

"If you were just checking in, why call her boyfriend looking for her? There's no record of July ever receiving a call from you that day."

"That's because her phone kept going straight to voicemail. Of course, there's no record of it. After several times of that, I got worried as most people would."

"Around what time were you getting her voicemail?" I said.

"I don't remember."

"According to July's boyfriend, you said you were supposed to meet July that night."

"Well that's not true," he said, getting a little huffy. "I'm not sure where he got that from. I just worried about her. That's all."

"Did you continue to give her money after she graduated high school?"

"What do you mean?" he said.

"You said you were like a father to her, that you worried about her. Fathers continue to support their children even after they're grown."

"I gave her gifts on Christmas, on her birthday. But she never really needed anything from me. You know how she was. She was very independent. She could always take care of herself."

"Did you give her any substantial gifts around the time she went missing?"

"Substantial?" he said.

"Say five thousand dollars or more."

"Heavens no."

"Do you know a man named Dave Massey?"

"Do I know a man named Dave Massey? You're just rattling off the questions aren't you." Pete bent down and grunted as he shoved a gloved hand under another rock. "There you are you little bitch!" He fiddled around under the rock a little and grunted some more, then stood up straight and pulled a dripping abalone out of the water—a large, black, fleshy foot topped with a white and red shell the size of a football. "I got one!" he said, grinning and turning to the other man. "Oh baby. Woo. You don't see many like that this late in the season." The abalone's black tentacles wormed out of the holes in the top of the shell and touched Pete's hands. He turned back to me. "You ever go for abalone?"

"I've gone with my dad a few times," I said.

"Little beauties aren't they?" He shook the abalone. "I almost feel sorry for them sometimes. They're so harmless. All they do is eat seaweed, but everyone wants to eat them. Poor little innocent creatures."

"I don't see how they're innocent," I said. "They're unconscious feeding machines. If they had the chance they'd eat all the seaweed in the world. They're much closer to evil than innocent."

Pete squinted at me. "That's one way of looking at it, I guess."

11

Avenue of the Giants

THE NEXT MORNING, I woke up in my futon with a man on top of me, shaking me. His face was six inches above mine. He had a big porous nose, bushy eyebrows, and a beard that hung down onto my neck and chin. He wore a nightcap, and his eyes were completely black.

I screamed.

The man jumped off the futon and said, in a woman's voice, "Do you like how my beard tickles?" then laughed.

"April?" I said. "Jesus Christ."

April hadn't stopped laughing. "I was—I was—"

"Stop cackling. Look at you. You're hideous."

She grabbed her stomach and doubled over. Her smile looked like it was trying to rip her face apart. Tears squirted from her eyes.

"Stop," she begged. "Don't talk."

I sat up and rubbed my eyes and waited for her laughing-fit to subside.

After repeating "Oh God," a few times, she recovered and said, "How you feeling, Drunky? Are you hungover again?"

"I'm fine."

"My rehearsal was canceled this morning, so I figured I'd come and wake you up since *you* woke me up the other night."

"Sorry."

"I forgive you, but now you have to come with me to see my dad. It's his birthday."

I shook my head. "I'm not doing that."

"Yeah. It's happening. Get dressed."

"No," I said.

"Come on. Come for a ride with me. You can tell me all about your gumshoeing." She opened my bedroom door. "Get dressed. I'll wait out here. Your mom made pancakes."

April left the room.

I lay back down on the futon for about ten minutes before feeling well enough to get up. My head was heavy from having drunk too much wine the night before, and I had to sit back down to put my pants on.

When I opened the bedroom door, Tuna jumped on me. I scratched her back for a minute, then walked down the hall. My mom and dad were both at the kitchen table eating pancakes with April. The morning light streamed through the windows. I could barely open my eyes. April had removed the prosthetics and make-up from her face, but she still wore a baggy, striped nightgown. She looked at me when I entered. Her face was clean and beautiful in the sunlight.

"What were you doing knocking on April's door at ten-thirty at night?" my mom said. "What is wrong with you?"

"I think he has a crush on me, Mrs. Kitchens," April said.

"Is that true, Timmy?"

"Oh Jesus," I said. "What is this, junior high? Look at her over there smiling, like a cat that plays with a mouse before she eats him."

"What a horrible thing to say about someone," my mom said. "Is that how you talk to women?"

"I speak truth to power. Is there any coffee left?"

"No," my mom said. "You have to make some more. The beans are in the fridge."

"I don't know how to use this coffee machine."

"You do too. Don't be a baby."

"What a little manipulator," April said.

"That's our son, the lawyer," my dad said. "I don't know where he got it from."

I threw up my hands. "I just want a cup of coffee."

"Now he's grumpy," April said. "Sensitive boy."

They all laughed.

After breakfast, April changed in my room while I brushed my teeth, then we both climbed into her small Nissan SUV in the driveway and drove off, while my parents watched from the front porch.

A neat pile of clothes and a carrot cake inside a plastic cake container were in the backseat. Kings of Leon played low on the stereo. An empty coffee cup from Dutch Brothers sat in one of the cup holders. The smell of April's perfume mixed with the smell of the nylon interior.

"This is like a sorority girl's car," I said.

"What? No it's not."

"Yeah. This is a quarter-life crisis car."

April laughed and said, "You're right. I miss my undergraduate years already. That explains why I'm still hanging out with loser guys like you."

"Exactly."

April's dad lived in Phillipsville, a small community about an hour and a half south of McKinleyville.

From my parents' house, we took Highway 101 South over the Mad River, through Arcata and Eureka, and smaller towns like King Salmon and Loleta. Between towns, cow pastures lined the highway, allowing clear views of the foothills to the east and Humboldt Bay to the west, until we turned into the foothills after thirty minutes.

At Rio Dell, we crossed the Eel River, then passed Scotia, the old mill town that had once processed the giant old-growth redwoods. Now it was relegated to second- and third-growth redwood trees. The mill was visible from the highway, with buildings the size of airport hangars, and yards filled with small mountains of logs and row after row of stacked lumber. The mill workers lived with their families in neighborhoods of indistinguishable company houses.

At each bridge we crossed, we caught glimpses of the Eel River's muddy water and wide gravel banks. We passed a sign showing the Eel's high-water mark during the 1964 flood, which had destroyed most of the small towns along this stretch of Highway 101. The residents had tried to rebuild afterward, but the towns were never the same.

After Scotia, the cow pastures were replaced by giant redwoods, and the road resembled a river cutting through a sheer, three-hundred-foot gorge.

I turned the stereo down and said to April, "July's old professor boyfriend called you *unconsciously self-deprecating*."

April laughed and said, "What? Really? That sounds like an insult."

"I think it was."

"That's great. What an ass."

"Then Ted told me July was calling him about gift taxes."

"Gift taxes?"

"Yeah. She was either planning on giving someone cash or receiving it. Any ideas which?"

"No. That's bizarre."

"Did she have a lot of money?" I said. "Was she spending a lot before she disappeared?"

"Not really. She had enough to put herself through community college without working, but I'm pretty sure it was all leftover from when she ran pot for Jared."

"Maybe she kept that in the safe-deposit box, and not bonds."

"Maybe," April said.

"You said she checked her safe-deposit box that day. That means she could have taken it all out then if that was where she kept it."

April turned off the stereo. "We should save this conversation for my dad," she said.

"Why?"

"Because he would like it, and it's his birthday. He's obsessed with finding my sister. When she disappeared, he kind of lost it. I mean, he was a drunk after my mom left him—you saw him—but after July, he got worse. He quit crabbing and moved to southern Humboldt just so he could be closer to where they found her car, so it would be easier for him to look for her. Every week he's out in the woods calling her name. He doesn't have a job. He lives off social security from an old back injury. All the growers know him, everyone down there knows him. That's how he doesn't get shot when he's wandering around on people's land. *He's the crazy old drunk looking for his daughter. Let him pass. Look how sad he is.*"

As we drove south, the highway veered farther and farther inland, skirting around the Lost Coast and the King Range mountains. We took the Meyers Flat exit onto the Avenue of the Giants, a thirty-one mile stretch of the old highway running parallel to Highway 101. The road was narrow and wound through groves of redwoods, some of which stood almost three-hundred-feet tall. The canopy blocked out the sun and there was a mist hovering overhead in the branches.

My phone vibrated in my pocket. I pulled it out. The number belonged to Becky, the woman Ted had told me took a picture of July in Mexico. She must've finally got my voicemails.

"Hi," I answered. "Did you get my message?"

"Yeah," responded a high-pitched, mousy voice. "I don't get good phone service out here."

"Ted told me you have a fairly recent picture of July."

"What?" April said, and pulled the car over.

I held my hand up to her and mouthed, "Hold on."

"I don't know," Becky said. "I never met her before, but that's what Ted says, and so does Jared, and he would know."

"Do you think I could take a look at it?"

"I don't care."

"Do you think you could email it to me?"

"No."

"Okay. How do you want to do it?" I said.

"These are very personal pictures. I erased all the digital copies. You can come over and look at it but I'm not letting it out of my sight. I wasn't even going to call you back, but Krista said you were her cousin and told me to invite you up."

"She said I was her cousin?"

"Yeah. Why? Was that a secret or something?"

I made a split decision to play along. "No, no. But I'd love to see her. You live out in Ettersburg, right?"

"Yeah. You got a pen? You're going to need directions."

I got a pen and an old receipt out of April's glove box and wrote while Becky told me when to take a left and when to take a right. She described bridges, odd-shaped rocks, burnt-out stumps, mailboxes . . . . I wrote it all down the best I could. "You're going to need to call before you come out," she said when she was through. "We get terrible phone service out here so you might need to call a few times. I check my phone twice a day usually."

"No problem," I said.

When I got off the phone, April scowled at me. "What picture are you talking about? And what does Krista Stapely have to do with it?"

"Ted told me someone he knows named Becky took a picture of July at a party in San Pancho, Mexico about two years ago."

"Did you see the picture?"

"Not yet."

"Ridiculous. What does Krista have to do with it."

"Not sure," I said. "Sounds like they live together, or something. Small world."

"That's Humboldt County."

"She told that girl Becky I was her cousin for some reason."

"Why?"

"Who knows? She's crazy. You remember her."

I hadn't seen Krista since high school. She had always acted like she and July were sisters, talking about how much she loved July and would do anything for her, even though the two had grown apart by high school. She used to ask July for outrageous favors, like rides to her boyfriend's house in the middle of a school night, or corroborating lies to mutual friends. One time she wanted July to be the decoy in a shoplifting scheme. When July refused, Krista lost her shit and yelled hurtful things about July's dead mother. Then, the next day at lunch, she asked for a bite of July's burrito like nothing had happened.

April said, "You're wasting your time looking at that picture."

"What if it's July?" I said.

"It's not her."

"I'd like to make sure."

"She wouldn't leave Sage. She just wouldn't."

12

Phillipsville

PHILLIPSVILLE WAS AT THE southern end of the Avenue of the Giants, where the ferns and old-growth redwoods gave way to oaks and madrones, and tall grass, still sun-scorched from last summer. The town took less than a minute to drive through. There was a volunteer fire department, a Post Office, an inn, a motor lodge, a market, a trailer park, and a twenty-foot-tall, carved wooden statue of a bearded, skinny man who looked like a prospector.

April pointed to a pear-shaped woman walking on the side of the road, wearing jeans and a purple and aquamarine windbreaker." That's Cricket. She's one of my dad's girlfriends."

"You want to pick her up?"

"No. She's got pills."

I looked. Cricket was holding a white pharmacy bag in her hand. The nearest pharmacy was almost ten miles away. She had either walked that distance or gotten a ride part of the way.

"I can't be there when my dad chops those pills up," April said. "Let's go get a coffee. We can come back after he's gotten high."

We drove a mile down the road and parked at the Chimney Tree Grill. Next to the grill was the Chimney Tree Inn, and next to that was the actual Chimney Tree, a redwood with a five-foot-tall door at the base of the trunk and two signs above that. One said, "Free," and the other said, "Hollowed out by fire and still alive! 92 feet tall in 1978."

The Chimney Tree Grill was a small place. There was one old man inside sitting at the counter. Since it wasn't raining, April insisted on sitting outside on the wooden deck, which had a view of the Eel River.

"It's freezing out here," I said after we had ordered our coffees. "Let's go back inside."

April said, "You should have worn warmer clothes. You look ridiculous in that fleece thing."

"This is a Patagonia fleece vest. My ex-wife gave this to me."

"People don't know what to think of you when you wear stuff like that. You confused the waitress."

"How did I confuse the waitress? What do you want me to wear, a flannel?"

"Sure," she said.

"This is called fashion. I can wear this for the morning commute or for brushing horses. It symbolizes my potential prowess as an outdoorsman while acknowledging my place in society."

She touched my arm and smiled. "Life isn't a J. Peterman catalog."

"Are you sure about that?"

She chuckled, then exaggerated a scowl. "Grown men don't wear things like that. You look like you killed a teddy bear for its hide."

The waitress came back with the coffee. April

dropped a spoonful of sugar into her cup and stirred.

"It pisses me off when people who don't know my sister say she's in Mexico fucking rock stars or something," April said, changing her tone. She brushed a few redwood needles off the table, then folded her napkin into a tiny square. "July never would have left Sage. If there was anyone on this earth that was born to have children, it was her. She used to spend hundreds of dollars on decorations for Sage's room. She changed them every three months or so, and that's not to mention the holidays. You should have seen Sage's face when he saw his room transformed into a jungle. Imagine that as a kid: seeing stuffed tigers and snakes and fake plants everywhere, and weird hats for you to wear, and toy guns and costumes. And July would dress up with him. She had a whole storage unit just for holding the decorations—pirate stuff, space stuff, cowboy stuff."

"Sounds like heaven for a kid," I said. "I always knew she would be a good mom. She used to treat me like her kid sometimes when we were in high school. She bought me presents all the time: video games, boxes of candy, baseball cards. She had that job at Kmart. I swear she must have been spending most of her paychecks on toys for me. She actually bought me action figures once, Ninja Turtles. I remember thinking it was kind of weird but . . . I don't know."

"She used to buy me toys too—My Little Pony— even when I was a teenager. I figured she was trying to make up for all the bad Christmases we had after Mom died. On my birthdays, she would plan treasure hunts for me just like our mom used to . . . ."

We finished our coffee, drove back toward Phillipsville, and turned onto a gravel driveway about a hundred yards before Deerhorn Market on the southern end of town.

"I have to warn you," April said, "Cricket's a little weird."

"What do you mean?" I said

"She's a psychic."

"Really?"

"My dad met her around when July disappeared. She had some theories about what had happened."

"I've never met a psychic."

"Working at the paper, you hear a lot from them. Every time someone goes missing, all the psychics come out of the woodwork."

A barking pit bull and a shepherd mix sprinted toward the SUV and followed us up the driveway to a one-story house with a green metal roof and plain wooden siding that had blackened in the sun. We pulled around back, gravel crunching beneath the slow-rolling tires, to a mother-in-law unit that matched the main house. There was a small garden in front of the porch with flowers and herbs and weeds.

April's dad, Rodney, opened the front door and studied the SUV. He must not have seen it before, because he didn't smile until he saw April step out with the cake container in her arms. He was missing a tooth and had pale blue, glassy eyes, a black and white mustache, and wiry, black and white hair that hung over the tops of his ears.

The Highwaymen song "American Remains," played from inside the house.

April set the cake on the porch and hugged her dad.

"Happy birthday, Daddy," she said.

"I can't believe it," he said, his voice high-pitched. He began to cry a little. "I can't believe it."

"I tried to call you but you don't answer your phone," she said.

He waved at the house. "I forget to take the damn ringer off silent."

The dogs were jumping on me and licking my hands. Cricket walked onto the porch, and I smiled and nodded at her. She urged everyone to come inside.

The front room had a small kitchen on one side and a living space on the other with a couch, end table, TV, and coffee table. The bedroom door was open across the room from me. A tin tray lay on the coffee table with a pair of short scissors and marijuana clippings inside. Next to it was an ashtray holding a few roaches and a pile of cigarette butts. Red curtains covered the windows. A yellow sheet covered the couch. There were black stains on the sheet. I could see and smell dog hair.

Cricket asked for April to sit on the couch, me to stand in the corner, and Rodney to sit on a kitchen chair in front of April. Everyone did what she said. Then, when I shifted my weight to one leg, Cricket noticed and said, "No. Stand up straight. You have to stand up straight for it to work." Her eyes were glassy too.

April said, "You remember Tim, don't you, Dad?"

Rodney looked at me for the first time. "Yeah, I remember."

"Happy Birthday," I said.

"I still got Ju-Ju's prom picture with you," he said. "Come sit down over here. Sit on the couch. Have a drink."

"No, he has to stand," Cricket said.

"Damn it!" Rodney said, spit flying out of his mouth. "My daughter's visiting. Don't tell my family what to do. I will knock you down. Get the hell out of here."

"Fine," Cricket said. "I'm taking everything with me then."

"I don't give a shit."

Cricket went into the bedroom and came out carrying something under her coat. "It was good seeing you April," she said before walking out the front door.

Rodney went over to the counter and grabbed a bottle of E & J Brandy and three glasses. He set the glasses on the coffee table and poured three drinks. "Have a drink. Don't be shy."

"I hate brandy, Dad," April said. "Why do you have to be such an asshole to Cricket?"

"No one tells my family what to do." He turned to me. "Just because some of these old ladies down here let me plug away at them sometimes, doesn't mean they can tell my family what to do."

I took my brandy in one gulp.

Rodney laughed at the face I made. "Now we're talking." He opened the cake box and fought back tears again. "Carrot cake. Your mother used to make this for me."

April got up and rummaged through some drawers and cupboards in the kitchen and came back to the coffee table with three plates, three forks, and a knife.

"Why are you slamming everything?" Rodney said.

April cut and served the cake, and said, "Tim's been looking into July's disappearance."

Rodney leaned back in his chair, stuck his chin into his neck, and looked at me. "Why?"

"I thought I could help."

"Why?"

"Because I want to."

Rodney stood up like he forgot something, went into the bedroom, and came out unfolding a large map. He laid the map over a pile of clothes on the floor next to us. Large areas had been shaded with a black marker. While April and I ate our first bites of cake, he pointed to the shaded areas and said, "These are all the places I've searched so far. Cricket thinks I should look here next, but a new guy just bought the property and I haven't been able to get a hold of him."

He reached over and scratched the shepherd mix sitting beside him. "I trained these dogs as cadaver dogs. They've been all over these hills with me. They found bones too, but not July's." He cackled a little. "You better believe they found bones in these hills. Good girls."

He got up and opened a cupboard in the kitchen and pulled out a bottle of wine. "This is a fifty-dollar bottle of wine. The owner of Whitethorn Vineyards gave this to me." Rodney couldn't find a corkscrew, so he pushed the cork inside the bottle with the handle of a butter knife and poured three glasses.

He said, "I talked to someone who saw a sheriff's car the night July disappeared, close to where they found July's car. If you're going to look into someone you should talk to Lou Da Rocha. He's a deputy. I never trusted that Portuguese fuck. Cricket says he has nothing to do with it, but . . . I didn't like how July acted when they were together. She was quiet around him. It wasn't right. I could tell, a father can tell. That guy was bad."

"I played basketball against Lou in high school. He always seemed like an asshole to me."

Rodney laughed and slapped me on the back and filled my glass to the brim. I took a long sip and said,

"How long was July with him?"

"About a year and a half."

"July broke it off?"

"Yes," April said. "When he went away for work. He was a corrections officer back then."

"How long had they been broken up before she went missing?"

"About a year."

I looked at Rodney. "You think he never got over the breakup?"

"No, I don't think he did," he said. "I know they said he had an alibi, but that can be faked. They just didn't find any evidence against him. They should have checked the mileage on his squad car."

April drank one glass of wine while Rodney and I finished the bottle in twenty minutes. Rodney got drunk fast. I don't think alcohol ever left his system, so it didn't take much. Add pills on top of that, and he was soon crying about his cat named Max, who had been missing for two days.

"You should lie down for a little bit, Dad," April said.

"I'm not lying down," he said. "Carter's supposed to meet me at the market to play checkers. I'm going down to the market." Rodney got up slowly.

"Dad. Come on. I'm visiting. Let's stay here."

"I told Carter I would meet him down there, Honey. Come with me. Let's all go." His eyes lit up. "We can have a tournament."

After Rodney threatened to walk to the market, April agreed to give him a ride. The first time we left, though, the dogs followed us, and we had to turn back and lock them in the house.

Rodney was trying to call Cricket on April's cell

phone when we pulled into the parking lot. He gave up after seeing a man on a bench with a few tall cans of beer in paper bags sitting beside him. The man was about Rodney's age.

"There's Carter," Rodney said. He got out and waved at Carter. "We drank that bottle of wine."

"No shit?" Carter said. "Where was I?"

Rodney introduced me and April to him, then the two of them made fun of each other for a few minutes, with Carter saying things like, "Your dad can't even cook Top Ramen."

April hugged her dad once more, and he cried a little but recovered quickly. He was smiling and waving by the time we drove off.

13

Fernbridge

AT TWO IN THE afternoon, we merged onto northbound Highway 101 and headed back.

"Thanks for coming with me," April said. "Sorry about my dad."

"No problem," I said. "I like doing things for pretty girls as much as the next guy."

She smiled. "Oh yeah? That reminds me. One of the dancers in the play had to drop out. You think you could take his place? You don't have to sing. You just have to dress up and hop around a little."

I shook my head. "I don't want to do that."

"Come on. It'll be fun. Your friend Levi's in it."

"Really?"

"His girlfriend talked him into it. She's one of the dancers."

"Wow," I said. "Levi must be hooked."

"What's wrong with that?"

"Nothing. She sounds nice."

"She is nice."

A few moments passed while we listened to the radio in silence. Then I said, "Sounds like your dad's got it in for Lou Da Rocha."

"I guess," April said. "That must be a new theory of his—maybe to annoy Cricket. I didn't want to argue with him, but Lou wasn't a deputy sheriff back then. He was a guard at the county jail. So if there was a sheriff's car in the area it had nothing to do with him."

"He was an ex-boyfriend, though. In my experience, it's very often the ex-boyfriend."

"Yeah, but they'd been broken up for over a year. Jared was the psychopath ex. And the one who had a baby with her."

"That's true," I said. "I'm just saying Lou isn't that outlandish a theory."

April shrugged. "No, I guess not. You want to go see him? I know where he lives. It's on the way."

"Sure. Let's go."

April looked at me with a smile. "I was just joking."

"Why not? It won't take long. How do you know where he lives?"

"He married a college friend of mine. I went to one of their kids' first birthday parties, but I lost touch after that. We're still friends on Facebook, but I don't really like Lou. He's kind of an ass. But we can go. Let's go. I want to."

We continued north for forty more minutes, then got off the highway at the Ferndale exit. When we reached the Humboldt Creamery building overlooking the banks of the Eel River, we took a left and drove over Fernbridge, which had been built out of concrete over a hundred years ago, and we headed toward Ferndale.

Ferndale had two nicknames: Cream City and the Victorian Village—Cream City because of all the dairy farms, and the Victorian Village because of the remarkable turn-of-the-century architecture. Going down Main Street was like traveling back in time. The beautiful old homes, with their gables and ornate trim, had been built with dairy money and were called Butterfat Palaces.

We drove past three miles of cow fields before reaching the Victorians, then we turned at the high school. Half a mile down the road, and out of sight of Main Street, the Victorians gave way to ranch houses. We parked in the driveway of a red one, got out, and walked through the front gate. Abalone shells lined the concrete walkway.

A neighbor checking his mail turned and hollered at us.

"What?" I said.

"They're not home," he said. "They went shooting down at the river bar."

"Thanks."

The river bar he was talking about was under Fernbridge. Locals went down there to shoot their guns and ride quads. High schoolers went down there to throw parties. In a few weeks, the rains would start in earnest, and the river would swell, and the locals would have to take their quads and guns somewhere else.

We got in April's SUV and drove back through the cow fields toward the Eel River. A frontage road led to a dirt parking lot at the foot of the bridge. April stopped the SUV at the top of the road leading down to the river. The road was wet and slick and had deep potholes.

"I don't have four-wheel drive," April said.

"What kind of SUV is this?"

"It's a crossover."

We parked and got out to walk. The sounds of

sporadic gun shots and revving two-stroke engines came up the banks from the gravel bar. We took small steps on the steep, slick, clay road. Overhead, cars and semis ka-chunked over each section of the hundred-year-old concrete bridge. Alders and river willows lined the bank.

We walked under the bridge. A line of trucks was parked on the gravel bar, each truck fifty yards from the next. Quads spun brodies closer to the water's edge. There were coolers, plastic fold-out tables, and people holding, loading, shooting guns.

We walked by the first two trucks, by a kid with a shotgun and one with a bow, by half-burned couches and mattresses, by broken glass and spent shell casings mixed in with the gravel. Various targets lined the bank. People shot at an old blown-out TV, a dartboard, a hairless doll, a football helmet, pizza boxes, cans, and bottles of beer and soda. Most people were smiling, though their expressions turned severe when they got ready to shoot.

Lou was leaning against the third truck in the line, a new Dodge truck, watching a black-haired boy around fourteen fire a pistol toward the bank at a poster of a featureless black body with concentric circles centered on the chest. A boy around four sat on the tailgate swinging his legs. There were yellow plugs in his ears. He tapped on an iPad or something lying in his lap, like he was playing a video game. Lou's wife, who was pregnant enough to cradle her stomach when she walked, recognized April and came over smiling. They hugged.

"How much longer?" April said.

"A month maybe."

"I bet you can't wait to get her out."

"Oh my God, I'm counting the hours."

April introduced us. Her name was Beth. We shook hands. She had beautiful, round, brown eyes and long eyelashes. Her skin was smooth and clear.

Lou grabbed two beers out of a blue cooler and walked toward us, smiling. He was swarthy and tall, maybe six-three, with thick black eyebrows and ten extra pounds around the waist. He had a cop's crew cut and bloated cheeks covered in dense stubble. In high school, he had been the best basketball player for Arcata High, our rivals. He had also been their starting quarterback. He was a year older than me.

Lou handed me and April a beer. "Look at you," he said, smiling at April. "Staying out of trouble I hope." He slapped me on the shoulder. "I remember this guy. He liked to throw the elbows."

"I did?"

"In the post. I remember you. Always with the elbows."

"That's part of the game," I said.

"It is the way you play. I heard about your little incident in San Francisco. I laughed so hard. I was like, man, I know that guy, and it seems about right too. How are you doing anyway? You still see big Ron around?"

"Sometimes."

"You guys should have come last weekend. We had a town-wide yard sale."

"That must have been fun," I said.

"Not for me. I had to work. Well, actually, volunteer. A few people drank too much. The same people every time. Not too bad though. Not too bad."

"What are you guys up to?" Beth said.

"We were just driving back from my dad's," April

said. "It was his birthday today." April looked at the ground and a pained smile twisted her face. "Um, I guess this is kind of weirder than I thought it was going to be. Tim has been looking into my sister's disappearance, and we were driving by and we just thought about . . . . We wanted to ask Lou a few questions if that was okay with you guys."

There was confusion in Beth's eyes at first, then nothing but sympathy. "Of course," she said. "Of course."

"I'm sorry," April said. "I wasn't even thinking about it being Saturday and family time and stuff."

"It's okay."

"I don't usually make a habit of talking about my ex-girlfriends around my wife," Lou said, and nudged me in the side with his elbow. "She might get jealous."

"Oh, stop it, Lou," Beth said. "Grow up. What if it was your sister?"

"I'm just kidding," Lou said. "Anything you want to know, just shoot." Lou slapped me on the shoulder. "Look at the gumshoe over here. You've always been a scrappy little guy, haven't you? Taking on the hard-luck cases, huh? Pro-bono as they say. Free of charge. Like Mother Teresa."

"I wouldn't go that far," I said.

April pointed to the fourteen-year-old with the gun. "Who's this?"

"That's my nephew, Kenny," Beth said.

April called to the nephew, "When's it my turn?"

Kenny gave a shy smile, and Beth and April walked over to him. He handed April the gun, and April squeezed off a rapid seven shots at the target.

"Goddamn," Lou said, and laughed. "Don't get her mad." He seemed like he was more than a few beers in.

While April reloaded, I said, "When was the last time you saw July?"

Lou looked at me, swallowed a gulp of beer, then looked up at the sky. "About a month before she went missing. At Lost Coast Brewery."

"You talk to her?"

He frowned, stuck out his lower lip, and shook his head.

"You ever meet Ryan Lowell? He was July's boyfriend at the time."

"No. Don't know him."

"He thinks July was cheating on him. She didn't tell anyone where she was going that night, and there was unopened liquor in her car. And she wasn't the type of girl to drive two hours into the woods to drink alone. She was meeting someone. Do you have any idea who that might be?"

Lou shook his head again. "It could have been anyone. July liked it fast and loud." He smirked and nudged me with his elbow again. "Life, that is. Fast and loud. She was in with the growers and their hangers-on: cokeheads, pill-poppers, hippies, psychopaths. She could have been meeting anyone out there."

"You think Jared Tidwell had anything to do with it?"

"Speaking of psychopaths. That's a start. But if the cops didn't find anything on him, you're not going to."

"Why do you say he's a psychopath?"

"I used to hear stories about that guy back in high school, and he didn't even go to my school. Stories about raping girls, stabbing people. He's been arrested a few times that I've heard of, usually for beating the hell out of someone at the bars. But no one ever presses charges. You talk to anyone who knows the guy and they'll tell you the same thing: He's crazy."

I took out my phone, found the picture of Don Tidwell with a woman, a boy, and two girls that I had taken in Don's office, and I showed it to Lou. "You recognize any of these people?"

"No. Who are they?"

"That's Jared's dad. And that's Jared, but the rest are a mystery."

"I would stay away from that family if I were you. Stay away from southern Humboldt in general. They don't like strangers out there, and they don't like cops. They tend to take care of problems in their own way, usually with a gun and a backhoe. There's a lot of wilderness out there, a lot. No electricity in some cases. No phone service. No police. Just guns and drugs and people who aren't afraid to use either."

"I'm not planning on going anywhere uninvited."

"No one invited you here."

I cocked my head and looked up at him. "I didn't realize an invitation was required."

He laughed and slapped a palm on my shoulder. "I'm just messing with you. You guys can come to dinner if you want. You want to come to dinner?"

"No, thank you," I said. "We ate already. Why did you and July break up, anyway?"

Lou smiled. "I transferred to Pelican Bay for a few months, and she wouldn't go with me. Then I came home one weekend to visit and she told me she'd found someone else. It was for the best."

"The person she left you for, was that Ryan Lowell, the professor?"

"I guess so."

"Where were you the night she disappeared?"

Lou shook his head. "Man, you sound professional,

almost like a cop. Maybe you should come be a sheriff with me."

"I wouldn't pass the background," I said. "Do you mind telling me where you were, or is it too personal?"

"No, not at all. I was at a dog training class with my old dog, Pinky. I would let you ask him, but he's been dead for two years." Lou laughed.

"Can I ask you one more question?"

"Sure."

"Do you think July's alive?"

Lou shrugged. "Anything's possible. It's possible she ran off with a member of the Mexican Mafia. Who knows? A girl like that doesn't want anything to do with normal. She wants to drink wine in the south of France and give handys in the back of Bentleys. She doesn't want to bake pies for her husband and watch Netflix on the couch. And there's a price to pay for that. There's a price to pay for everything. You know that."

Lou walked toward the truck. I followed. He grabbed another beer from the cooler and popped it.

April had finished shooting and moved on to the four-year-old on the tailgate. She asked the little boy questions like, "What are you playing?" and "Is that your favorite?" while Beth looked on, smiling.

We walked over.

"Frank," Lou said to the little child. "Frank. This is Tim. Shake his hand."

Frank looked up, showing me his big cheeks and button nose. When I put out my hand, Frank jerked his head away. I laughed and let my hand fall to my side.

"Ahh, he's shy," April said.

"Frank," Lou said. "Shake his hand."

Frank didn't budge.

"Frank."

"Oh, just leave it," Beth said.

"The boy needs to learn," Lou said. Then, in a lower tone: "Shake the man's hand, Frank."

"Oh God, Lou," Beth said.

Lou raised his voice: "Frank."

Frank turned to me, head down, and stuck out his hand. I grabbed it with a thumb and two fingers. He shook, let go, and said in a tiny voice: "You shake like a girl."

Lou laughed like the joke was new to him and patted Frank on the back. "That's my boy," he said. "That's my boy."

"Well," April said, facing Beth. "We should leave you guys alone now. Sorry to bother you on your Saturday."

"Nonsense," Beth said.

April and Beth hugged and promised to keep in touch. Lou shook my hand and said, "Hey, my kid was right." Another slap on the back. "Just messing with you. You guys have a good one, huh."

April and I walked back toward the dirt parking lot. We passed two families packing up their trucks, and a laughing group of men building a fire. The light was fading, and the naked willows and alders lining the banks were silhouetted black against the pale blue sky. The gun shots were farther apart than they had been when we'd arrived.

14

Redway

ON THE MONDAY BEFORE Thanksgiving, I left work at 11 a.m. and called Becky to let her know I was on my way, having already okayed it with her the night before. She answered on the first try this time, reiterated the most important landmarks to look out for, and said it would take me about two hours to get to her place from Eureka.

I merged onto Highway 101 and followed the Eel River south through the redwoods, as April and I had done on the Saturday before. The fog was thick, and I took it slow. I drove for an hour before getting off the highway at the Redway exit, five minutes past Phillipsville and April's dad's house.

Redway was one of the larger towns in southern Humboldt, with a grocery store, hardware store, a diner, a small pizza joint, and two garden supply centers, catering to the local marijuana industry, with pallets of soil stacked outside the gates. The Green Rush had dramatically increased the demand for soils, pots, drip lines, insecticides, and all the rest of the items needed for a successful crop. Garden supply stores were popping up everywhere. Trucks carrying pallets of soil and huge water tanks ran constantly up and down the highways. Growers sought out the advice of fertilizer gurus and compost-tea wizards, anything to get an edge.

I turned west on Briceland-Thorn Road, heading toward the Lost Coast. The road cut through a residential neighborhood before crossing the south fork of the Eel River and passing through a small redwood grove. The road was windy and narrow. In several turnouts, I saw torn trash bags and scattered garbage. Occasionally, the trees lining the road thinned, and I caught glimpses of the surrounding hills.

I passed a cluster of houses called Briceland and a sign for a vineyard that went by the same name. The vineyard where April's dad had gotten his nice bottle of wine was farther up the road.

I drove up and down hills, following curves and switchbacks. There was very little traffic. The vehicles I did see were all pickup trucks—massive ones with all the aftermarket extras: brush guards, customized grills, bolt-on fender flares, rims, roll bars, bed liners, lift kits. Levi called them grow-dozers, because in Humboldt County, for the most part, only marijuana growers could afford them.

The oncoming grow-dozers squealed their tires around turns and drifted into my lane. The ones behind me rode my ass until I pulled over.

Every five miles or so I passed a makeshift memorial lying on the side of the road—flowers, candles, a sign saying, "We love you Kate," or "We miss you David"—marking the spot where someone was killed in an accident.

July's missing posters were on every fourth telephone pole. Her father didn't let anyone forget. I saw one with writing on it and pulled over to take a look. Someone had scratched "whore" across July's face. I ripped it down. Looking at her pixilated face, into her pixilated eyes, I choked up. I felt irrational, like a part of her was in the poster, like we had left her out here, on the side of the road, alone, undefended.

About twenty minutes from Redway, I came to a fork in the road and a sign with an arrow pointing left for Whitethorn and Shelter Cove, and another arrow pointing right for Ettersburg. Like all the road signs I had seen out here, it was peppered with buckshot and bullet holes.

I turned right, and the road climbed and narrowed even more. I drove over jarring, traction-stealing potholes. There was an embankment on my side and an increasing drop on the other—no guardrails, no centerline.

As I went into a turn, a grow-dozer came in from the other side. I tightened my grip on the steering wheel and hugged the embankment. Underbrush scraped the side of my BMW as the truck roared out of the turn, spewing exhaust. There had barely been enough room for both of us. From then on I crept around each corner, craning my neck and straining my ears.

There were no signs for residential roads out here, but Becky had given me good directions. I turned right onto the dirt road just before the first bridge after the fork. I took another right after crossing a creek over a one-lane wooden bridge that looked like a deck that belonged in someone's backyard. The road wound up the hill for a mile and a half, and I took the first left after seeing a small water tower. After a while, a truck came bouncing down the road in front of me. The man driving hung his head and arm out the window. When he got close, he raised a palm, and we stopped beside each other. I rolled down my window. He scowled at me. He was young.

"This is a private road," he said. "You can't be here."

"I'm meeting someone," I said.

"Who?"

"Krista Stapely."

"There's no Krista Stapely on this road."

"Okay. Do you know which road she's on?"

"This is a private road. You need to turn around." The young man held up a handgun next to his face.

"All right," I said.

I drove ahead a ways, performed a seven-point turn, and followed him back down to the bridge. He pulled aside, and I passed and turned back onto the main road. I parked at the first turnout I came to and tried to call Becky, but there was no signal. I did not find a signal again until I was back in Redway.

I parked at the grocery store in town and sat in my car for thirty minutes, getting Becky's voicemail over and over, while I watched a group of transients on the corner sitting with their dogs, drinking forties out of paper bags and holding a sign that said, "Got Trimmers?" Levi called them trimigrants. They came here during harvest season, looking for work trimming the excess marijuana leaves from the bud.

A lot of people from all walks of life trimmed during the fall harvest to pick up a little extra cash. Levi did it between gigs. Growers paid two hundred dollars for every pound of trimmed bud. The best trimmer Levi had ever seen could trim a pound in five hours.

As I tried Becky for the twentieth time, I remembered something else Levi had told me. Ron, the drummer in my old band, and the one who had gotten Levi the job installing satellite dishes, lived in Redway.

I called him up, and we caught up for a bit: he had a wife and two daughters, and I was a disgraced lawyer. After trading a few funny stories about Levi and trying to analyze his behavior, I told him what had happened to me in Ettersburg.

"What were you thinking?" he said.

"The girl invited me up."

"Then have her meet you at the bottom of the road."

"She doesn't have service up there."

"Jesus. Who is it?"

"Her name's Becky. I don't know her last name. But Krista lives there, too. You remember Krista?"

"Oh yeah. I know where you're talking about. I set up their system."

"Maybe you could give me a ride up there," I said. "No one will stop us in your work truck, right?"

"No, they won't. They all know me around here. I can give you a ride in the morning if you want. I'm going up that way tomorrow anyway. Come over. I'm barbequing. You can stay the night in my RV."

It sounded like a plan to me. Ron lived in the neighborhood across from the garden supply center on the north end of town. I drove five minutes to his house and parked behind his RV in the driveway. He heard me pull up and greeted me at the front door. There was a lump in his upper-lip where he kept his tobacco, and an old plastic Pepsi bottle in his right hand where he kept his chew-spit. He wore a camouflage baseball cap, and he smiled at me, but not all the way. He didn't want to disturb the tobacco.

I hugged him, and he introduced me to his wife,

Carol, and their two daughters, Emma, four, and Melissa, nine. The girls were both shy and spied on me from behind doors, tables, and chairs, while I got the tour of the house. When we reached Ron's bar on the back porch, Carol told us she was leaving for the store. She took the girls with her, and I could hear them broaching the subject of ice cream as they walked out.

Ron scooted behind the bar and asked what I was drinking. I told him whiskey and beer, and he poured a serving of each for both of us. We drank that round and had another, and then another, while we told old stories. An hour later, we were on the present:

"So you move back home," he said, "and instead of looking up your old girlfriends like everybody else, you start looking up your dead girlfriend." He laughed.

The sun was going down when Carol came home with the groceries. Ron got the charcoal going and barbecued chicken thighs, corn, and hot dogs.

"It's never too cold to barbeque," he said after his youngest daughter, Emma, had complained. "I'm going to barbeque Christmas dinner this year."

"Noooo," she said. "You can't do that."

"Why not?" he said teasing her.

After dinner, Ron and I started talking about the old band, and Carol escaped to the bedroom to watch TV. The girls stayed and watched while I tried to play our band's original songs on the piano in the living room, and their father struggled to remember the lyrics. We spent twenty minutes on that before Ron got up and grabbed an accordion out of the hall closet.

"I picked this up at a garage sale," he said. He strapped it around his neck and began to play. He didn't sound bad. I asked him what key he was playing in, and he shrugged, so I accompanied him on the piano the best I could.

His oldest daughter covered her ears and yelled, "Mommm. Dad's drunk. He's playing the accordion again."

Ron lifted his chin and closed his eyes. The corners of his lips curled into a smile as he pumped away. I smiled with him. His daughters ran out of the room.

15

Ettersburg

THE NEXT MORNING, RON woke me up banging on the RV door, then entered holding a coffee mug.

Forty-five minutes later, we were on the road, with me crammed into the passenger seat of Ron's little work truck, a tool belt and drill resting against my left arm, and boxes beneath my feet.

"I can't believe how long you took in the bathroom," Ron said, driving down Briceland-Thorn Road faster than any of the grow-dozers I had seen the day before. Around each turn, the equipment stored in the bed of the truck crashed against the camper-shell walls.

Ron pointed to a car parked in a turnout just before the fork between Whitethorn and Ettersburg. "You could have called me from there," he said. "That's the only spot with service on this road. Everyone comes down to make calls there."

I tried to call Becky again, but Ron was driving too fast and the signal was already gone. I had been trying her since I woke up with no luck.

Ron had two dish installations in the Ettersburg

area that day. Because I didn't want to show up at Becky's before nine in the morning without getting ahold of her, I asked Ron if I could tag along for the first install. He didn't mind, and we made a quick plan for him to drop me at Becky's on the way to his second job and pick me up on his way home.

There was no town of Ettersburg that I could see, only a small grammar school surrounded by forest. We passed it and Becky's road, crossed the Mattole River, and drove almost ten miles toward the town of Honeydew before turning onto a gravel driveway shaded by oak trees. We rolled up to a long ranch house with a large parking area in front that sloped into a pond the size of half a football field. I assumed the greenhouses were located farther down the driveway.

Ron gave me a company hat so I looked official, and he put me to work digging a posthole. I had been digging for ten minutes when men pulled up from down the driveway in a tractor, two four-wheelers, and two souped-up, four-wheel-drive golf carts with roll cages called UTV's. They parked next to Ron's truck. Six men got out and walked to the house, speaking what sounded like Russian to each other.

The installation took almost two hours, and when we were done, a man in sweatpants gave us each a plastic bag full of marijuana—about two eighths all together. "We have party soon," he said in his strong accent. "On thirtieth. You come back. Big harvest party. We have good hookers this time. You come."

I nodded, and to be nice, Ron said he would if his wife was out of town that weekend. Then we both got back in the truck and drove off.

We stopped at the nearest turnout for a piss and a snack, then continued toward Ettersburg, crossing back over the Mattole River, and taking a left onto Becky's road. We got a little farther than I had the day before when a truck appeared from over a hill and drove toward us, swaying gently over the potholes. The truck kept its slow pace, and the driver nodded as he passed.

"So you never get hassled?" I said.

"No. Never. I've installed or fixed most of the dishes in these hills. These people know me. They know where I live."

Becky's driveway was the first right after a burnt-out stump that looked like, in her words, "a vagina or an evil fairy castle, whatever floats your boat." It looked like neither to me, and I don't consider myself lacking in imagination. If I had been alone, recognizing that stump might have lost me hours.

Ron parked near the opening of the driveway, outside a heavy-duty, steel barrier gate.

I checked my phone for a signal: nothing.

"What now?" I said.

"We wait," Ron said. "It shouldn't be long." He pointed to a white plastic cylinder attached to a small tree on our side of the gate. "That's a motion sensor." He let off the brake and the truck lurched forward. "Every time we move, an annoying alarm goes off in their house."

No more than five minutes later, a black grow-dozer pulled up to the gate and two men hopped out. The driver walked toward us, smiling, while the passenger walked toward the gate. "You Tim?" the driver said. He was of average height, with a small gut and a wide face. He wore board shorts, a red plaid shirt, sunglasses, and a green baseball cap. His arms were covered in tattoos.

I got out of the truck. "Yeah," I said.

"Becky said you were coming yesterday," he said and stuck out his hand.

We shook.

"I'm Mike," he said. "Krista's boyfriend. I own the place."

"Nice to meet you," I said. "I tried coming yesterday but I got stopped by your neighborhood watch."

Mike turned his palms up. "Comes with the territory, man, sorry. Who stopped you? What did he look like?"

I described the man.

"That was probably Craig." Mike turned to Ron, who was resting his forearms on the roof of the truck. "What the hell is this guy doing here? I don't need my TV fixed."

Ron smiled. "I run a taxi service now. Didn't you hear?"

"I asked him to give me a ride," I said. "We're old friends."

"I'm heading over to Kev and Nat's place," Ron said to Mike.

A few minutes of small talk was exchanged about Kev and Nat, then Mike grabbed a walkie-talkie from his truck and said, "Someone tell Becky to come to the gate and give Tim a ride down." Then he looked at me. "I'd give you a ride but I gotta make a supply run to Eureka. Thank God for Costco. Nothing like giant chocolate cakes to tame the womenfolk."

I nodded like I knew what he was talking about.

Becky arrived on a UTV shortly after Ron and Mike had left. She was skinny and young, between maybe twenty and twenty-three, with a small head and blond hair in a ponytail. She wore sheepskin boots, a zip-up hoodie, and sweatpants with the waist rolled down to her panty line so that, even sitting down, a small strip of skin below her bellybutton was exposed.

"Why didn't you come yesterday?" she said, sounding put out.

I told her what had happened.

"You should have come anyway," she said. "I told you you could."

"The guy had a gun."

"Yeah, but I told you you could come."

I thought on that for a brief moment and decided not to respond.

As I climbed into the passenger seat of the UTV, Becky popped it into gear, and we took off with a jerk. She did not swerve or brake for potholes. I was bounced out of my seat and slammed back down over and over.

After a quarter-mile, we came out of the trees and into a clearing. The driveway split at a white, two-car garage with what looked like a living space above it. Four tents were set up on one side. A truck and another UTV were parked out front.

To the left, the driveway turned one hundred and eighty degrees down a steep hill, then veered right and stopped at a large, two-story house with a green metal roof, plain wood siding, and a wrap-around deck. A forest of oaks and firs grew behind it.

The driveway to the right of the garage continued toward more trees.

Becky parked at the garage next to a running generator. The exhaust mixed with the pungent, skunky smell of marijuana.

"I have to do something here for a second," she said.

"Okay," I said.

She walked to the side door of the garage and turned to me. "Don't sit there like a weirdo. Come in."

I walked into a small foyer, with a door on my left and a narrow staircase ahead that had naked drywall on either side. A cloud of smoke lingered at the top of the stairs. I could hear reggae hip hop playing while people laughed and talked.

I followed Becky up toward the smoke and noise and into an open room. A bathroom and kitchen shared the wall to my left. The counters were cluttered with paper plates, frozen pizza boxes, liquor bottles, Hot Pocket sleeves, and a cardboard tray full of muffins. Two windows on the far wall looked onto the driveway, so that anyone could see who was coming and going.

In the center of the room, over a dozen men and women between seventeen and thirty, with haircuts ranging from dreadlocks to shaved heads, sat at three foldout tables trimming pot out of trays. Paper grocery bags full of buds sat at their feet. Names had been written on the bags in black marker. Small pot leaves were strewn all over the tables and floors, and each table had two foam cups that had been cut in half and filled with what looked like oil.

"This is Krista's cousin, Tim," Becky said.

Everyone sitting at the tables looked up at me.

"Krista's cousin's kind of hot," one of the women said.

"Shut up you slut," another said.

Everyone laughed.

"I'm weighing you guys up real quick," Becky said. She placed a notepad and an electronic scale on the end of one of the tables. After calibrating the scale with an empty paper bag, she weighed the bag belonging to the woman closest to her. "One ounce," she said, and marked it on her notepad. A few people ribbed the woman, saying she was lazy and smoked more than she trimmed. Becky moved to the next bag.

I sat in an empty chair next to a kid who handed me a pair of trimming scissors and a branch that was heavy with buds.

"Thanks," I said. I had nothing better to do while Becky worked, so I picked up the scissors and the branch and started cutting.

The trimmed buds were light-green, lumpy, and on average two inches long with the circumference of a small egg. They were sticky to touch and covered in reddish-blond hairs and tiny white crystals.

While I cut the buds from their stems and trimmed off their dry leaves, I talked to the kid who had given me the scissors. His name was Philippe, and he was from France. He had heard about the Humboldt trim scene back home and had planned his backpacking trip through California to coincide with it. He wore black carpel tunnel braces on his wrists, which he had brought from home, having read on the internet that trim work involved repetitive motion of the wrists and hands.

"You're lucky," Philippe said in a French accent. "The last batch was larfy. This is much better."

A man sitting across the table laughed and said, "Yeah Philippe. Catching on fast. You guys hear that? Philippe said *larfy*."

A few people laughed.

"What's larfy?"

"It means the bud has too much air, too many leaves," Philippe said. "It's harder to trim, and it takes longer, and it's light so it pays less."

While I trimmed, my fingertips and scissor blades became coated in sticky pot resin, which was black and olive, and the scissors started mashing the leaves instead of cutting them.

"Do this," Philippe said to me, dipping his scissors in the half-cup of oil on the table. "It helps. It cleans them."

The man across the table weighed in again: "Hell no. Just roll that shit up like this, man. It's finger hash." He rubbed his fingers together until the resin balled up, then he added it to a black, marble-sized lump sitting beside his tray. His eyes were half-closed, and he had a haughty smirk on his face. "This is the master blaster," he said. "You don't waste that shit." He pinched a chunk off of the black lump, placed it in a pipe, and smoked it.

When Becky was done weighing the bags and noting the results, she picked up two large plastic totes and told me to take one and follow her. The totes were empty except for a few dry twigs and marijuana leaves. We carried them downstairs and into the garage, where Becky turned on the lights. Half of the garage was empty. The other half was full of marijuana, row after row of branches weighted with buds that had been hung upside down from clothes hangers to dry. Along with the pungent, skunky smell, I could smell hay, which must have come from the dried stalks and stems.

"Aren't you guys trimming this stuff a little late?" I said. "It's almost Thanksgiving."

"So what?" she said. "The outdoor market's flooded after harvest, so we let a lot of it hang a while. We get a better price that way."

She picked the branches from the hangers and

tossed them into the totes until they were both full, and we carried them up to be processed.

I gathered the buds I had trimmed and threw them into Philippe's bag.

He looked concerned. "You don't want them?" he said.

"No, I'm just visiting."

He smiled. "Thank you."

On the way out, Becky had me pick up two trash bags full of stems and leaves. I carried them to the UTV and threw them in the back. "You're kind of bossy," I said to her.

"You should have come yesterday," she said. "We were partying yesterday. Now it's time to work."

I raised my eyebrows. "I guess I should have come yesterday."

We drove down to the house. Two men were on the lawn in front of the porch. One was working on a four-wheeler while the other watched. Becky emptied the bags into a burn pile.

"I don't know where Krista is," she said. "She might be inside."

"Do you think I could see that picture now?" I said.

"Why do you want to see that picture so bad? Are you some kind of pervert?"

"What? Why would that make me a pervert? I told you on the phone, July's family wants to know if she's alive."

"Well, it's in the house," she said, like the house was a bank vault.

"Okay. Can I see it?"

Without a word, she turned and walked toward the front door. I took that as a yes and followed. When we reached the porch, she told me to wait outside, so I sat down on one of the benches.

The two men occupied with the four-wheeler engine were on the lawn below me to my left.

"How's it going?" I said when they looked up.

"Bueno," one said. The other said nothing.

Besides the humming generator, everything was quiet. The sky was overcast, and the air was crisp. I could smell a fire burning inside.

I waited on the porch for ten minutes before Becky came out and handed me a black-and-white copy of the picture, which had been scanned and printed out on a letter-sized sheet of paper. The picture was of five naked adults having sex in a living room. A woman sat on a couch alone with her hand on her clitoris. Another woman lay on her back on the same couch with a man on top of her. A different man sat in a chair, peaking over the shoulder of a third woman, who was on top of him and facing the camera. Becky had blown up the picture so that it filled most of the paper. She had also scratched out the faces of both men and two of the women, along with their breasts, using a blue ballpoint pen. The only face not scratched out belonged to the woman on top of the man in the chair. There was an expression of both pain and pleasure on her face. She didn't look like July to me, but I wanted to show the picture to April to be positive.

"Now I see why you thought I was a pervert," I said. "Can I keep this?"

"No," Becky said.

"Who is the man having sex with the woman you think looks like July?"

"I didn't say she looked like July. I never met July. Ted and Jared said she looked like July."

I pointed to the man sitting in the chair. "Do you

know this man?"

"No."

"How did you get this picture? Did you take it?"

"No, a friend took it."

"Are you in this picture?"

"No, Jesus."

"Sorry, I'm just trying to figure out how I can double-check this. Would you mind if I talked with the friend that gave it to you?"

"That's not going to happen."

"If it has any chance of clearing up a missing person's case, of course you should show it to me. Did you give this to the police?"

"Fuck the police. I don't want those pigs sweating over this. Fuck them."

"At least let me keep this copy so I can show it to July's sister. You scratched out everyone's face."

"No."

"Here," I said. "Let's do this." I tore out the woman's face. "Now I just have her face. I'll throw it away after I show it to July's sister. What do you say? Can I keep this?"

Becky frowned. "Okay, but you better throw it away after you show it to her."

"I'll send you a video message of it burning," I said, and I slipped the torn-out face into my wallet. Then I handed Becky what was left of the picture.

"I told Krista you're here," she said. "Have fun on the porch." She walked down the steps, got in the UTV, and drove back up the driveway.

The two guys working on the four-wheeler looked at me.

"Was that a metaphor, or was she being literal?" I said.

16

Tidwell Property

A SOUND CAME FROM the end of the deck to my left. The door to a small wooden shed connected to the corner of the house swung open and steam poured out. Krista emerged from the steam and walked toward me. Her robe was open enough that I could see the bikini she wore underneath. She had a slightly upturned nose and thin, manicured eyebrows. Her bleach-blond hair was in a ponytail, and frizzy from the steam.

As she walked toward me, the eyes of the two mechanics never left her. The one that had been doing all the work crept over to a hose, picked it up, and sprayed Krista's bare feet with water. Krista squealed and jumped, then grabbed a brush from her robe pocket and flung it at the man, missing by four feet. She smiled and said, "Fuck you, Miguel."

The two men giggled.

Krista turned and appeared to see me for the first time. "Tim," she said. "You made it. I'm so glad."

I stood up, smiled. "How's it going?"

She hugged me. "I really missed you."

"Come on Krista. We didn't know each other that

well."

"I still missed you. Did you see the picture? Did Becky show it to you?"

"Yeah. Just a minute ago."

"What do you think?"

"It didn't look like her to me," I said, "but it's hard to tell with the face the girl's making."

"What, you never saw July make that face? You must have been doing it wrong then."

I laughed. "Do you think it's her?"

"No, of course not. July wasn't going to leave her son." Krista squinted and smirked while she talked, like a parent listening to their kid tell a harmless lie. "So Becky told me you were looking for proof that July was alive?"

"Or dead," I said.

"And that's because of some kind of assets?"

"Yes."

"Have you talked to Pete yet? You should talk to him. If anyone knows about July's assets it would be him."

"What do you mean?"

"He paid for everything for July. That man paid her rent, her cell phone, even for her community college classes. What kind of assets are we talking about anyway? And why now? Did April find some cash or something?"

"I can't talk about that Krista," I said, and waved my arm at the yard. "Looks like you're doing pretty well. This place is beautiful."

She nodded. "Oh yeah. For sure, for sure. I love it here. I have my sauna, you know, and it's just wonderful." She opened the front door of the house. "Come in."

There were two staircases, one on either side of the foyer, leading to second-story bedrooms. The sunken living room had vaulted ceilings and tall windows that looked onto the forest. A Harley Davidson motorcycle was parked next to a green wraparound couch that faced a flat-screen television.

Becky took off her robe and hung it in the closet by the front door, and I pretended not to watch her walk up the stairs in her blue bikini. Her skin was tan, and she had kept her body in shape.

"Take a seat on the couch," she said over her shoulder. "Just don't touch the Harley. That's Mike's baby. I swear he'd let that thing sleep in the bed with us if he could."

I sat on the corner of the couch next to an end table supporting three bongs, each a different size, shape, and color-pattern. Dozens of DVD and Blu-ray boxes were scattered across the coffee table and couch cushions.

"Why did you tell everyone I was your cousin?" I said, raising my voice so Krista could hear me from the second floor.

She laughed. "Did you like that? It was the only way I could help you. And I wanted to help you. For July. You would have never seen that picture if I hadn't told Becky that. People are very suspicious around here, especially during this time of year, and especially Mike, too. He gets a little jealous. And Becky is very protective of him. She's a little bulldog. They're cousins, but they're more like brother and sister."

"That's nice," I said.

When Krista came back downstairs, she was wearing a black puffy vest and black yoga pants. "Do you want something to drink?"

"No thank you," I said.

Krista grabbed a mug from the kitchen, sat next to me on the couch, and crossed her legs. I began asking her questions about July. She was fidgety, touching her hair, tapping her mug, rearranging the items on the coffee table, but she answered. I asked her about Don and Jared Tidwell first. They lived up the hill from her. She thought they were crazy, but they let some of the neighbors go on part of their property where the cell reception was good. Jared had a thing for Becky, but Becky didn't want anything to do with him. Krista had warned her about his fetish, which she had first heard about from July, who had stopped seeing him because of it. Jared was a crusher, someone, Krista explained, who got turned on by watching people crush random things, like cake or insects, against their body.

I asked her if she had ever heard of them abusing Sage, and she said she hadn't. Then I pulled up Don's photo on my phone, the one I had taken at his office in Stone Lagoon, and showed it to Krista. "Do you recognize any of these people?"

Krista took the phone from my hand and started pointing. "This is Don," she said, "and this is Jared. He has those crazy eyes even as a kid. And these two girls, I think, are his sisters, but I'm not sure. Mike says they live here, but I've never met them. And this woman—I recognize her from the grocery store in Redway."

"Is she Don's girlfriend? Wife?"

"No, his wife's our age. And Jared's mom is dead, I think. But there was a second wife between those two, and that could have been her. I don't know. You could ask her. She works at the store. She's there every time I go in. Her name's Candice. She's a real sweet old lady."

"When was the last time you saw July?" I said.

Krista leaned back. "A couple months before she went missing. I saw her in a grocery store. She was buying poppy seeds to make a cake."

"Did she ever say anything about cheating on the professor?"

"No. Never. She loved him as far as I know."

"She was meeting someone in secret that night," I said. "Do you have any idea who she was meeting? She wasn't found too far from here."

"I really have no idea. I wish I did." She took a sip from her mug.

"April thinks she might have been on her way to meet you."

Krista swallowed her sip just in time to laugh without spitting up. "Why? Because she had the stuff for Manhattans? Lots of people drink those."

"Yes, but none of her friends. Where were you that night?"

"Oh geez. Camping with my family." Krista stood up. "If you want to find out what happened to her, you should figure out a way to get a search warrant for the Tidwell property. Me and Miguel found this creepy little shack the other day, just up the trail from where we get cell reception, with rope in it like someone had been tied up there. Who knows what goes on up there. I think July is buried on that property somewhere."

"How far is it?" I said.

"Not too far. You want to see it?"

"Yes."

"You're the guest."

She led me out and around the side of the house, where another UTV was parked. We got in, and she drove us back up the driveway, through the gate, and up the gravel road a ways, then turned off onto a trail through trees and underbrush. Branches thwacked against the windshield and scraped over the roof. A trickling creek ran through the center of the trail. After a few minutes of slow climbing, we passed a "No Trespassing" sign, crossed the creek, and came to a small meadow.

"This is where half the hill comes to make calls," Krista said.

We followed another trail on the other side of the meadow into the trees along the crest of the hill. After a few bumpy minutes, we reached a one-room, windowless shack with walls made from one-by-six wood boards. Weather had bowed the wood over the years, partially prying some of the rusty nails out of the studs. Oak trees shaded the flat roof, which was covered in soil, dead leaves, grass, and dandelions. The door was held shut by a broken shingle that had been nailed to the threshold. I swiveled the shingle vertical and the door swung open toward me.

There was a filthy blue couch on one side of the room, with dingy white stuffing hanging out of tears in the cushions. Black garbage bags full of something had been piled across from it. A large, black ceramic cross hung on the far wall, surrounded by little drawings.

A rat darted into the garbage pile and made a rustling noise as I walked inside to get a better look. The cross was six feet from the floor, and the drawings were actually carvings, thousands of them, each no bigger than a nickel. They spread out from the cross four feet in both directions and a foot above and below. The outer carvings had yet to fade. They were all the same: a snake-like line with two small circles on either side.

Below the cross, near the floor, a steel handle had

been bolted into a stud. A rope was tied to the handle.

I took pictures of everything I saw and walked out, leaving the door how I had found it. Krista was not waiting for me in the UTV.

"Krista?" I said. "Krista." I searched around the shack. "Krista."

"What?" she said, coming out of the bushes near the trail. "I was going to the bathroom."

"We should go," I said.

"Did you see the drawings?"

"Yes."

"Creepy huh?" she said.

"Yeah. I don't know what to make of it. Come on, let's go."

Krista's eyes got big, and she smiled and made her whole body shiver. "You got the heebie-jeebies, don't you?"

"No." I lied. "Let's go."

We took the long, bumpy trail and road back to her place. As we pulled up, I heard a loud buzzing noise, like an old doorbell. Krista said it was the gate alarm. I told her it was probably Ron, and she agreed to give me a ride back up.

When we passed the trimmer garage, I heard a man yelling curse words from farther up, around the corner. After a few seconds, the cursing stopped, and Becky's voice crackled through the walkie-talkie sitting in the center console: "Krista, come to the gate now. Miguel, you too."

We turned the corner. Two men stood in front of a red truck parked outside the gate. Becky stood inside the gate next to a UTV. As we pulled up behind her, I recognized one of the men as Don Tidwell, and the other as his son, Jared, whose crazy blue eyes gave him away. They were the same as those of the boy in the picture.

Jared was my age, about five-eleven in height, with shoulder-length brown hair, sunken cheeks, and lean, sinewy arms I could see because he wore an old tank top. It was not warm out.

Krista and I both got out of the UTV.

"What's going on?" she said.

Don looked at me and smiled knowingly, then looked at Krista. "My daughter saw a man and a woman trespassing on our land," he said. "Scared the shit out of her. Do you know anything about that Krista?" He didn't wait for a response. He pointed at me. "Did you bring that cunt-rag onto my land?" He turned to his son. "That's the fucker who broke into my office."

Jared's facial muscles tightened as he stared at me.

"We were just making a call," Krista said. "I thought it was okay." She looked like she was about to cry.

"Don't lie to me girl," Don said. "What happens to this man now is on you."

Jared placed a palm on the gate, swung his legs over, and stomped toward me with his fists hanging at his sides. Don walked around the gate.

"Hey," Becky said. "Get back."

Jared was five yards away from me. "Stay out of this, Becky," he said. "I don't want you to get hurt."

Two yards.

"No," I said. "He just wants to crush beetles on you." It was the first time my instinct to make a joke had saved my life.

Jared stopped in front of me with a hurt look in his eyes. He turned to Krista, the one who gave up his secret, showing me his left cheek, and said: "You fucking bi—"

Before he could finish, and while his mouth was open, I reared back and whipped my right fist into his chin. His head snapped back, and he went limp and fell backward into the dirt. When I looked up, Don's fist was sailing toward my face. I ducked in time to catch it above the ear. The pain was sharp where the knuckles made contact, then dull and roaring as it spread through my brain. The next punch dropped me to one knee. I covered my head with my left arm, blocking the third punch, and threw my right fist into Don's crotch. He doubled over long enough for me to tackle him. As he tried to roll onto his stomach to get up, I knelt at his side and landed two solid punches near his left ribs and kidney.

He groaned.

He was moving slower now. I stood up and kicked him in the ribs.

"Tim," Krista said in a calm and measured voice. "You need to get out of here. When Jared wakes up he's going to kill you."

I looked at her. "Give me a ride," I said.

She got back in the UTV and fired it up.

"Krista," I said. "Give me a ride."

Miguel and his partner pulled up carrying rifles.

"Just in time," Becky said, and scoffed. Then she turned to Krista, "Where's he going to go, Krista?"

"He's got a ride coming," Krista said.

"When?" Becky said.

Krista ignored the question and performed a three-point turn.

"Fuck it," Becky said. She walked around the gate to Don and Jared's truck, pulled a knife from one of her sheepskin boots, and jabbed it into the sidewalls of both passenger-side tires. Then she turned to me and said, "Hopefully your ride comes soon. I don't know what else to tell you, dude. You better go. Sorry."

I looked down at the Tidwells. Don had rolled onto his side, and there was a small puddle of puke on the ground beneath his open mouth. Jared was stirring, but barely. Neither one of them was going anywhere for a while.

"Thanks," I said to Becky as I walked past her. My voice was a little shaky.

She gave me a thin smile, and I turned and walked up the road in the direction Ron had taken after dropping me off.

When Becky was out of sight, I started running— not sure why I waited that long, but I did. I passed two driveways before coming to a fork in the road. Afraid of taking one and missing Ron, I scrambled up an embankment, hid in the underbrush, and waited. I could smell the damp soil and decomposing leaves beneath me. Blood dripped down the side of my face and from my chin into my lap. My clothes clung to my sweaty skin, and my heart thumped in my ears.

As I watched for Ron's truck, I kept thinking of what Lou Da Rocha had said to me about the people out here: "They tend to take care of problems in their own way, usually with a gun and a backhoe."

I only had to wait five minutes before I saw Ron's dish truck barreling down the left fork. I jumped into the road and waved, and when Ron stopped, I ran around to the driver-side window.

"Jesus," he said. "What the fuck happened to you?"

"I got in a fight," I said. "The Tidwells came at me. They might be looking for me, I don't know. I should probably ride in the back till we get to your place."

"Jesus, Tim."

Ron got out and opened the door to the camper shell. I crawled in, and he shut the door behind me. With no windows, the camper was dark inside. I stretched my legs over a few boxes and leaned against the camper wall. The metal dish parts piled next to me clanked and clattered as we drove over bumps.

I was starting to come down from the adrenaline. My hands shook, and every fifteen seconds my whole body quivered. My wounds began to throb.

Then the truck stopped.

I heard Don's voice muffled by the camper walls. "There's a thief on the road," he said. "You seen anyone?"

"No," Ron said.

"Let out a honk if you do."

We started rolling again.

After twenty minutes, the road was less bumpy, and the truck stopped again. Ron opened the camper door and dropped the tailgate. "Come on up front," he said. "They're not following us. Mike's the only one who knows I gave you a ride anyway."

We got in the truck. The passenger seat wasn't much more comfortable than the back.

"You know," Ron said, "in a few days everyone in these hills will know about this, and they'll know I gave you a ride. Customers are going to be asking me questions for months."

"Sorry," I said.

"What the hell happened? I saw the truck with the tires slashed."

I told Ron the story.

"What is wrong with you?" he said when I was

through. "You're too old to be getting in fights. You're in your thirties now for Christ's sake."

"They were coming at me," I said.

"Yeah, because you were trespassing. That's kind of a big deal out here." He laughed. "That's pretty awesome you nut-punched Don Tidwell though."

Back at Ron's house, his wife, Carol greeted me with heavy gasps, bulging eyes, and hands over her mouth, like I had lost a limb. "I got in a fight," I said, rather than going into the whole story again.

"Oh Jesus. You boys," she said, shaking her head.

While Ron and I sat at the kitchen table, she went looking for some bandages. I asked for, and was promptly given, a glass of whiskey to settle my nerves. Ron joined me, and while we drank, I showed him the same picture of the Tidwells I had shown Krista.

"Krista says this lady works at the grocery store here in town," I said, pointing. "Her name is Candice. Do you know her? I need to talk to her."

"Sure," he said. "Nice lady. She just retired, I think."

Carol came back in the kitchen with a bandage roll and began wrapping my head with it.

Ron said, "Hey Honey, do you know how to get a hold of Candice from the grocery store?"

Carol said, "Ehhhh, not really. I know she joined that protest group to Save Richardson Grove."

When Carol finished wrapping my head, I stood up and thanked them both and apologized. Patting the gauze on my head like it was a bouffant hairdo, I said, "What did you do, Carol, make a turban?"

She laughed, and she and Ron saw me to the door. "Where are the girls?" I said, wanting to say goodbye.

"They saw the blood and got scared," Carol said.

17

The Old Creamery Building

AN HOUR AFTER LEAVING Redway, I parked in front of April's house in Arcata. The sun had gone down, and my head had stopped hurting. Her living room light was on. I knocked on the front door.

She answered in the costume she had worn to my house the other day, minus the prosthetics and makeup.

"Do you wear that thing all the time?" I said.

"Oh my God," she said, looking at the gauze on my head. "What happened?"

"I got in a bar fight." I didn't want to tell her about the shed just yet and worry her unnecessarily. What I'd seen in there could've meant the Tidwells were performing ritual abuse or it could've meant nothing. Before I had left Redway, I sent the pictures of the shed to Child Welfare and the sheriff's office, along with my statement, just to get ahead of things in case the Tidwells decided to charge me for trespassing.

April opened the door wider. "Come in."

I sat on the couch and recounted most of my experiences in Ettersburg while she did her makeup at the kitchen table. When I was finished, she said, "So you think this Candice might know something?"

"I think so," I said. "It shouldn't be too hard to find her. She's part of some group trying to save Richardson Grove."

April set down one of her makeup brushes, went to the bathroom, and returned with fresh gauze and a brown bottle of peroxide. "Let's see what you got," she said, and reached for my head.

I pulled away. "What are you doing?"

"I want to see the wounds. Relax."

"No. They could start bleeding again."

"Then I'll make them stop. Did you clean them?"

"I'm not sure. Ron's wife took care of it."

"Let me clean them. Don't be a pussy." As she unwrapped the gauze, I watched her delicate hands and wrists circle my head. Her perfume reminded me of her sister. She piled the bloody gauze on the cushion next to me. "You're not bleeding anymore," she said. "But these cuts haven't been cleaned."

"Do you want to see the picture that's supposed to be your sister?" I said.

"No."

The peroxide stung in my wounds and was cold as it ran down my neck.

"You're wiping kind of hard," I said.

"It has to be clean. You want an infection?" She gathered up the used gauze, stepped back, smiled, and said, "Your hair looks crazy," then threw the gauze in the trashcan and went back to her makeup. "I'm leaving for rehearsal in fifteen minutes. Are you coming? Levi's gonna be there with his girlfriend, Sandy."

Just then, fifteen minutes seemed like such a short amount of time. I wanted to be with her longer, have her company. I knew it was a mistake. I knew I was tired and needed to go home. I felt the anxiety, the maniacal energy coming on. But I ignored it. "Okay, I'll go."

"Really?" She stretched her neck out and turned her puckered smile on me. Will you wear a costume?"

"Yes," I said, surprising myself.

She clapped and let out an excited laugh.

When she had her fake nose and beard in place, and I was wearing a long, blond wig, blue-striped nightgown, and slippers, we left her house and walked ten minutes to the old creamery building, which took up half a square block and had concrete brick walls, gridded windows, and a fifty-foot-tall central tower. A sign above the entrance read "Arcata Playhouse."

We walked inside, and I followed April across a dark lobby, past an unattended concession stand, and through a heavy gray curtain into a theater. The house lights were on, and over a dozen people, including Levi and his girlfriend, Sandy, were gathered between the stage and bleachers. They were all wearing street clothes.

"How come we're the only ones in costume?" I said. "I thought this was a dress rehearsal."

"I never said that."

"Then why are we in costume?"

"For fun."

Everyone was staring at us.

"This is Tim," April said. "He's going to take Aaron's place."

Two people said "yay."

Levi walked up to me, smiling. "You look like shit," he said.

"I've had a bad week," I said. "I don't think I've brushed my teeth in two days."

"Here," he said, pulling out a flask. "I got some gin. Rinse your mouth out with this."

"Gin's not a substitute for mouth wash, Levi."

"Sure it is," he said. "It cures depression too, and constipation, and gingivitis. Where have you been?"

A tall, lean man with big ears backed away from the group, raising his arms and performing one-handed claps. "I need the dancers for the bedroom scene over here," he said. April, Sandy, and two other women followed him. "And I need the extras in the back. And Travis, you come up front."

As we walked over, Levi whispered: "That's Todd, the choreographer. He's Sandy's dance instructor. I think he has a thing for Sandy."

"Really?"

"Yeah. I'm worried, man. Sandy's always doing these dance recitals. I keep thinking Todd, or some other dance guy is going to seduce her."

"Why?"

"They spend so much time together."

"Ahh," I said. "You're worried about being cuttlefished."

Levi snorted. "Maybe I would be if I knew what that was."

I stopped walking, and so did Levi. I whispered, "During cuttlefish mating season, the bulls fight over who gets the right to mate with the females. But sometimes the smaller males disguise themselves as females to sneak by the bulls and mate right under their noses. This Todd guy is the human equivalent, a guy who pretends to be your girl's friend, then undermines you every chance he gets."

Levi looked at me sideways, like he knew I was slipping. "You might want to keep those thoughts to yourself."

"What? Why?"

"I don't know. Sounds like some kind of misogyny thing is going on with you."

"Misogyny?" I said, raising my voice. "What? I'm just pointing out the successful evolutionary practices of the more devious members of our gender."

"Are you okay?"

"I don't know, are you? Maybe you're the cuttlefish."

Now Levi raised his voice. "Don't call me a cuttlefish."

"Accusing people of misogyny is cuttlefish behavior, man. Plain and simple."

"Guys!"

I looked over. April was scowling at me. The rest of the group stared with a combination of confusion and amusement. "Sorry," I said.

"He's an idiot," Levi said, and we joined the group.

While a stereo played a song called "Link by Link," Todd instructed me and Levi and the other extras to stalk around the stage, pretending like we were drunk, zombie ninjas. When he was satisfied with our performance, he turned his attention to the lead actors. We went over everything five times.

Because the next number didn't involve many extras, I sat in the bleachers with Levi and watched April dance with Sandy and another man.

Twenty minutes in, as they started the scene over for the third time, Pete Holloway, in black slacks and a tucked-in dress shirt, walked through the gray curtain, carrying five pizza boxes. A woman followed two steps behind, cradling a bulging, paper grocery bag.

"Surprise," Pete said. He walked through the

middle of the dancers and dropped the pizza boxes onto the stage.

While his companion put the bag down and began unloading paper cups and two-liter bottles of soda, Pete turned and addressed his onlookers: "I thought you guys might need a little snack. Now, this is just a small gesture to thank you for the tremendous job you guys did putting on that play for my fundraiser. It took everyone's effort to reach our goal of ten thousand dollars and you guys did it. So I just wanted you guys to know you were appreciated. And as part of that appreciation, I have taken care of the rental fees for the rest of your rehearsals. Now dig in."

Everyone clapped and converged on the pizza. April hugged Pete, and they began chatting.

Pete had a mischievous look in his eyes, and his lips were curled at the ends in a perpetual smirk. Looking at him then, I imagined he had been his mother's favorite child, and that over the years he had used his charm to weasel out of thousands of scoldings, first from his mother, then from his wives. He had the look of someone who was never properly punished.

I kept thinking of what the creepy professor had told me, that Pete had been way too close with his former stepdaughter. The more I looked at the guy, the more I worked myself up. I should have left right then. I should have gone home and gone to sleep. Instead, I fed the fire.

I walked over to the foot of the stage and stood beside April, in front of Pete, and said, "You told me you didn't give July money."

"Excuse me?" Pete said.

"I have been told by someone close to July that you paid for her school, her rent, and her cell phone bill.

Why did you lie to me?"

"What do you mean?" he said.

"Did you give her money occasionally to help her out with her bills?"

He squinted at me. "Why do you ask?"

I scoffed. "Because it's important. Apparently, she came into some money around the time of her disappearance."

His smirk turned into a smile. He raised his hands and looked at April. "What is this?"

"I just want to know if you gave her cash before she disappeared," I said, feeding my anger, my manic energy with outrage that I may or may not have manufactured. He was evading me, like a squid squirting ink. "Did you?"

"Who are you?" he said. Then turning to April, "Who is this guy?"

"My name's Tim. We met the other day on the beach, remember? And I'm just trying to clear some things up. I would like to get one statement out of you, that's it. Can you do that, or are you going to keep answering my questions with questions? Because I can do that too."

"Why do you need a statement from me? Is this a deposition?"

"Have you been to many depositions? Have you been to Hawaii? Are your grandparents still alive?"

"This is ridiculous," he said.

"There it is. There's a statement. And you're right. This is ridiculous. You can't answer a simple question. A week before July disappeared, she asked her accountant for advice on what to do with a large gift of cash. I just want to know if that gift came from you."

"I need to talk to you, Tim," April said, walking

away.

"Do you drink Manhattans?" I said to Pete.

He laughed. "Am I in the Twilight Zone? I'm reliving a moment I had five years ago. Who are you? What is wrong with you?"

"I ask you two questions and you act like you're being persecuted. And you act like you don't know me. What is wrong with you?"

"Tim," April said.

I turned and followed her across the room to the bleachers. "What?" I said.

"Pete has been like a father to me," she said. "You're acting crazy."

"I'm acting crazy? I don't think I am. That guy's a liar, and he's acting like he doesn't know who I am. Who's really crazy here?"

"You are," April said. "You're losing control. We talked about this. Pete's a public figure and you are embarrassing him in front of the public. What do you expect him to do?"

"I expect honesty and integrity from my public figures. I don't know about you."

"You should go, Tim. You're exhausted and you need some sleep."

I stared at her for a moment, then sighed. "Maybe you're right." Then I pointed toward the stage. "But I don't fucking like that guy."

"You don't even know him."

"Oh, I know him. I know his kind. He's a squid. He plays the victim. I can't respect that."

18

Richardson Grove

I WOKE UP TO my cell phone ringing. I tried to ignore it and fall back to sleep, but whoever it was called again. I rolled to the edge of my futon and grabbed my phone off the floor. It was April. I answered.

"Guess who called in sick today," she said.

"You?" I said.

"No. Matt. Guess what his assignment was."

"I don't know. Who's Matt?"

"He was assigned to a protest rally at Richardson Grove. And guess who they called in to cover for him."

"The day before Thanksgiving?" I said.

"The news doesn't stop for Thanksgiving."

"Yeah, but why are they having a protest today?"

"Think about it: All the people going home to visit family today have to drive right through the grove. That means a lot of exposure."

"I thought you just did the graphics?" I said.

"I do but there's no one else to cover. How about it? I bet Candice will be there."

"I bet she will. Are you picking me up?"

"I'm in the driveway."

"Jesus. I just woke up."

"Hurry up."

I got out of bed and walked down the hall to the bathroom. Before I could make it inside, my dad caught me.

"We're going for baitfish today," he stated.

"I can't today," I said. "I'm going to a protest with April."

"A protest. Why are you going to a protest? It's the day before Thanksgiving. And what happened to your eye?"

"What do you mean?" I looked in the bathroom mirror. There was a pool of blood in the white of my left eye. "I'll tell you about it later," I said.

"So you're too cool to go fishing with your old man. You know I could die tomorrow. Imagine how terrible you would feel for not going fishing with me."

"Thanks, Dad. But you can talk to April about it. She's in the driveway."

"April's in the driveway?" he said, excited, and he turned and walked out the front door.

After I finished in the bathroom, I poured a cup of coffee from a pot my mom had made and took Tuna to do her business on the lawn. April and my dad were talking outside her vehicle.

"Here comes the famous pit bull," he said and laughed.

"You love this dog," I said.

"I don't love that it shits in my yard."

After I put Tuna back in the house, April and I took off in her SUV.

For the third time in five days, I was taking the hour-and-a-half trip to southern Humboldt, driving south on Highway 101, and following the Eel River through the redwoods and the mist and fog. Nine miles past Redway and Ron's house, at ten in the morning, we reached Richardson Grove State Park. The four-lane highway became two lanes, and the shoulder disappeared. We weaved around giant old-growth redwoods that grew right up to the edge of the road. Their roots made cracks in the concrete. Reflective signs had been planted in front of their trunks, which had deep gashes and scrapes from vehicles crashing into them. The redwood canopy turned the day into twilight.

"So what are they protesting?" I said.

"Caltrans wants to cut down these old-growths so bigger trucks can come through," April said.

A large white sheet hung thirty feet above the highway between two trees on the southern end of Richardson Grove. The words, "Save the Old-Growths/Stop Caltrans Lies," were painted on the sheet in red. We passed under it and entered a clearing that ran flat for one hundred yards before climbing into more trees. The sky was overcast, and the ground was still wet from the rain that had fallen earlier in the morning. An RV park and a gas station were on the right, and two gift shops were on the left, one with the "Famous Grandfather Tree," and the other with the "Famous One Log House." On display in front of both were burl carvings of bears, Bigfoots, gnomes, and totem poles.

April slowed to ten miles an hour, and I let my window down. The road was lined with a few dozen protesters dressed in layers, holding signs that read, "Yield to Nature," "Caltrans Stay Out of R. Grove," "No Police State," "Resist Invasion from the South/No

Road Widening," "More Grove, Less Road."

Two young men with dreadlocks sat cross-legged playing bongo drums. An older man patrolled one side of the highway on a Segway, while a stout woman in a black sweatsuit and a leather cowboy hat patrolled the other. She carried a trumpet and stopped every few steps to play three to four melancholy notes.

April parked next to a Sherriff's car. Two officers were leaning against it, pointing and smiling. They both wore sunglasses. Next to their car was an old Ford pickup riddled with dents and rust. Bundles of sage were laid out in a row on the hood. A homemade sign in the windshield said, "Wild Sage $5."

"I'm going to go find some interviews," April said. "You coming with me?"

"No, I think we should split up," I said. "Otherwise, people will think I'm a narc. I need to go undercover."

She laughed. "Then you shouldn't have worn that fleece vest again. I told you about that thing."

"What are you talking about? Everyone trusts a man in a fleece vest."

"No. No they don't." She turned and walked away.

One of the cars driving by honked, and the protesters shook their signs and cheered. I jogged across the highway when it was clear and approached the first person I saw, a woman holding a sign that read, "No Big Box Stores."

"Hi," I said. "I forgot my cardboard. Do you have any extra?"

She looked confused.

"For the signs," I said.

"Oh," she said. "No. sorry."

"Candice called me last minute to tell me about this

thing, and I forgot to make a sign. Has she got here yet?"

"Candice?" she said. "I don't think I've met her yet. Joe probably knows her though." She pointed to the man on the Segway.

"Thanks." I walked over to Joe, who was five yards down the line. He had a gray beard, hound-dog eyes, and a ponytail. "How's it going?" I said. "Nice day, huh? I don't know what's going on with the trumpet player though. It sounds like a funeral out here. The trees aren't dead yet, right? How about a little optimism?"

Joe turned his Segway 180 degrees and glared at me. "I think Susan's doing a great job," he said.

"No, of course," I said. "It's just a little sad, that's all. But real. Real stuff." I looked around. "Have you seen Candice? I'm Tim, by the way."

"Candice is in the grove getting ready to take the photo with everyone else," he said. "If you want to do it, too, you still have time. The more people the better. The shuttle's picking everyone up over there." He pointed across the highway to a group of three protesters standing in front of the gas station.

"Okay. Thanks, Joe."

I jogged across the highway again and found April talking to a woman in a pantsuit holding a microphone. A man with a large camera sitting by his feet stood next to them.

"Hey," I said, getting April's attention. "Candice is in the grove. I'm going to take the shuttle they got. I'll be back in a little bit."

"Are you getting in the picture?" the woman in the pantsuit said, smiling.

"I don't know," I said. "Maybe."

"I'll be on the next shuttle," April said. "I'm not finished here yet."

I walked over to the three protesters Joe had pointed to—a woman and two men—and stood beside them.

I greeted them: "How's it going?"

"Are you getting on the shuttle?" the woman said.

"Yeah."

"It should be here soon."

"What's going on in the grove, some kind of photo op?"

"Yeah. And a prayer ceremony. Mountain Sorrel's going to lead it."

"Who's that?"

"He's one of the original eight who delivered supplies to Julia Butterfly while she was living in Luna. He's a spirit guardian now."

"I remember her." Julia Butterfly had lived in an old-growth redwood for something like a year to save it from being logged. Her protest had made the national news when I was a kid."

"She lived in Luna for 738 days," the woman said. "The original eight had to battle loggers just to get her food."

A green minivan pulled up, and we all piled in and took a ride back into Richardson Grove. Less than a mile in, we turned left at a sign that said, "Richardson Grove State Park" and drove by a park ranger in a kiosk, then down a hill and under the highway. We parked in front of a sign that said, "Dawn Redwood Group Camp."

The campsite was located between the highway and the Eel River, and it had two fire pits, four tables, and an outhouse, all shaded by redwood trees. Sword ferns grew around the border. The ground was covered in fronds and leaves that had turned red.

At the center of the site, near the outhouse, about fifty people stood in a lopsided circle around a man and a woman. I assumed the man was Mountain Sorrel because he was holding a burning bundle of sage in one hand and a wooden staff decorated with black feathers in the other. He was tall and lanky with curly red hair, a curly red beard, and pale blue eyes set deep in their sockets. A colorful blanket with geometric patterns on it was wrapped around his shoulders.

The woman had a similar blanket around her shoulders, and she was holding a baby. She had long black hair and caramel-colored skin.

I joined the circle, along with the three protesters I had ridden with in the shuttle. Mountain gave us each a river rock the size of a softball, which he had taken from a pile next to the woman with the baby, and he told us to write our names on our rock with a black marker that we passed around. When I was done, he waved his sage around the rock and in my face. The smoke got in my eyes and lungs, and I coughed. The bundle of sage looked the same as the ones I had seen for five dollars on the hood of the old Ford parked in front of the gas station.

When my eyes cleared, I looked around the circle and saw that everyone was holding a rock with their name on it. I scanned the names and faces for Candice. The only woman of retirement age was ten people to my right. She was on the back half of sixty, with long, thick gray hair. She wore a rainbow-colored, knitted beanie, and a purple, knitted poncho. I could not see the name on her rock, so I pulled out my phone. The man to my left glared at me and sighed, but I ignored him. The picture of Don and Candice I had taken from Don's office in Stone Lagoon was at least twenty years old, but after comparing the faces, I was almost certain I had found the right person.

When I looked up, Mountain Sorrel was dancing and waving his staff in the air. The only sounds accompanying his dance were the traffic from the highway, the fussing baby, and his feet sliding in the dirt. When he stopped, he looked around the circle, nodding. "All right," he said. "Good stuff. Powerful stuff. I think it's time for the photo. Is everyone ready?" He smiled.

People said "Yeah," and "Woo-hoo."

"Okay," he said. "Just bring your stones and follow me."

He walked out of the campsite, across a driveway, and stood on one side of a trailhead. The woman with the baby stood on the other. The circle broke up and formed a line in front of them. I found the woman I thought was Candice near the head. No one objected to me cutting in beside her. They were busy chattering amongst themselves. They sounded nervous and excited.

"Hi, I'm Tim," I said. "Are you Candice?"

She looked at me, confused. "Who are you?" she said.

"Tim. Are you Candice?"

"Yes?" she said. "Do I know you?"

"I'm looking into a potential child abuse case. I was hoping you could answer a few questions for me about Don Tidwell."

"Are you a cop?" she said.

"No. I'm a lawyer."

"I don't know anyone named Don Tidwell. Sorry."

I got out my phone and pulled up the picture. "Is this you?"

She looked. "No."

"Are you sure?"

"Yes, I'm sure. I don't know who told you it was, but this is really weird of you to come at me like this."

I heard wood beating on wood and looked up to see Mountain Sorrel at the front of the line holding up his staff. "Okay," he said. "Now's as good a time as any." He dropped the blanket from his shoulders and took off his sweatshirt, exposing his pale, naked torso. Then everyone in the line began removing their clothing.

"What's going on?" I said.

Candice took off her poncho. "If you're not going to take off your clothes like the rest of us, you're going to have to leave."

"Why do I have to take off my clothes?" I said.

"For the picture."

"What kind of picture is this?"

"We're taking a picture in our natural state with the trees to show solidarity. It's to raise awareness for the Grove."

I looked over and saw Mountain Sorrel and a few other people completely naked. "I think it's going to work," I said.

More and more people were naked around me. Their clothes were in small piles on the ground with their name-stones on top of them. Candice was down to her underwear.

"Well, I'll get out of here," I said. "I don't want to make anyone uncomfortable. Could you just give me your number so we can finish this conversation later?"

"No," she said.

"Why not?"

"I don't know Don Tidwell. And I'm not the person in that photograph."

The line began moving past Mountain Sorrel. He stayed at the entrance to the trail with his arms folded over his chest, like a rancher watching his cattle skip into the corral.

"It's possible that Don is abusing his grandson," I said to Candice as we reached Mountain Sorrel. "I know that's you in the picture, and I can tell that you're scared, which leads me to believe that any suspicions I might have are well-founded. But I need evidence against him. Any evidence. It could be years old. I just need a witness. Just give me something. Please."

She ignored me and kept walking. I tried to follow but Mountain Sorrel put a hand on my chest.

"You can't go up there with clothes on, man," he said. "If just one guy has his clothes on it will ruin the picture."

"I just need to talk to Candice for a second," I said.

"Respect the rules, man. Have honor."

"Have honor? I just need a second. I'm not going to get in the picture."

"It's not just about the picture. It's about trust and no judgment. There is a man here who is not naked. Can he judge? Absolutely he can judge. You know what I mean?"

"Fine," I said, and stepped aside and started taking off my clothes. When I was done, I threw them in a pile on the ground with my stone and went back to the trailhead, but Mountain stopped me again.

"Sorry, man, but your energy's not right," he said, and offered me a fresh bundle of sage. "Here, take this back to the campsite and cleanse yourself. I'll check on you in a minute."

"I'm fucking freezing," I said. "Are you kidding me? My energy's not right? I'm naked, aren't I? What else do you want from me?"

"Just take a minute, and I'll come and check on you. Be peaceful, brother."

I was thinking about making a run for it when I heard April's voice: "What is going on? Do you have Alzheimer's? I can't leave you alone for a second without you taking off your pants and yelling at people?"

She was grinning.

Seeing her made me feel modest all of a sudden. I stepped away from the line, grabbed my pants out of the pile on the ground, and held them in front of my crotch. "He won't let me through," I said. "First he said I had to be naked, now he says my energy's bad."

"Why do you need to get through?" April said. "Are you trying to get in the picture?"

"No. Candice is up there. And she lied to me. I just want to figure out why."

"Why couldn't you just wait until she comes back down again?"

That was a good question. Suddenly, I felt foolish. "I don't know. I got upset."

April set down her notebook, took off her jacket, and began unbuttoning her shirt.

"What are you doing?" I said.

"Helping." She smiled. "Besides, it will make my story better."

"To get naked with a bunch of *hippies*?" I whispered the last word so Mountain Sorrel wouldn't hear.

"Don't watch me undress. Turn around."

I did as I was told, and a few seconds later she

walked by me, naked. She turned and looked at me. My mouth must have been open, because she said, "Keep it together, Kitchens. Come on."

By then everyone but Mountain Sorrel and the woman with the baby had gone up the trail. The woman and the baby had remained clothed.

April said to Mountain Sorrel, "Sorry about him. Do you mind if we go up together? I'm a reporter and he's helping me. I think his energy's good now. I'll look out for him."

Mountain Sorrel looked at me. "Be peaceful," he said. "And don't forget to take your shoes off when you get up there."

"Okay," I said.

He stepped aside and let us pass.

As April and I walked up the trail side by side to the highway, I said: "That was easy. I guess Mountain Sorrel approved of your energy. I think he could sense you do yoga."

"You should do yoga," April said. "It might help with your anger issues."

The November air was cold and crisp. We were both shivering by the time we made it to the top and joined the rest of the naked people, about fifty of them, standing around giant redwood trunks on both sides of the highway. Cars driving by honked and passengers leered. When semi-trucks passed, they created a forceful wind that reached every crevice in my body.

Some people in front of me were looking over my head. I turned around and saw a man halfway up one of the smaller trees, climbing with a rope, a camera case strapped around one shoulder.

I spotted Candice a few yards away, talking with another woman. "There she is," I said, pointing, and

April and I walked over to her.

"Should I go talk to him?" I heard Candice say to the woman.

"That didn't work the last time," the woman said.

"Talk to who?" I said.

Candice took one look at me and frowned.

The woman next to her had no such prejudice, however. "Ken," she said. "He's staring at the women again. I can't make him stop."

"Sounds like Ken isn't here for the trees," I said. "Go tell Mountain Sorrel. He seems to be the regulator around here."

"Oh, that's a good idea," she said, and walked away.

I looked Candice in the eyes. "There are only two reasons that I can think of for you to lie to me," I said. "One: you're ashamed of having been with Don. Two: you're afraid of him. Most likely it's both. But how do you think a child feels around him? Can you imagine what his grandson is going through?"

"I don't know Don," she said. "Leave me alone."

"Please," April said. "If you know anything that could help my nephew, please tell us. He could be in danger."

Candice looked at April, whose eyes glistened with tears. Then Candice looked down, sighed, and said, "I was only with Don for three months. I never witnessed any abuse."

"Can you tell me who the other people are in that picture I showed you?" I said.

"Don and his son, Jared, and his daughter, Mary. And the one on the end is my daughter, Simone." Her voice wavered. "I never witnessed him doing anything, but I suspected it. That's why I left. He had property out in Ettersburg that he never took me to the whole time I knew him, but he took my daughter, and without asking me. She was twelve." Candice choked down a sob. She spoke slowly, struggling to maintain composure. "When he finally brought Simone home, she was very quiet and scared. Terrified. And she wouldn't tell me what happened. And she still won't. But we left that day and never went back. I can't believe I left her alone with him so many times. I just—"

She began to weep, and April hugged her. The people nearby stared.

"What's going on here?" a man said behind me.

I turned around and saw Mountain Sorrel standing with his arms crossed.

"Nothing," I said. "We're having an emotional conversation."

One of the women nearby stepped forward and said, "That's not true. They're bullying Candice. I heard them."

"You're ruining this event for everyone," Mountain Sorrel said to me. "You have to go, man. You're ejected. You and your friend."

"We're not ruining anything," I said.

The people nearby started chanting together: "Go home. Go home . . . ."

"This is ridiculous," I said.

"Have some honor," Mountain Sorrel said. "Leave. We don't need your poison here."

"Come on," April said. "Let's go."

"We don't have to go," I said. "We're not trespassing."

"Calm down," she said. "Let it go."

I threw up my hands. "Fine."

Mountain Sorrel followed us back down the trail to make sure we left. We got dressed at the trailhead, waved goodbye to him, and walked to the day-use area on the banks of the Eel River, where April had parked her SUV. When we got inside, she opened her notebook, tore out a page, and handed it to me. There was a phone number written on it.

"Candice gave me her daughter's number while you were arguing with Mountain Sorrel," April said. "She lives in Los Gatos, down in the Bay Area."

"Really?" I said. "Good job. Now maybe this whole day won't be a waste of time."

"I can't believe you got me kicked out of the protest."

"I'm sorry. Are you going to be in trouble?"

"No. Tom will think it's funny. I already have enough to write a good article anyway."

I called the number on the page while April started the engine and drove out of the park.

A woman answered.

"Hi," I said. "I'm looking for Simone."

"This is she."

"I'm investigating Don Tidwell, and it is my understanding that you were his stepdaughter for a short period. Is that true? . . . Hello?"

"What happened?" April said. "She hang up?"

"That happens to me a lot. I have an extremely attractive phone voice. Most women just aren't prepared for it."

April rolled her eyes, then I called again. "Hi, this is Tim again. I think we got disconnected."

"I'm a mother," she said. "I don't want the memory of that man defiling my house. Please don't call here again."

19

Mouth of the Mad River

ON THE WAY BACK, April and I stopped in Fortuna, a small town just south of Fernbridge, in the lower Eel River Valley. We ate lunch at the Eel River Brewing Company, near the riverbank, then we left a little after one o'clock and reached my parent's house at two. As I stepped out of the SUV, April said, "I'll be back in a few hours. I have to go home and finish this article first."

I leaned over the door. "Are we having dinner together too?" I said.

"Oh. I forgot to tell you. Your dad invited me to go fishing with you guys tonight."

"Really? Tonight?"

"Yeah."

I smiled. "Okay."

When I walked inside, I found my dad on the couch watching TV and my mom at the kitchen table opening a can of pumpkin. The tabletop was covered in flour. The house smelled like apple pie.

"We're going fishing tonight?" I said to my dad.

My mom didn't wait for him to answer: "He wants

to go fishing the night before Thanksgiving. I can't believe it."

"Nature waits for no man," my dad said. "How many times do I have to tell you? The time is now. The fish won't be there in two days. They don't care if it's Thanksgiving. They don't know what Thanksgiving is."

"Why do we have to go at night?" I said.

"Because that's when the night fish are out," he said.

"What are night fish?"

"They're the same as day fish only they spawn at night instead of the day?"

"What are day fish?"

"Little surf smelt. They live in the surf. But the rednecks say only the night fish are running right now."

"These sound like mythical creatures, Dad. What rednecks told you this?"

"No. They're real. I've seen pictures. The rednecks fill up the beds of their trucks with these things. They come in huge schools. They're the best bait around, and they're free. If you want to, we can fry them up like French fries, like the Vietnamese do."

My dad went to the garage and came back with two wood boards wrapped in netting under his arm. The boards were two inches square, four feet long, and bolted together at one end.

"What are you doing?" my mom said. "Don't bring your disgusting fish stuff in the house."

"Relax, would ya," he said. "My disgusting fish stuff feeds this family." He opened the net by pulling apart the boards at one end to make a V shape. He placed the open end on the living room floor. "I got this at a garage sale. I bought two of them. You put them in the surf like this and the little fishies just swim right in.

Then you close the net. The tricky part is finding the schools. The mouth of the Mad is a good spot. You look for birds. If the birds are in the surf, then there's a school there. If there are no birds then you build a fire. The night fish are attracted to the light."

"Like moths?" I said.

"That's what the rednecks say."

While my dad put his disgusting fish stuff back in the garage and my mom went into the other room to get something, I snuck a slice of apple pie from one of the four cooling on the kitchen counter. I finished before they both came back, which was difficult, and I sat on the couch and fell asleep watching the History Channel with my dad.

When I woke up, all the lights were on in the house, it was dark outside, and my dad was opening the front door, smiling.

April walked inside wearing jeans, an oversized hoodie beneath an oversized snowboarding jacket, and a blue Dodger baseball cap that made her blue eyes almost glow in the shade of the bill. Her hair was tucked behind her ears, and her face, amid the big clothes and hat, seemed small. The hat looked similar to one her sister used to wear in high school when we went to beach parties or camping.

"Are you ready," April said to me.

"Yeah," I said.

"You don't look like it." she turned to my dad. "What beach are we going to?"

"Mad River," he said. "But you guys have to go on your own."

"What?" I said.

"I have to help your mother with something. She's overwhelmed. Thanksgiving's tomorrow. She has a lot to do."

"This was your idea."

"Relax," my mom said. "I made some sandwiches for you guys." She handed April a brown paper lunch bag. "You guys go. Have fun."

Holding the lunch bag, April smiled and gave me a suspicious look, and I realized we had been set up on a date.

"I loaded the truck already," my dad said. He handed me a set of keys and showed me which one would open the gate at Mad River Beach. "When you get to the beach turn north. The mouth won't be far."

"This was your idea," I said.

"I know but you can still go get some fish for your father. You'll have fun."

April and I said goodbye to my parents, and they watched from the porch as we climbed into my dad's old Chevy LUV pickup and took off. The cab smelled like burning oil. There were spider webs in every corner and the gears ground when I shifted into second.

We rattled and clattered south on Highway 101, took the first exit to Arcata, and drove through the Bottoms and its maze of cow fields. Air whistled into the cab through rusted-out holes around the windshield. April and I had to shout when we talked. Even so, our conversation was stilted. We talked about the weather.

A quarter moon illuminated storm clouds to the west. The pineapple winds whistled through the trees, and though they had traveled across the ocean from Hawaii, they smelled like land, and they were warm and full of energy. They carried the power of the pending storm, and when I parked at Mad River Beach and got out to unlock the gate, and I breathed in the electric air and looked up at the night sky, my eyes welled with tears, and for a moment I wasn't afraid of dying, and I felt free.

Sometime before morning, the clouds would reach the shore and burst, and the temperature would drop, just as it had done countless times when I was a kid.

I opened the gate, locked the hubs on the front tires, put the truck into four-wheel drive, and drove over the dunes. When we hit the beach, I rolled down the window and turned north. The warm wind and the sound of the roaring surf filled the cab. After a few hundred yards, I spotted the Mad River shimmering in the silver moonlight. The beach narrowed as the river veered north and ran parallel to the shore. We followed it to the mouth and parked.

As I unloaded the firewood, I could hear seals barking on the opposite bank. I cut some kindling with a hatchet and piled it on top of newspapers, and April did her best to block the wind while I lit the paper.

"What now?" April said when the fire was strong enough to leave unattended.

"We wait," I said. "If the birds come, then that means there's fish."

"There's a storm coming. The birds are all inland."

"Maybe there's some stragglers. I don't know. I've never done this before. What kind of sandwiches did my mom make?"

April grabbed the bag out of the truck, pulled out a sandwich, and made a face. "Meatloaf," she said.

"You don't like meatloaf?"

"No I like it."

April spread out a blanket and we both sat in front of the fire and ate our sandwiches.

"This is why I never left Humboldt," she said.

"Because of meatloaf sandwiches?" I said, kidding around. "You can get these anywhere."

She smiled. "No. This. Everything: the beaches, the storms, the rain, the fog, the redwoods. If I feel like having a fire on the beach, I'll have a fire on the beach. I love it here. People come from all over the world just to see this place, and I get to live here."

"What do you mean, *you get to live here*? Anyone can live here. This is America. People can live wherever they want."

"It's not the same. I grew up here. It's different for me than for someone who moves here or retires here. It just is. I'm a part of this place. It's a part of me."

"I don't know if that's such a great thing."

"Why not?" she said.

"That's how people get stuck. That's how people end up trying to renovate their parent's old Dodge Dart."

She shook her head. "You think I'm stuck? Being connected to a place has nothing to do with how people get stuck. You don't think you're stuck? You left Humboldt and you're the most stuck person I know."

"I am? How?"

"You don't stop and think about your own shit. You just bulldoze ahead, like that will solve everything."

"What shit are you talking about?" I said.

"Come on, Tim. What shit? How about losing your law license? How about getting a divorce? How about getting a DUI and continuing to drive drunk, or getting kicked out of a boutique in Old Town and getting kicked out of a protest rally. I mean, this is just stuff that I'm aware of. Obviously, something's going on with you that you don't want to deal with. Look at how you're going after the Tidwells."

"What about it? You asked for my help."

"Yeah, I did, kind of. But that's not the point. This is beyond help. You're getting obsessed, like my dad or something."

I threw up my hands. "I'm not obsessed. I just don't like to see people get away with shit, especially people like the Tidwells. You let that happen, then everything falls apart. The guy who murdered my sister was accused of rape twice before he even saw my sister. Twice, and both times the DA decided not to prosecute. And as bad as that was, as bad as losing her felt, I can't even imagine what you went through, what you're going through. Not knowing what happened. I can't imagine. So maybe you're right. Maybe I am stuck. Maybe I never got over my sister's murder. But I don't think you ever get over something like that. Do you?"

We both had a little extra moisture in our eyes.

"No," she said.

I wrapped up the remaining half of my sandwich and put it back in the bag. I wasn't hungry anymore. As I picked up another log to throw on the fire, I thought I heard a seagull, but with the barking seals and pounding waves, it was hard to tell. My eyes had adjusted to the firelight, and I could see only darkness beyond it. I went to the truck, which faced the ocean, and turned on the headlights. Dozens of birds, mostly seagulls, were jostling and scrambling in the surf.

"They're here," April said.

I unloaded two nets and two pairs of waders from the back of the truck. We put the waders on over our clothes and trudged through the shifting sand with the nets under our arms, and we waded into the ocean until we were knee-deep. The birds squawked at our arrival and rose into the air. Some were carried away by the wind into the darkness, outside the circle of yellow light beaming from the truck onshore. Others glided in place above our heads, their feathers quivering in the wind. When they landed in the water again, they were farther out but still visible.

The surface of the water was alive with a frenzy of jumping smelt. Light reflected off their thin, silver bodies. We put our nets down and a large wave crashed into us. Cold, salty foam sprayed into my face and mouth and dripped down my waders. Before the wave receded, I closed my net. Hundreds of glistening, flopping night fish were trapped inside. I threw the net over my shoulder and turned to April.

"Mine swam out," she said, shouting over the excited birds and roaring surf.

"You have to close the net before the wave goes back," I said.

Another large wave came and nearly knocked me over. I heard April squeal, and when I looked over, her hat had fallen off and her hair was soaked, but she had closed the net in time. As I snatched her hat out of the foamy water, the receding wave stole the sand beneath my feet, and I fell to one knee. April helped me up, and we retreated to shore together.

At the truck, I grabbed a large cooler out of the back, and we emptied our nets into it.

"I think the waves are too rough to be doing this," April said.

"Yeah," I said.

She smiled. "There are definitely fish flopping around in my pants right now."

We took off our waders and shook them upside down over the cooler. After a half dozen fish fell out, I found a towel in the truck and handed it to April. She wrapped the towel around her waist and shimmied out of her jeans. She laid the jeans on the hood next to me, then turned and placed a palm on my stomach. She raised her mouth, and we kissed.

Her lips tasted like strawberry Chapstick, the same flavor her sister had worn in high school. I pulled back.

"What?" she said.

"Nothing," I said, and kissed her again.

We lay down on the blanket next to the fire. I unwrapped her towel and ran my hands over her thighs and hips and down her back. Her stomach clenched, and she pushed out a breath. I kissed her neck and felt her skin against mine.

We spent most of the night there.

When the rain woke us up just before dawn, the air was cold, and the fire was smoldering. We packed up in a hurry. I started the truck and turned on the heater. We huddled together in the cab, surrounded by foggy windows, with the fan blowing and rain pelting the roof. We both smelled like campfire smoke.

When the windows cleared, we left the beach, drove back through the Bottoms, and stopped at Toni's, a small hamburger joint with a breakfast menu and enough parking for semi-trailers. April let out a cheer when she saw they were open on the holiday.

We sat at one of the brown booths and ate omelets and tater tots, and when we finished, we ordered pie and coffee. We were tired and punchy and quick to laugh. After our second cup, we wished the woman behind the counter a happy Thanksgiving and left for my parent's house.

When we parked in the driveway a little before nine, April kissed me on the lips and said, "I'll call you tonight when I get home from my dad's."

"You're not going to come in and have some pie?" I said.

"More pie?"

"Yeah."

"No, I can't. It would feel weird to see your parents right now." She kissed me again. "I'll call you tonight."

I carried the cooler full of smelt around to the backyard and set it on the patio. My dad came out of the house, and when he saw the fish, his eyes got big. "It worked," he said. "You got 'em."

"Yeah," I said. "We would have got more too but the waves were a little too rough."

"Now we just have to freeze them and we'll have free salmon bait for the whole season. I got to make room in the freezer though, and that's a whole 'nother battle with your mother."

My mom walked out the backdoor on cue and tiptoed toward us. "What are you doing out here?" she said.

"Talking," I said. "What's wrong? Why are you whispering?"

"Oh, I forgot to tell you," my dad said.

"There's a woman waiting for you inside," my mom said.

20

McKinleyville

"A WOMAN?" I SAID. "Who?"

"She said her name's Krista. She came about an hour ago and asked if she could wait for you. I couldn't get a hold of you, so I said it was okay. We've been watching the parade on TV together. It's really awkward."

"Why do you put your mother through this?" my dad said. "Why are strange women always coming over here for you?"

"What strange women?" I said. "This is the first time this happened."

"That we know of."

"I don't know why she's here. My phone's been dead since last night."

"She said you promised to give her legal advice," my mom said.

"Well that's not true," I said.

I walked inside the house. Krista was sitting on my parent's couch with her legs crossed, wearing a black pants suit.

"What are you doing here?" I said.

"I tried to call you," she said, "but you didn't answer, so I decided to stop by."

"On Thanksgiving?"

"I'm sorry. I honestly forgot about that until I came here and saw the pies. My mommy's memorial service was yesterday. I've been up all night."

"Jesus. I'm sorry to hear that."

"Thanks."

My mom and dad walked in through the back door. I told Krista we could talk in my room, and she stood up and followed me there. I closed the door behind us and sat in my dad's office chair. She sat on the edge of my futon.

"I'm sorry about the other day," she said. "They're our neighbors. I didn't know what to do."

"You could've given me a ride," I said. "You just left me there. Those guys could've killed me. Lucky Becky slashed their tires. I should send her a thank-you card."

"They're my neighbors. You made a lot of drama for me. Jared is shooting guns off every day now. No one can go up there to use their cell phone anymore. Mike is pissed at me."

"And that's my fault? How do I know you're not the one who called the Tidwells in the first place? You disappeared for a while out there."

"Are you crazy? Why would I cause this drama for myself?"

"I don't know, Krista. I don't know what's in your head. Why are you here anyway?"

She leaned her back against the wall and rested her boots on my unmade bed. "I have evidence of who July's murderer was," she said.

"Really. What kind of evidence?"

"I'll show you. But first, you have to help me with something."

"What?" I said.

Krista sat up. "I want twenty thousand dollars as a reward. That's fair, right? They offered an award five years ago."

"That was ten thousand."

"And I want twenty," she said.

"I don't have twenty thousand. And neither does April or her father."

"Then that's too bad."

"Where did this evidence come from all of a sudden, anyway?" I said.

"I can't tell you. That's part of the evidence."

"Okay. Maybe we can figure something out, but you'll only get paid if your evidence leads to the capture and conviction of July's murderer."

"Not good enough. I want it upfront."

"That's impossible. You're crazy if you think anyone's going to give you twenty thousand dollars, without assurances, for evidence that might turn out to be nonsense."

She stood up, walked to my sister's piano, and sat down. "You know Chopsticks?" she said.

"No."

"Sit down. I'll teach you."

"Krista—"

She hit the opening notes to Chopsticks. "Your mom said you play piano. Is that true?"

"Sometimes."

"Then come over here."

"I'm tired, Krista."

She turned back around and stared into my eyes. "I can tell. You look like you've been rode hard and put away wet."

"Thanks. You know, I can propose some type of contract if that will make you feel better, but no one is going to give you a reward unless the information leads to a conviction."

Krista raised her chin. "Hmmm. That's an interesting concept. I'll have to sleep on that."

In my head, I rolled my eyes—*interesting concept?* I stood up and opened my bedroom door. "I hope you change your mind, but if you're not going to tell me what you know right now . . . I need some rest."

She frowned, then shrugged and walked over to me. "If I was your girlfriend," she said. "I'd never put you away wet."

As I blew air out through my nose, she stood on her tiptoes, pressed her breasts against me, and kissed my mouth. "Promise me something," she said.

"What?" I said, annoyed by her little games.

"Think of me the next time you play piano." She smiled and turned and left out the front door.

My mom, who had seen the kiss from the couch in the living room, said, "Is that my next daughter-in-law?"

"The wedding's tomorrow," I said. "Is that okay?"

"That's fine. Go take a shower. Everyone's coming over in a few hours."

21

Los Gatos

THE MONDAY AFTER THANKSGIVING, my ex-wife, Madeline, left a message on my phone while I was at work. I called her back on my lunch break and learned that she had gotten me an informal interview with Hunley, Davis, & Runiyon, LLP, a San Francisco law firm specializing in high-dollar, often headline-grabbing, personal injury cases. It was a small firm lead by old-fashioned trial lawyers disposed to sitting on nonprofit boards and being frequent guest speakers at charity luncheons. Mitch Runiyon ran in the same circles as Madeline and knew her father. He was well-known in the Bay Area and throughout the state. He was also a member of several Bay Area bar associations and professional development committees. I had talked with him briefly a few times at bar association events, but I was fairly certain he wouldn't remember me. I even had him as an instructor once for a continuing legal education course on ethics. He was prone to impromptu pontificating on the virtues of the American right to civil jury trials and the historical developments leading to—and benefits of—the modern contingency fee system. Fortunately, for his firm, and the rest of us, his values were closely aligned with his financial interests.

He knew about my history, according to my ex-wife, and he didn't seem to think it would be a big problem, especially since my license was being reinstated in a little over a month. He had a long history of hiring former assistant district attorneys, my ex-wife said, which seemed to ring a bell to me.

"Mitch wants you to come in on Wednesday at two," Madeline said over the phone.

"I'll be there," I said. "Thank you again. I appreciate you thinking of me."

"I still care about you, Tim. You're not a bad person. You deserve good things."

"*I deserve good things?* What's going on with you? Have you joined a church or something?"

She laughed. "No. I'm just . . . happy to make you happy."

I planned to leave a day early and stay the night in San Francisco, so I wouldn't have to do an interview after driving five hours. If I had time on the way down, I would drive the extra hour or so to Los Gatos, where Candice's daughter, Simone, lived, and see if I could get any information out of her in person.

I called Candice to get her daughter's address, but Candice hung up on me.

That night I went over to April's house for dinner. She answered the door in a floral print, A-line dress that went down to mid-calf. She wore stockings, heels, an apron, and her hair was done up with bobby pins. I was given a newspaper and a pair of brown leather slippers and told to sit on the couch and wait for my dinner. I did as I was told. She was definitely unique.

After I told her my plans to interview Candice's daughter, she said, "What if you drive all that way and she still won't tell you anything?"

"Interviewing someone in person always works out better," I said. "There's a good chance she'll give me something. And even if she doesn't, the trip won't be a total waste. I was going to stop in San Francisco on the way back and see some old friends."

"Oh. Okay. When are you coming back?"

"Probably Thursday. Maybe Friday."

"We have rehearsal on Friday," she said.

"Okay. I'll be back by then."

In the morning, I gave April a long kiss goodbye and drove south on Highway 101. I was out of Humboldt County in an hour and a half. The dense green forests eventually disappeared, replaced by a more Mediterranean landscape: craggy, dry hills dotted with small trees and shrubbery or covered in row after row of grapevines. I skirted away from the edge of Napa Valley and through the more populated corridor of Sonoma County, over the Golden Gate Bridge, through San Francisco, and around the South Bay. I took Highway 17 west from San Jose and got off in downtown Los Gatos at three in the afternoon, a little more than six hours after I had left April's.

I found parking and walked to a small cafe on a narrow street lined with trees. I could see the foothills of the Santa Cruz Mountains to the west. About half of the buildings were stucco with red tile roofs. Well-groomed white people with straight white teeth walked the streets. Most of them wore fleece jackets.

I ate a sixteen-dollar turkey sandwich, and when the bill was brought to my table, I picked it up and said to the waitress, "Oh no. Simone will take care of this. Put it on her tab, please. I'm her brother."

The waitress looked confused. "I don't know who Simone is," she said. "And we don't keep tabs here."

"I've done it before. Let me talk to your manager. He knows Simone. Everyone knows Simone."

"Just a moment," she said, and walked to the back.

A minute later a tall, burly man in a red-striped polo shirt walked up to my table. "I'm sorry, sir, we don't keep tabs here."

"You do for Simone," I said.

"I only know one Simone, and she definitely doesn't have a tab here."

"Simone Papsburg?".

"I don't know her last name."

I didn't either. "She lives on Second Street?"

"I don't know where she lives, sir," he said.

"I must be in the wrong town." I paid my bill in cash. When I got back in my car, I called the number Candice had given April for Simone. I used a burner phone I had bought just in case Simone recognized my number and decided to ignore my call.

"Hello?" a woman answered.

"Hi, is Simone there?"

"This is she."

"I am the manager at the Los Gatos Cafe and we are having a situation here. A man is claiming that you will pay his bill. He says he's your brother."

"What? I don't have a brother," she said.

"Is your name Simone Papsburg?"

"No. Simone Huntley. You have the wrong number. How did you get this number anyway?"

"The man gave it to me. I'm sorry to bother you."

I pulled up Google on my phone, looked up the number for the sanitation company for Los Gatos, and called it. "Hi, yes, this is Simone Huntley and I am having trouble with my garbage service. No one came to pick it up this week and this is the second time in a row. I'm beginning to think you have the wrong address on my account."

A woman's voice: "Where do you live, sir?"

"Twenty-two twenty-two Second Street."

"Let me just look that up real fast . . . . I'm not showing any account associated with that address."

"This is crazy. I've been dealing with this for two weeks now. Do I even have an account with you guys at all?"

"I'm sorry you're having so much trouble. Let me see if I can look you up another way. What was your name again?"

"Simone Huntley."

"And your phone number?"

I gave her Simone's number.

"Okay," she said. "There you are. We have you listed under two-seventeen Jones Road. I can change that for you right now if you like. What was the other address again?"

"Thank you so much. I have to run, but I'll call you back."

Jones Road was a narrow street five minutes from downtown, with trees and a view of the foothills. The homes were large but modest considering the average income in Los Gatos. I put on one of the blazers I had packed, walked up the steps of two-seventeen, and knocked on the front door. After thirty seconds, a woman around my age answered. She had curly black hair, big brown eyes, and thin, dark eyebrows. She wore jeans, a black blouse, and a long, gray cardigan.

"Good afternoon," I said. "My name is Tim

Kitchens. Are you Simone Huntley?"

"Yes?" she said.

"We spoke on the phone about a week ago. I was hoping I could ask you a few questions."

"Oh, you're the guy who's been asking about Don. Are you a cop?"

"No. I'm a lawyer."

"Is there a case against Don?" she said.

"Not at this moment. Right now I'm just investigating."

"Okay, well, I told you over the phone I didn't want to talk about it, and I meant it. And now you show up at my house?"

"I'm very sorry to bother you." I pulled up a picture of Sage on my phone that April had sent me, and I showed it to Simone. "This is the boy I believe is being abused by either Don Tidwell or his son. We want to help the boy. It would really mean something if you could give us any kind of information at all."

Simone's lips tightened around her teeth. "You want to look at pictures?" she said and turned and walked away from the door. "Come on in, let's look at pictures."

I went inside and stood beside her in front of a mantle with a line of framed photographs on it. Two were of a man in a suit shaking hands with other men in suits, and the remaining four were of children, two boys, and one girl, at varying stages of development. Simone pointed to them. "These are my children," she said. "And if I have to choose between their future and the future of someone else's children, I'm going to choose mine every time."

"What does answering a few questions about Don Tidwell have to do with their future?"

"Everything. When or if Don and his little compound out there in Ettersburg get exposed, it's going to be a national story, and I don't want my name or my family's name attached to that—to have my children deal with that at school. What if we have to move? Do you know how good the schools are in Los Gatos? This is my family's life we're talking about, and I'm not going to let something that happened to me twenty years ago ruin it."

"What do you mean a national story?"

"You know what? I can't even talk about this here. I won't contaminate my home with this. Did you drive here?"

"Yes."

"I'll tell you what. I have ten minutes before I have to pick up my girl at basketball practice. I will answer your questions until I have to leave, but only in your car."

"Okay," I said. She followed me to my car, and we got inside.

"Were you abused by Don Tidwell?"

"Yes," she said. "By him and Jared."

"What's going on at the house in Ettersburg that you think is going to make the national news?"

"Inbreeding."

"Inbreeding?"

"Don has at least two kids by one of his daughters. I saw them when I was there. I also saw his other two daughters, pregnant with their own brother's kids. Have you ever seen a pregnant twelve-year-old girl?"

"No."

"That was twenty years ago. Who knows how many inbred children are running around that property now? I know they didn't stop trying to make them. It's part of their belief system. Don's crazy. He used to make me recite this crazy prayer every night, and I'm not going to repeat it because I'm never going to say it again in my life. But basically, Don believes mankind should go back to being how Adam and Eve were before God kicked them out of paradise. He thinks we shouldn't feel shame when we're naked, and other nonsense like that. That's why he let his two inbred kids get away with everything. He said they were like Adam before he ate the fruit. He treated them like princes. They were a little slow in the head, but they were nasty."

I had seen appalling crimes and criminals as an assistant district attorney, but nothing like this. "I need that in a statement," I said.

"I already told you I'm not getting involved."

"How can you not get involved when you have the power to stop this?"

"As a mother, you have to make hard choices."

"Come on. That's bullshit."

"I have to go," she said, and opened the car door. "If you come here again, I'll call the police. And stop bothering my mother, too. If she wants to be oblivious let her be oblivious. I've made my peace with that."

"I'm glad you're at peace," I said.

She stepped out and walked away without shutting the passenger-side door, then she climbed into a Cadillac Escalade.

I drove back to San Francisco. After checking into a hotel off Gough Street in Hayes Valley, I called April. I told her I was unable to find Simone and would try again in the morning. I didn't want to give her the truth over the phone. I wanted to be there for her, in person, when she learned that Sage was in the worst situation imaginable, and we were running out of legal options.

22

The Bottoms

I RECEIVED A TEXT from Madeline Wednesday morning, two hours before my interview: "Mitch has to reschedule for Friday at eleven a.m. Is that okay?"

I sent back, "It will have to be," then finished brushing my teeth. As I undressed to take a shower, a call came in on my phone. I answered, "Krista. Good morning."

"I've changed my mind," she said. "I'll give you the evidence on your terms, but it has to be twenty thousand. You can pay it in installments if you want, but the first installment has to be five thousand."

After very little haggling, I got her down to fifteen thousand. She seemed desperate. I didn't have fifteen thousand, but I figured April and I could handle installments if her information led to finally knowing what had happened to July.

"But I want it in writing," she said. "I want a contract, and I want you to bring it to me tonight."

"That's not going to work," I said. "I'm in San Francisco until Friday at least. How about I draw up the contract, sign it, and have someone bring it to you?" I

194

considered asking April, but she hated Krista and had thought her "evidence" was a lie from the beginning. "I'll have Levi come by with it."

She said, "That's fine. He can find me at the Eureka Inn, room one-five-seven."

After I got off the phone, I drew up the contract and emailed it to Levi, then called him and convinced him to run the errand for me.

I spent the rest of the day drinking and eating with old friends. I passed out in my hotel room early that night. When I woke up in the morning, I had two missed calls from April, but none from Levi. I called him after breakfast.

"She wouldn't give it to me," Levi said. "She said you have to come."

"Jesus Christ."

I called Krista and got her voicemail. I kept trying every hour after that, without success, throughout another day of drinking and eating with friends. By Friday morning I was primed for my interview. I left my car at the hotel, took a bus downtown, and met Runiyon in his office on Fremont Street. He was a slow-talking man with a long, sallow face and a smile that occupied only half his mouth. We got along fine and the interview went well.

Afterward, I called Madeline to thank her again for the opportunity. She offered to take me to lunch, but I declined. I drove over the Golden Gate Bridge around noon and reached April's house five and a half hours later.

"What are you doing here?" April said after answering the door. The tone in her voice was flat and her face was expressionless. She turned and walked away, leaving the door open. I followed her inside.

"I thought you wanted me to come over today?"

She stood in the threshold of the kitchen with her arms crossed. She was wearing sweatpants. There was a bowl on the coffee table with dry, crusted bits of cereal inside. The TV was on. "How was your interview?" she said.

"Fine," I said.

"Why did I have to hear about it from your mom? Why didn't you tell me?"

"What's the big deal?"

She pushed a breath out of her nose and shook her head. "Did you get the job?"

"I don't know yet. It was just informal. If they liked me, there will likely be multiple interviews."

"But if you do, you're moving back?"

"I'm moving back no matter what."

She nodded slowly. "This might sound corny, but I like you, and it's only getting worse. If you're just going to move away, I don't think we should see each other anymore. Besides, I don't think we're good for each other anyway. You're obviously still unstable, and I'm . . . I don't know what's wrong with me."

"You're fine. I'm fine. I'm not ready to end this. I really like you too. That's not corny. We can figure something out."

She stared at me for a moment, then sighed and said, "I got a letter from Child Services. They said my claim was unsubstantiated. They said that it had come to their attention that I had hired a private investigator who had trespassed on Don Tidwell's property twice. Don has filed harassment charges against me, and he told me he is seeking a restraining order. He says I'll never get to see my nephew again."

"There's no way—" I said but was quickly cut off.

"Shut up," April said. "I thought we talked about you keeping yourself under control. You promised me. What did you do?" Her eyes and eyelashes were wet and shiny and beautiful.

I told her the whole story of what had happened in Ettersburg, then I repeated the account Simone had given me of the abuse she had suffered at the hands of both Don and Jared. After I was done, she stared through me for about thirty seconds, then turned and walked down the hall. When she came back, she was holding a revolver.

"What are you doing?" I said.

She put the gun in her purse and grabbed her coat. I stood in front of the door.

"This is not how to handle this," I said.

"What else can I do?" she said. "You said yourself, Simone won't talk."

"There are other options. Don't do this. You could get killed. Sage could get killed. Just give me a day to think of something. Can you do that? Can you wait?"

She sat down on the couch, set her purse on the cushion next to her, put her face in her hands, and began to sob.

I went to her and placed a hand on her shoulder.

"Don't touch me," she said in a soft voice.

All I wanted to do was hold her, comfort her, but I had lost that privilege, and it hurt.

"Please leave," she said.

23

Eureka Inn

WHEN I WAS BACK in my car, I called Krista one more time. But her voicemail picked up, so I drove twenty minutes south to the Eureka Inn, where she was staying. I parked on the other side of the street between the old Carnegie Free Library, with its Greek-inspired pillars and facade, and the abandoned Downtowner Hotel, with its fenced-off parking lot and boarded-up windows.

The Eureka Inn occupied a city block and was four stories tall. It had several gables and was painted white with green trim and green skirting. I walked through the glass doors into a lobby with high ceilings, chandeliers, and a brick fireplace. A twenty-foot-tall Christmas tree stood next to the fireplace, and poinsettias had been placed on each table. "Little Drummer Boy" played over the lobby sound system.

As I turned down a hallway to search for Room 157, hoping Krista was still there, I recognized a voice coming from the lounge. I walked inside and found Levi sitting at the bar.

"What the hell are you doing here?" I said.

He turned and smiled when he saw me. "What's going on?" he said.

"I'm going to see Krista. What's going on with you?"

His smile widened. "Nothing. Just hanging out, enjoying a drink with my friend Phil here." Levi waved his glass toward the bartender, a tall, skinny man. "Phil plays keys for me sometimes."

I nodded to Phil. "How you doing? I'm Tim." I shook his bony hand, then sat down beside Levi. "I thought for a second you were here to see Krista."

"No, I am," Levi said.

"Oh, really? How long's that been going on?"

"I don't know. We've been on a tear since that first night. I hope this doesn't screw things up for you."

"It doesn't," I said. "Does Sandy know you're here?"

His smile disappeared. "We broke up."

"What happened?" I said.

"I got cuttlefished, like you said."

"Todd?"

"Yep." Levi raised his glass, as if to a fallen comrade.

"You're kidding me? Shit. I'm sorry, man."

"It's alright. I'm moving away in a few months anyway. It was never going to work."

"I guess you're not doing that play anymore then," I said.

"Fuck no."

"I'm not sure I am either," I said.

"Why not?"

"I had kind of a falling out with April."

"You too, huh? Was it a dancer?"

"No. It was all me."

Levi took another drink. He looked and smelled like he had been on a three-day bender. "Have you ever eaten ice cream out of the same bowl you just ate fried rice out of?" he said.

"No, I don't think I have."

"Sometimes the rice kernels left in the bowl stick to the ice cream."

"I can imagine."

"That's what we are," he said. "We're the fried rice stuck in the ice cream. We were good in our time, but now we're fucking with desert, and no one likes that."

"That sounds about right," I said in a patronizing tone he was too drunk to recognize. Then I got up. "I'm going to go see Krista. You want to come?"

He finished his drink in one gulp and said, "Yep."

I followed him down the hall, and when he found Room 157, he knocked on the door. No one answered. He knocked again. Nothing.

"Is she supposed to be here?" I said.

"Yeah," Levi said.

"Do you have a secret knock or something?"

He smiled and pulled a keycard out of his wallet.

"You already have a key? Things are moving fast, huh?"

He slipped the card in and out of the slot and pushed the door open. He took one step inside, then stopped. "Holy shit," he said.

I looked over his shoulder, then stepped by him.

The room had been ransacked. The mattress and box spring had been overturned. The sheets had been stripped and thrown on the floor next to the drawers from the TV cabinet, desk, and nightstand. Women's clothes were scattered around an empty suitcase. One of the windows was open.

I walked deeper into the room and found Krista lying under the mattress that was propped up on the table next to the window. One of her shoulders leaned against the built-in bed frame, and the other was flat on the floor. Her T-shirt had been pulled up over her mouth, and her sweatpants had been pulled down to her knees, revealing black, thigh-high stockings and black, sheer lingerie. There were three dark, small holes in her chest, and her eyes looked empty.

Levi stood beside me. "Oh my God," he said, and reached to lift the mattress looming over Krista's body.

"Don't touch it," I said. "She's dead. Don't touch anything."

Levi let his arms drop to his sides, and I squatted down and pressed two fingers against the inside of her wrist just to be certain. Her skin was cold, almost damp. I kept my fingers there for a minute but felt nothing, then called 911.

Levi left the room and I followed him into the hallway. When I got off the phone, he said, "I just saw her a few hours ago." His eyes were unfocused and pointing to my right.

"Where?" I said.

"Here."

"You guys were just hanging out?"

"Yeah."

"From when to when?"

Levi placed a palm on his cheek. "I came here around two and left at four."

"You guys have sex?"

"Yeah."

"Did you wear a condom?"

"No," he said. "Just give me a second." He leaned against the wall, slid down into a crouch, and rested his arms on his knees and stared at the carpet.

I waited a minute or so before I said, "I'm sorry Levi, but you have to tell me what's going on. I need to know before the police come. You're going to be a suspect. Why did you come back? Did she call you?"

Levi sighed. "No. She told me to come back before I left. She had to go do something with her family and she wanted me to meet her here around seven with some coke."

"You have the coke on you now?"

"Yes."

"Okay. Forget about that for a second. What did you do after you left here?"

Levi rubbed his face. "I went home and took a shower, then I called my coke guy and went over to his house."

"What time was that?"

Levi looked on his phone. "I called him at four-forty-three and went over to his house right after that. He lives about ten minutes from me."

"How long were you there?" I said.

"Not long. I just picked it up and went home."

"Did anyone else see you there?"

"His girlfriend and some other dude were there. They saw me."

"Then what?"

"I did a little coke and played guitar and drank beer. Then I came here and saw my buddy and had a drink at the bar. I was a little early. I was only there a few minutes before you came."

"Did you call anyone since two?"

"I called one of the guys I play music with but he didn't answer."

"What time was that?"

He checked his phone again. "Five-fifteen, just after I got the coke."

"Did you leave a ninety-minute voicemail?"

"No."

"Then your alibi isn't that great."

"Can't they track my phone or something?"

"Just because your phone's at home doesn't mean you are."

Levi rubbed his forehead, then looked up at the ceiling. "This is crazy. You think the cops are going to think I killed her?"

"It's going to cross their mind. We're both going to be suspects. They're going to question us. Don't go to the station if they ask, and don't offer any information, just answer their questions. Don't say anything about drugs or alcohol, and try to say very little about hooking up with Krista. You knew her and were friends. Now go to the bathroom in the lobby and flush the coke down the toilet. Make sure it all goes down. And take my phone. While you're in there, call your coke guy and tell him to leave out the coke when the cops talk to him, although I'm sure he will, but you never know." I handed Levi the burner phone I still had on me, and he walked down the hallway toward the lobby.

Two uniformed Eureka Police arrived first. They cordoned off the hallway with tape and asked me and Levi a few basic questions. Then the evidence techs arrived, followed by the coroner, the sergeant, three more uniformed officers, and two detectives.

Levi and I were questioned by Detective Westbrook. Westbrook had small blue eyes, big lips, a short white beard, and a forehead like a beluga. His hair was the same length and color as his beard.

After going over the answers we had given the

uniformed officers, Westbrook said, "At this point, I would like to invite you guys to come to the station for further questioning. It's a little quieter, a little more comfortable. We can go in my car, or you can follow me, whichever you like."

"We would rather just finish up here," I said.

"Are you sure?"

"Yes."

"Okay. No problem." He pulled a small, black audio-recorder from his pocket. "I'm terrible at taking notes, so I'll be recording our conversation. It's just for me. I have a bad memory. And I'd like to talk to each of you separately."

"I'm sorry, but we won't answer your questions if you're recording, and we will not be talking to you separately."

Westbrook furrowed his brow and stared at me for a long moment. "Okay," he said. He slipped the recorder back into his pocket and pulled out a pen and notepad. He asked us detailed questions about where we had been in the last twenty-four hours, our relationship with Krista, and how we had come to discover the body. He repeated some of the questions in different wording two-to-three times. He was interested in Krista's "evidence" and wanted to know April's phone number. I gave it to him.

"That's it for now," he said. "I'll be in touch."

Levi and I walked to the lounge, sat at the bar, and ordered straight Jim Beam from Levi's keyboard player. After gulping half of mine down, I called Ted Nadler, the accountant who was Krista's ex, and Jared Tidwell's friend. I wanted to hear his reaction to Krista's death, get his first impressions on who might have done it, and maybe get Krista's boyfriend's phone number, but

Ted wasn't picking up his phone.

"That was brutal," Levi said when I put down my phone.

"It might get worse if they don't find another suspect," I said. "You want to go over to Lost Coast Brewery?" After finishing our drinks, we walked through the lobby and out the back door into the parking lot.

"There's Krista's car," Levi said, pointing to a newer Toyota 4Runner with a policeman standing in front of it and two evidence techs milling about inside. The front, driver-side window had been shattered.

24

Lost Coast Brewery

THE BREWERY WAS PACKED with the Saturday-night crowd. Growers in their flat-brimmed hats and contractors with their cell phones attached to their hips sat at the bar, while men and women dressed in cotton earth-tones drank and ate at the tables. Levi called them Yippies, a combination between Yuppies and Hippies. The air was humid. Loud, drunken conversation blended with laughter and clinking cups and plates.

I recognized the bartender from the last time I had been there. She was Jared's ex-girlfriend, according to Ted. I found a small opening at the bar, wedged myself in, and tried to get her attention. While I waited for her to see me, I scanned the room for Ted. He wasn't there. The bartender came over ten minutes later. "Have you seen Ted Nadler?" I said.

"Yeah, but he left," she said.

"Did he say if he was coming back?" I said.

She gave me a look like I was crazy.

"Okay, thanks," I said. "Can I get a pitcher of that?" I pointed to a tap handle with a sculpture of a cat on it.

She poured the beer, and I took the pitcher and two glasses to a table by the hallway that had just opened up.

"What's going on?" Levi said.

"Ted was here earlier. I want to see if he comes back. If he's not here by the time we finish this pitcher, we'll leave."

Levi poured a glass for himself, took a drink, and shook his head. "Poor Krista," he said. "I can't believe she's dead." He smiled. "She was fun, man. She was great. Why would anyone kill her?"

"To keep her quiet," I said. "I think she was blackmailing the Tidwells."

"With what, that evidence you were telling me about?"

"Yeah. You saw her room—and her car. Whoever killed her was looking for something specific. Did you notice anything weird while you were with her? Angry phone conversations, anything like that?"

"No, nothing weird. She talked with her sister a few times. That was about it. Then she went to see her sister. That was yesterday."

"Did you go with her?"

"No."

"Did her boyfriend know about you?"

"She had a boyfriend? She never said anything about that."

Levi and I talked for an hour, taking our time with the beer. When the pitcher was finished, I stood up and walked toward the bathroom. As I reached the end of the hall, I recognized two men standing next to the back door. I stopped.

"We've been looking for you," Don said. His son, Jared, stood next to him, staring at me with his unsettling blue eyes.

"Nice to see you," I said.

Don pulled a small pistol from his coat pocket, then slipped it back in. "Let's go to the bathroom for a second," he said.

I did not move.

"If you run," he said, "I'll shoot you in the back."

My legs felt unsteady beneath me, but I managed to turn the corner and reach the bathroom. Jared kindly held the door open for me, then I heard him shut and lock it. As I turned to face them, Jared punched me in the gut, and I doubled over. I could not breathe. I felt like my insides had grown too large for my body. Then Jared slapped me on the ear, hard. I heard ringing.

"Don't leave a mark," Don said.

Jared kicked me in the thigh, and I went down. Don stood over me and held the gun to my head. "Death is pure," he said, "and you are undeserving of it, but I will give it to you before your time if you continue to contaminate my thoughts and my family. Do you understand?'

"Yes," I said with a dry mouth.

Don put his gun back in his pocket, turned, and opened the door. Jared bent over and screamed in my face, then walked out, followed by his father.

I struggled to my feet, hobbled over to the sink, and washed my face with shaking hands. The pressure in my bladder was painful. I went to the urinal and stood for five minutes before my muscles relaxed enough for me to pee. Levi found me as I was finishing.

"How long does it take you to take a piss?" he said. "Jesus Christ."

I zipped up and turned around. "I just had a gun pulled on me," I said.

"What?"

"Don pulled a gun on me and threatened to kill me."

"Jesus. You're limping."

"I'm aware of that."

"How did they know you were here?" he said.

"The bartender is Jared's ex-girlfriend. I'm assuming she told them."

Levi followed me into the parking lot, and we climbed into his truck.

"Your ear is red," he said, after turning on the dome light.

"Good," I said, and handed him my phone. "Here. Take a picture. Get one close-up and one of the side of my face."

Levi held up my phone and snapped the photos. "You going to the police?" he said.

"Yeah. I'm going to report this. I'd like to get a real drink first though."

"I got whiskey," he said, handing me a paper bag that had been sitting between us on the bucket seat. "I forgot all about it. Krista asked me to pick it up before I came over."

I opened the bag and saw three bottles inside: a fifth of whiskey, a fifth of sweet vermouth, and a small bottle of bitters.

25

Bayshore Mall

AS I ATE CEREAL Monday morning at my parent's kitchen table, I received a text message from Becky: "Meet me at bayshore mall food court at 10. I have something from Krista."

I texted back, "What do you have?"

After five minutes without a response, I called her, but she didn't answer, which wasn't surprising considering the reception where she lived.

I drove to Eureka, to work, and reached the Law Offices of William J. Rafferty at nine. Melissa, the receptionist, said "Good Morning" as I entered. Her smile was full of pity. I could smell the fresh lilies on her desk from the front door.

"Bill wants to see you," she said.

I dropped my bag at my desk, knocked twice on Bill's door, and walked through. A small plastic Christmas tree sat on his desk. He wore a Santa hat. "Please sit down," he said.

I sat.

"I'm sorry to have to do this," he said, "but I think you knew this was coming. I'm going to have to go in a new direction with the paralegal position." He pushed an envelope to the edge of his desk. "Here is your final paycheck."

I leaned forward in the chair. "I didn't know this was coming at all," I said. "What's the problem?"

"It's hard for me to believe you don't know the answer to that. You barely come to work."

"I get my work done on time," I said. "I do everything you ask."

"That's true. But being on time and available in this office is just as important. Just doing the tasks that I give you as you're running out the door isn't enough. You have to be a part of the team. We're a team here."

"Is this because I wouldn't wear Hawaiian shirts on casual Fridays?"

"No, but now that you mention it that could be symbolic of a larger issue. If I felt like you were part of the team I might have been willing to make exceptions. This is a small office, and we're like family here. I don't think you ever quite grasped that."

I was on the brink of throwing a temper tantrum, but I held it in. Part of me understood his position. I took the news like a gentleman, shook Bill's hand, and thanked him for the opportunity. I cleaned out my desk in two minutes and said goodbye to everybody. Melissa hugged me on the way out.

"We'll always have sticky buns," I said.

She nodded, on the verge of tears. She had ignored, or failed to detect, the sarcasm in my voice.

"It's okay," I said. "I'll be all right."

"I can't believe he did this to you so close to Christmas," she said.

"It's okay. I'll be okay. Have a Merry Christmas." I hugged her again and left.

I had less than an hour before I was supposed to meet Becky at the food court. Because April still wasn't answering my calls, and I had a little time, I drove one block past the courthouse and parked on Sixth Street, outside a two-story, stone building where the *Times-Standard* kept their offices. I walked through the front door and asked the receptionist if April Morrison was available. He took down my name, and I sat in one of the chairs by the door.

Five minutes later, April came down the hall wearing gray slacks and a black collared shirt. She stood in front of me with her arms crossed. "What's going on?" she said.

I stood. "Sorry to bother you at work but you weren't answering your phone."

"Okay?" she said.

"Did you hear about Krista?" I said.

"Yes."

"I think Krista was the one your sister was meeting that night five years ago. I think she had something on the Tidwells and was blackmailing them."

April closed her eyes, placed a hand on her forehead, and said, "You think maybe she knew they killed my sister?"

"Maybe. I'm looking into it today."

"I told the police about the woman in Los Gatos. They said they're going to talk to her."

"That woman's not going to tell the police anything."

"I'm sorry, I have to go back to work," she said in a somber tone. She sounded exhausted.

"I'll call you," I said.

She turned and walked away.

I left the *Times-Standard* building, got in my car, and

drove to the Bayshore Mall on the southern end of Eureka. The parking lot was full. A light rain was falling. People hurried to and from their cars.

I set an alarm on my phone and took a nap in my car until a quarter to ten, then I walked into the food court, ordered a coffee at Starbucks, and sat down at a table in front of Burger King.

The mall seemed busy for a Monday. The food court was decorated with Christmas lights, ribbons, wreaths, garlands, and ornaments. The employees at the pizza place wore Santa hats. Christmas music played over the sound system.

I was nearly done with my coffee when I spotted Becky walking through the doors on the other side of the food court. She wore sweatpants and a tight zip-up hoodie. She carried a manila envelope under one arm and a small, silver purse under the other.

I stood up and waved at her, and she came over, sat down, and put the envelope on the table.

"I'm sorry about Krista," I said.

"Me, too," she said, pushing the envelope to my side of the table. "She left this for you."

I opened the envelope and pulled out two items: a twenty-four-month lease for a house in Shelter Cove signed by ten people, including Krista's mom, Winona Stapely, and a bulky flip-phone that would not power on and was too old to record video.

"What is this stuff?" I said. "Why did Krista leave me an old lease that belonged to her mom?"

"I don't know. I thought you would know. She gave this envelope to me and said it was her inheritance from her mom, and she was afraid her family was going to steal it or something. She told me if anything ever happened to her to give it to you because you were her lawyer and you had the rest of her inheritance, and you would know what to do. And when I asked her what was going to happen to her, she told me nothing was going to happen, she would be fine, that this was just in case, but then someone killed her, and I don't know what to do. I don't know what this stuff is, and I don't know if someone's going to try to kill me because of it, and I'm just doing what she asked me to do."

"Okay," I said. "It's okay. No one's going to kill you over this stuff. You'll be fine. But none of this makes any sense. I wasn't her lawyer, and I don't have any part of her inheritance. Does her boyfriend know anything about this?"

"No. Krista broke up with him a few days after you got in that fight with the Tidwells."

I leaned back in my chair. "Where was Mike on Saturday?"

"Mike didn't kill Krista. Mike was in Idaho. He still is."

"All right. When did Krista give this envelope to you?"

"She gave it to me after her mom died about two months ago."

"Two months ago? Krista told me her mom's memorial service was the day before Thanksgiving."

"It was. They had to wait for family to get into town."

"Who do you think killed her?"

"I don't know. How am I supposed to know?"

"You knew her. She never said anything?"

"She said a lot of things, but she didn't tell me who killed her."

"You never noticed anything alarming?" I said. "Arguments? Threats? Feuds? Anything?"

"There were people she didn't like, mostly girls out in SoHum. But nothing serious, just catty shit. Not even any fights. She did get a little mad at her mom's funeral, though. We had to leave early. She got in an argument with her mom's old boss."

"Pete Holloway?" I said.

"Yeah."

"Her mom, Winona, was his secretary right?" I said.

"His personal assistant, for like twenty years, or something crazy like that. The guy gave a speech at the funeral and cried and everything."

"Did Krista tell you what the argument was about?"

"Not really. She just said he was an asshole, basically, and he didn't really care about her mom. It just sounded like family stuff to me. People were sad. It was a funeral."

I hunched over and tapped my forehead against the table over and over in four-four time.

"What's wrong?" she said.

I looked up at her. "I don't know what to do. I'm trying, Becky. I'm really trying here, and I'm lost. I don't know what to do."

I put the two items back in the envelope, and as I folded it to put in my pocket, a man and a woman walked up to the table. The man was short with a solid build. The woman held shopping bags. She looked familiar.

"Are you Tim Kitchens?" the man said.

"Yeah," I said.

The man threw a punch that landed just above my right eye and knocked me out of my chair. The pain resonated throughout my brain.

"No one calls my wife a dolphin rapist," the man said.

As I got up, I saw Becky push the man, God bless her, but he ignored her and pointed at me. "I don't ever want to see you near her store again," he said. His wife I knew now was Heidi Gerhardt. She had a smile on her face as they both walked away.

I sat back in the chair.

Becky grabbed some napkins from Burger King and handed them to me. "You're bleeding," she said. "Hold this on your eye. You might need stitches. You should go wash this in the bathroom. Who was that guy?"

I held the napkins in a bundle against my eye. "I think he was the Moonflower lady's husband."

"Who's Moonflower lady?"

"The owner of Moonflower in Old Town."

"The shoe store? I love that place."

I gave Becky a look.

"Why did you call her a dolphin rapist?" she said.

"I didn't. I compared her actions to dolphin rape. But I guess the distinction got lost somewhere. Thanks for sticking up for me though. I appreciate that."

Becky's eyes were wide with excitement. "No problem," she said. "That guy sucker-punched you."

I smiled. "You're kind of a brawler aren't you? You know, I still owe you for slashing those tires that day. If you hadn't done that the Tidwells might have killed me. Krista said you guys had some trouble with them after that."

"It wasn't that big a deal. Mike was madder than anyone. I don't know why. He never liked the Tidwells that much anyway. They were always Ted's friends. I think he was just mad he wasn't getting free abalone anymore."

"Don used to give him abalone?" I asked.

"Yeah. All the time."

"That's a pretty expensive gift. Were they close?"

Becky shook her head.

That didn't add up. People don't usually give abalones away to just anyone. I took my phone out of my pocket and looked at the picture I'd taken of the Tidwell family photo that had been in Don's desk in Stone Lagoon. Underneath the photo were the three abalone cards I had found. When I looked closer, I saw they were all for the same year. Fishermen were only allowed to have one abalone card per year.

I stood up and smiled and held out my hands. "That's it," I said. "I'm an idiot." I could feel the blood dripping down my cheek, but I didn't care. "They're poachers!" I said, and I laughed. "They're fucking poachers. I'm an idiot."

26

Founders Hall

AFTER GETTING SEVEN STITCHES above my left eye at St. Joseph Hospital, I went to the Department of Fish and Wildlife office on Second Street and spoke with Warden Tomlin, a man with a wide face, low forehead, and bushy mustache. I told him about Don's extra abalone cards, showed him the picture, and warned him that Don and his son were dangerous. Tomlin seemed undaunted, thanked me for the tip, asked me to send him a copy of the picture, and said he would check the records. I shook his hand and left.

April still wasn't answering my calls, so I stopped at the *Times-Standard* building again. When the receptionist told me April had left early, I took a shot and drove to her house in Arcata, where I found her sitting in the back seat of the rusty, old Dodge Dart parked on her front lawn. I walked up to the back door and pulled on the handle. The hinges croaked as the heavy steel door swung open. I sat next to April on the bench seat. The cab smelled like dust, oil, and vinyl. April's eyes were red and swollen.

"Hey," I said.

"Hey," she said.

"You thinking about Sage?"

She nodded.

I said, "I just reported Don to Fish and Wildlife for poaching abalone. I think there's a chance it could lead to something."

"What do you mean?" April's voice was soft and low.

"Fish and Wildlife take abalone poaching very seriously. If they have reason to believe Don's been poaching, they're going to search his property, and if what Simone told me is true, if they go out to Ettersburg and see pregnant twelve-year-olds with no Social Security numbers, then it's over. The Sherriff gets involved, Child Welfare gets involved, and all the kids get taken away."

April squinted. "Do you really think that will happen?"

"There's a chance. Again, if Simone was telling the truth."

"Are you sure he's been poaching? I mean, do you have proof?"

"Yes. I saw his extra abalone cards. There were at least three. And I have a picture of them. I was an idiot not to see it sooner. You're only supposed to have one. My dad knew a guy once that got two by saying he lost his original. If that's how Don got all of his, then there'll be a record of it. All Fish and Wildlife has to do is look it up."

She was silent for ten seconds. Then she said, "How soon will we know if they found something?"

"However long it takes them to do a preliminary investigation and get a search warrant. Two weeks. A month, maybe. I'm not sure how fast they work."

April leaned in close and hugged me. I could smell her perfume and the shampoo in her hair. "Thank you," she said, and drew back. Our eyes met for a long moment, then she turned away.

I reached in my coat pocket and pulled out the phone Krista had left for me. "I need an old phone charger," I said. "Do you have anything that would fit this?"

April looked at the phone, said "I think so," and got out of the car. I followed her into the house and waited by the door while she searched the hall closet. "I still have all my old phones," she said. "I keep meaning to transfer the pictures to my laptop so I can get rid of them, but I never do." She closed the closet and walked toward me with the phone and a charger. "This one should work."

I took them from her. "You mind if I plug it in real fast?" I said.

"Go 'head. Why do you have such an old phone anyway?"

"Krista wanted me to have it," I said, fiddling with the charger.

"What do you mean she wanted you to have it?"

I recounted my meeting with Becky. When I was done, I said, "Whoever killed her was looking for something. I think this was it. I think this was the evidence she was trying to sell us."

April hovered over me as I knelt and plugged in the phone. I held the power button down until the Verizon logo appeared on the screen. Three successive tones played through the scratchy little speaker, and the home screen popped up with a flat teal background. I searched the call history, messages, photos, and contacts. Everything had been erased except for one contact under the name of July and one brief exchange of text messages:

To July: **Your boyfriends here**/Sent: 6:40 pm Oct 18, 2011

From July: **You mean dick pants?**/Received: 7:11 pm Oct 18, 2011
[Under the message was a grainy picture of a man's body, from the chest to the knees, wearing only women's pantyhose.]

To July: **Dont make me laugh. Hes really mad. He wants everything out by tonight**/Sent: 7:12 pm Oct 18, 2011

From July: **Tell him no problem**/Received: 7:14 pm Oct 18, 2011

To July: **Hes throwing things!!! where are you?**/Sent: 7:14 pm Oct 18, 2011

From July: **Almost there**/Received: 7:15 pm Oct 18, 2011

From July: **Nevermind. i dont want to see him. tell me when he leaves**/Received: 7:15 pm Oct 18, 2011

To July: **K**/Sent: 7:16 pm Oct 18, 2011

To July: **Hes gone**/Sent: 8:06 pm Oct 18, 2011

To July: **Hello?**/Sent: 8:17 Oct 18, 2011

I rested the phone on my thigh and looked up at April. "These were sent the night she disappeared," I said.

"That can't be her," April said.

"Why not?"

"I have her cell phone records. She didn't text anyone after three o'clock that day."

"Maybe she had a burner phone."

"Why would she have a burner phone? She wasn't a criminal."

"She ran pot for Jared before. Maybe she got involved in something else. This is Humboldt County. There's plenty of shit to get involved in."

"May I see that?" April said, reaching her hand out.

I gave her the phone and she began rereading the messages. When she was done, she turned to face me. She had a hurt look in her eyes. "Do you really think this was her?"

"I don't know," I said. "I think it could be."

Her eyes fell back to the phone.

"Are you okay?" I said.

"I don't know."

"Do you want to see what else Krista left me?"

She nodded. "Okay."

I pulled the folded lease and envelope out of my coat pocket and handed them to her. As she looked over the lease, I took the phone with the charger and opened the front door. "I'll be back in a little bit," I said.

"Where you going?"

"I want to catch the Professor before he leaves work for the day, see what he thinks of this phone."

Humboldt State University was on the other side of town, across the highway. The drive took five minutes. I parked on B Street, dropped two quarters in the meter, and walked across campus, up five flights of stairs to Founders Hall. I was hot and breathing through my mouth when I got inside. The halls were empty and quiet. I took off my coat, walked around the courtyard to the back of the building, and found Ryan Lowell's office. The door was closed and locked. Hoping he was still on campus, I stuck my head through an open door across the hall. "Sorry to bother you," I said to a woman sitting behind a desk. "I got a call from Professor Lowell about a projector not working, but I forgot what room he said he was in."

The woman squinted one eye. "I'm not sure. Ask Diane next door. She's a member of that tribe."

"He's in the lecture hall," Diane said through the wall.

The woman smiled. "You heard her."

I found the back entrance to the lecture hall on the second floor and snuck in without anyone noticing. There were over a hundred students in the class. Professor Lowell stood in front, twenty rows down, wearing jeans and a V-neck sweater without an undershirt. When a young woman in the middle of the class raised her hand, he threw a small blue football at her. She giggled when she caught it, then asked a question about conclusion paragraphs.

I leaned against the back wall and watched Lowell lecture and throw that football around for thirty minutes. After class, a dozen or so students lingered to ask him questions and laugh at his jokes. I waited for them to leave before I approached him.

"What can I do for you, Mr. Kitchens?" he said without looking up from his laptop.

"I was hoping to ask you a few more questions about July?"

He raised his eyes to meet mine and smiled. "Is this a hobby for you?"

"Something like that."

He checked his watch. "I have a birthday party to go to, but I can give you ten minutes." He tossed his little football to me, and I caught it. "Ask your questions and I shall endeavor to satisfy," he said.

"I appreciate that. I found some strange text messages I'd like to get your opinion on." I pulled out Krista's phone and held it up. "You mind taking a look?"

"I am here to serve."

I walked up beside Lowell and showed him the messages. When we had gone through them all, he turned to me and said, "These are from July?"

"Yeah, I think so, sent the night she disappeared."

"Who's she talking to?"

"I'm not sure. I was hoping you could help me with that? Let me just read a few quotes back to you: 'Your boyfriend's here,' 'He wants everything out tonight,' 'He's throwing things.'"

"I get it," he said. "I realize how that sounds. But July and I weren't breaking up. We were moving to Paris together."

"The last time we talked you said you thought she was cheating on you."

"But not at the time. I didn't really start believing that until after she left."

I pulled up the picture of the naked man again. "Is this you?"

Lowell snorted. "No. Pantyhose has never been my thing."

"Who do you think July was cheating on you with?"

"I don't know."

"Come on," I said. "Someone popped into your mind just now. Every man knows their rivals. There's always someone that makes her laugh too much, a coworker, an ex-boyfriend. There's always someone."

Lowell chuckled. "That's true, but we're talking about a long time ago here. There was someone, but I don't think July was cheating on me with him."

"Who?"

"Her old step-father."

"Pete Holloway, the Supervisor?"

"Yeah. She called him her second father. And he was, in a way. He would give her money sometimes, and find her jobs. He got her that office job at the property management place. Then sometimes he would text her late at night, which always kind of bothered me. I don't know. They seemed more like brother and sister than father and daughter to me, like a really close brother and sister."

"So you don't think they were sleeping together."

"No."

"But it crossed your mind."

He shrugged. "I guess it did, but a lot of things cross my mind. That doesn't make them true. Sometimes jealousy can make you think crazy things."

"True enough," I said. "Thank you for your time, Professor. I really appreciate it."

I stuck out my hand and Lowell shook it.

"No problem," he said. "Tell April I should have July's suitcase for her in a few weeks. I'm going down to see my parents for Christmas, and I'm sure it's there."

"She'll be happy to hear that," I said, and tossed his little football back to him.

I drove back to April's and found her sitting in the back seat of the Dodge Dart again. When I stepped inside, she turned off the music that had been playing on her phone. The lease was on the seat between us.

"How much time do you spend in this car?" I said.

"It's comforting to me," she said. "Don't make fun of me."

"I won't."

I rehashed my conversation with Lowell, and when I was done, April picked up the lease and pointed at the company name in the header, which read Lost Coast Property Management. "This is the place where July worked for a while," she said, then turned to the signature page. "Do any of these names pop out at you?"

The page had been signed by the agent, Tammie Campbell, the landlord, Dave Massey, and eight tenants. Each signature was dated April 1, 2010, eighteen months before July's disappearance.

"Dave Massey," I said. He was the one whose number April had found in July's last cell phone bill. In early November, Massey's widow told me the call must have been made by mistake because neither she nor her late husband had known July. "This doesn't necessarily mean Dave knew July," I said.

"It's a pretty big coincidence, though, don't you think? And what about this?" April pointed to one of the signatures of the seven tenants.

I took the lease from her. "Samantha Diana Francis," I said. "That was the name July had on her fake ID in high school."

"I think Krista is trying to tell you something," April said.

27

Shelter Cove

WHEN I GOT HOME that night, I tried to call Dave Massey's widow, Evelyn Massey, but her number was no longer in service, which seemed strange since I had just spoken with her a month earlier. The disconnection had been so recent, though, that she was still listed under that number on the Yellow Pages website, with an address that matched the property in the lease.

The next morning, I decided to make the trip to Shelter Cove to see if I could track her down.

Before I left, I made copies of the lease and saved the messages from Krista's phone onto my laptop. Then I put the lease and phone in a box, along with a signed statement containing everything I knew about the items and where they had come from, and I addressed it to Detective Westbrook.

Taking Tuna with me, I drove south to Eureka, dropped the box off at the Post Office, and stopped at the Lost Coast Brewery to see if Jared's ex-girlfriend, Rayna, was working. I walked in twenty minutes before noon. The lunch crowd had yet to arrive and only a few people sat at the bar. Rayna was cleaning one of the tables.

"You remember me?" I said.

Rayna looked up, a blank expression on her face. "No."

"Someone called Jared Tidwell on Saturday night and told him I was here. Was that you?"

"No. I would never call him."

"But you were his girlfriend at one time, right?" I said.

Rayna stopped cleaning, stood up straight, and shifted her weight to one leg. "Who are you?"

"My name's Tim. I'm a friend of Ted Nadler's."

She raised her eyebrows. "Oh, you're the guy who was looking for him the other night. I called Ted and told him, but I didn't call Jared."

"Then Ted must have called him," I said.

Rayna walked to the bar. "Why does it matter?"

"That's why I came to see you," I said. "It's a little embarrassing actually. I think my wife's been cheating on me with Jared. I found a picture on her phone. There's no face in it, so I can't tell if it's Jared or not. Do you mind taking a look? It's a little graphic."

"What do you mean by graphic?" she said.

"It's a picture of a man's penis."

She laughed. "And you want me to tell you if it belongs to Jared?"

"Yes. I would appreciate it. You guys used to be together, right?"

"Yeah, unfortunately. Go 'head, show it to me."

I took my phone out of my pocket and pulled up the photo of Dick Pants, which I had emailed to myself before leaving the house. When I showed the photo to Rayna, she laughed again. "That's not him," she said.

I thanked Rayna, walked back to my car, and got

back on Highway 101 South. I drove for an hour, following the Eel River through the redwoods to Redway, where I took Briceland-Thorn Road west. Instead of turning right to Ettersburg at the fork, I turned left onto Shelter Cove Road.

A few miles past the Whitethorn Post Office, the road climbed up the King Range. I passed fewer and fewer gravel driveways. I knew houses stood at the end of them, but I couldn't see them through the trees. Not many people lived out here between Whitethorn and Shelter Cove.

Most of the county's population lived in the towns around Humboldt Bay, but the rest lived in the surrounding hills and mountains, on large plots of land cut out of the wilderness. There was no sprawl out here, no new development save for sheds, garages, greenhouses, pump houses, and cabins, built without permits because no one would enforce the building codes out here. This was still the West, or what was left of it.

I stopped at the turnout where July's car had been found. It was on the westbound side of the road, adjacent to a sharp bend. There were no driveways in either direction, only trees. There were some flowers on the ground I assumed Rodney had left.

I got out of the car, gave Tuna some water, then walked around with my cell phone, looking for a signal for five minutes without success. I noticed only one person drive by in that time.

I loaded Tuna back into the car and drove up and over the King Range. The road on the western slope was steep and full of switchbacks. I slowed to ten miles an hour, five miles an hour. By the time I reached Shelter Cove, I could smell my brakes.

As with most of Humboldt County, Shelter Cove survived mainly on tourism and marijuana. It was a small town, less than a thousand people, with three restaurants and five small inns, a harbor, a market, a golf course, and a small airport with a short runway and no tower. Boxy two- and three-story houses with wraparound porches lined the beaches and dotted the forested foothills.

The sky was clear, and the ocean glistened with sunlight. Tuna had been cooped up in the car for two and a half hours and deserved a walk, so I found the beach where my sister and I had played as kids. My parents would take us there nearly every summer, and we would camp nearby. Heather and I would walk up and down the creek that ran through the campground, hunting for frogs with flashlights in the dark, giggling when we caught them, then running back to camp wet, with plans of scaring Mom.

I let Tuna out of the car and walked north along the shoreline, away from the glare of the low winter sun. Tuna ran ahead, wagging her tail and sniffing everything that had washed ashore: seaweed, shells, jellyfish, even a seal carcass. She rolled in the seaweed, but thankfully not the carcass. The beach was ecstasy to her.

We made it back to the car after an hour or so. I punched the address on the lease into my phone and followed the directions up the foothills above Shelter Cove, then down a long, gravel driveway that led to a small, blue house that had been built on a steep hill in a small clearing. An older Subaru Forester was parked in the only flat spot on the property. There was a narrow view of the ocean at the horizon through a break in the tree line.

I parked behind the Subaru, tied Tuna to a tree with

shade, left her a bowl of water, and walked across a high, front deck to the front door, and knocked. I heard shuffling noises inside, then a woman's voice through the closed door: "Who is it?"

"Tim Kitchens," I said. "I'm looking for Evelyn Massey."

"You've found her. What do you want?"

"We spoke on the phone last month about July Morrison. You invited me to coffee."

The door cracked open and the face of a woman in her mid to late eighties appeared. "I remember you," she said, smiling. "You're the lawyer. What a surprise. Come in. Hurry up. I don't want the cat to get out."

Mrs. Massey had white hair, gray-blue eyes, and thin, papery skin. She wore a purple sweatshirt and white slacks.

She sat me down in the living room, which had a nautical theme: wallpaper with pastel seashells, a coffee table made from a ship's wheel, and small ceramic statues of a lighthouse, a boat, and a fisherman. Family pictures occupied most of the flat surfaces and wall space.

An old golden retriever watched me from his bed in the corner while Mrs. Massey made me coffee in the kitchen.

"Did you drive from Eureka?" she said.

"McKinleyville."

"McKinleyville. Wow. What is that, three hours?"

"About two, two and a half."

Mrs. Massey brought a cup of coffee and a Tupperware tub full of cookies into the living room and set them on the coffee table with a few napkins. "These are peanut butter chocolate," she said, opening the lid to the Tupperware. "You have to eat them so I don't get fat." She laughed and sat in the chair across from me.

I took a bite of one of the cookies, which turned to dust in my mouth. The batch must have been at least a month old. I set the cookie on a napkin.

Evelyn said, "So you came all this way just to see lil ol' me?"

"I tried to call first but your number was disconnected."

"Oh, that's my daughter's fault. She finally talked me into getting one of these smartphones. She says I don't need a landline anymore. When you get old like me, everyone starts making decisions for you."

"How long have you lived here?" I said.

"Here? Ummm . . . let's see. I moved here in the fall of two thousand twelve, so about four years now."

"I'm a little confused. The phone number that showed up on July's cell phone bill in two thousand eleven was the same number I called you on a month ago."

"That's because I had them transfer my number when I moved here."

"But that number was for this area. Did you use to live nearby?"

"Oh, yes. I have another house on the beach, about ten minutes away."

"So you have two houses in the same town?"

"Yes."

"Why did you move to the one not on the beach?"

She laughed. "That's what everyone asks me. Everyone thinks I'm crazy, but I never liked living on the beach—too much wind, and tourists always walking in front of the house. Dave was the one who loved it there. When he died there was no reason for me to stay.

I leave the other house empty now. I see a lot more of my grandchildren that way. Their parents can't resist a free stay at a beach house. They actually fight over who gets to visit me." She laughed again. "It's an old lady's dream."

"When your husband was alive did you rent this place out?"

"Yes, we did."

"Do you remember who the last tenants were?" I asked.

"No. My husband always dealt with that stuff." She cocked her head and looked me in the eyes. "You remind me of him, by the way. You have the same build." She stood up, grabbed a framed photo from the end table, and handed it to me. The photo was of a thin, middle-aged man in a gray suit, with a wide smile that made deep creases in his cheeks. "He was a beautiful dresser," Mrs. Massey said. "He had beautiful clothes. I still have most of his wardrobe. I can't find anyone to give it to. Everyone's too fat nowadays, especially my sons-in-law. You should try something on. I bet you're the same size."

"No, thank you, I have plenty of clothes," I said, but she was already leaving the room.

She returned a moment later with a tweed blazer, a white collared shirt, and black slacks draped over her arm. "Here, try these on," she said.

"I have enough clothes, Mrs. Massey. Trust me."

"Not like these. Didn't you say you were a lawyer? A lawyer would be lucky to have these clothes. If you don't try these on, I'm going to be offended."

"Okay." I stood up, took off my fleece, and put on the shirt and blazer. Mrs. Massey tugged on the sleeves and lapels, asked me to raise my arms, then patted my sides, hips, and lower back.

"Try on the pants," she said.

"That's okay. I'm pretty sure—"

"Try on the pants for heaven's sake. You can change in the bedroom."

I took her late husband's pants into the bedroom, changed, and came back out. Mrs. Massey patted my hips again, grazed my butt with her palm, and bent over and tugged at the inner and outer seams of the pants. "Oh my God," she said, stepping back, her gray-blue eyes sparkling. "It's a perfect fit. I can't believe it."

The blazer was a little tight around the shoulders, and the pants were a little too long, but I wasn't going to argue with her.

"What size shoe do you wear?" she said.

"Eleven."

"Unbelievable," she said, raising the pitch of her voice. She left the room and came back with black, leather dress shoes. I tried them on as well, and she stood back, put her hands on her hips, and stared at me with her mouth open. "You know," she said, "I have coffee once a week with a few of the other widows in town. To hear them talk you'd think their lives began when their husbands died."

I smiled. "They must not have liked their husbands."

"Few of us do."

I reached into the pocket of my pants, which were draped over the back of the couch, pulled out the lease, and handed it to Mrs. Massey. "This is a lease for this address," I said, "signed by your husband in April of two thousand ten. The lease ended in April of two thousand twelve. The tenant was Winona Stapely. Does that name ring a bell at all?"

"No. Like I said, my husband dealt with all of that stuff."

"How many bedrooms does this house have?"

"Only two. I guess three if you include the den downstairs."

"This lease says there were eight people living here."

"That can't be right," she said. "You see this place. Where would they all fit? That's silly. I don't even think one person was living here. Both of the bedrooms were used to grow pot."

"Really? How do you know?"

"They left this place a mess. I had to hire a contractor. Carpets were ripped out. There was water damage. And someone had tampered with the electrical box. They ran extra wires. There were wires just lying on the ground. It wasn't safe. I'm surprised we didn't lose this house to a fire."

"Did your husband keep any records? Files or anything?"

"He did. Why do you ask, anyway? What does my house have to do with that poor girl that went missing?"

"I'm not sure yet," I said. "Do you think I could take a look at your husband's records?"

"Sure."

Mrs. Massey took me down to the den, which had a window looking out onto the steep, grassy clearing. There was a table in the center of the room cluttered with albums, loose photos, a pair of scissors, a glue gun, and scraps of paper.

She pointed to a desk in the corner with two boxes stacked under it. "All his records are over there," she said. "But you're on your own. I don't feel like crying today." She walked back upstairs.

I searched the drawers first, then the boxes, rummaging through letters from the Health and Benefits division of the Department of Veterans Affairs, old W-2s and tax returns, newspaper clippings, deeds, a license for a charter boat named the *Karley Anne*, and so on. After an hour, I came across a folder with several leases inside, one of which resembled the lease Krista had left me. It had the same address and dates but was missing seven of the tenant signatures. I could tell the lease was an original copy by the color and impression of the signatures. When I looked closer, I found a clause on page nine prohibiting more than four residents without the landlord's consent. That clause was missing from the lease Krista had left me.

Saying goodbye to Mrs. Massey turned out to be a twenty-minute process. By the end of it, I had agreed to take the tub of cookies, and she had agreed to let me have the original lease.

28

Lost Coast Property Management

WHEN I GOT HOME later that evening, I looked up Lost Coast Property Management online. According to its website, it was a "family-owned and operated company" headed by Tammie Campbell, who had been in "real estate and property management for over fifteen years."

Tammie Campbell was the name of the agent on both of the Shelter Cove leases.

The following morning, after eating breakfast with my parents and fielding questions about my next career move, I drove to Eureka. Lost Coast Property Management's office was on Broadway Avenue, a four-lane stretch of Highway 101 running through the south end of town, lined with gas stations, fast-food joints, local businesses, vacant buildings, and rundown hotels. Its sidewalks hosted an unending parade of meth addicts and hard-luck cases.

Just north of the Bayshore Mall, I pulled into a small shopping center and found Lost Coast Property Management across from a sporting goods store, between a car insurance broker and a vacuum cleaner supply shop. When I walked inside, I smelled citrus and noticed two yellow candles burning on the receptionist's desk. The receptionist was a young woman in her early twenties. She still had baby fat in her cheeks, and her lips were shiny with lip gloss. Two palm plants stood in pots on either side of the desk. The brown carpet looked new. Large framed photos of kids and puppies playing in grassy yards hung on the walls.

"Good morning," I said, smiling.

The receptionist pointed behind me. "Our available properties are posted on the wall over there and they're also online," she said. "Our applications are in the box by the door. You can fill it out here if you want or you can take it with you and bring it back."

"Thank you, but I'm here to see Tammie Campbell. Is she in today?"

"What's your name?"

"Tim Kitchens."

"What is this regarding?"

"A property she used to manage a few years back."

"And you want us to manage it again?" she said.

"No. I just have a few questions for Tammie about it."

"Okay? What's the address?"

I gave it to her, and she walked to the back and disappeared through a door. Less than a minute later, she returned. "Tammie's busy right now. She said to come back in an hour."

"Okay," I said. "If you don't mind, I'll wait here."

The receptionist responded with a heavy sigh. After I sat down in one of the chairs by the door, she began watching a TV show on her computer with the volume up loud enough for me to hear. The show was about a group of women who organized fundraisers and events and often got angry with each other over trivial things.

After spending exactly one hour listening to that, I walked up to the desk and said, "Do you mind checking if Tammie's available now?"

The receptionist glared at me and curled her upper lip. "If she was ready for you, she would have said something."

"Do you mind checking anyway? Maybe she forgot about me."

"She didn't forget."

"How do you know?"

"If she was ready to see you, she'd tell me. You don't have to wait here, you know. You can leave your number and I'll have her call you."

I took both leases out of my pocket and straightened them out on her desk. "Could you please just show these to her? It's important."

"Absolutely," she said.

"Thank you." I sat down again.

Instead of getting up, she crossed her legs and went back to watching her show.

"Excuse me," I said. "Do you mind showing them to her now?"

"She's busy right now."

I took a deep breath. "I don't think you understand. If I don't get this resolved today I'm going to hire a lawyer." I stood up and flailed my arms. "My son broke his ankle falling through one of your rotten porches. Do you know how much a broken ankle costs? Are you going to pay for it? I'll sue this place for a million dollars."

The receptionist scowled at me for a moment, then grabbed the leases and walked to the office in the back.

The door closed, and I could hear muffled voices. When the voices stopped, the receptionist came out and sat back down at her desk. "Go for it," she said.

"Thank you," I said, and walked across the room to the open door.

Tammie Campbell stood as I entered. We shook hands, and I sat on the green loveseat in front of her desk. She was in her late forties, with blond highlights in her hair and mascara clumped in her eyelashes. She wore a silk or rayon jungle-print blouse. Her teeth were white, and her skin was tan with an orange tint.

There were six framed photos on her desk facing me. The frames had words like "Love," "Family," and "Friendship" carved into them. Two of the photos were of Tammie and three middle-aged women with a middle-aged man I recognized as Pete Holloway. In one, they were posing in front of a bar, wearing oversized football jerseys. In the other, they were posing in front of a dugout, wearing oversized baseball jerseys. The remaining photos were of three young boys I presumed were Tammie's sons.

"Now what is this about a broken ankle and you wanting to sue us?" Tammie said.

"I'm not sure what you're talking about," I said. "I don't want to sue anyone."

"I'm confused."

"So am I. Who broke their ankle?"

"I don't know. You're the one who said someone broke their ankle."

"I never said that. This is bizarre. I just wanted to ask you a few questions about those leases. Did your secretary give them to you?"

"Yes. So no one broke their ankle?" she said, squinting at me.

"I think there was a serious miscommunication. Do you remember those leases?"

The bracelets on Tammie's wrists jangled as she picked up a lease and thumbed through its pages, looking up at me now and then with suspicion in her eyes. "Not particularly," she said. "We rent out a lot of properties. This is six years old, looks like. What is this about?"

"I'm helping July Morrison's family investigate her disappearance. She worked here during that time, didn't she?"

"Yes, she did, about once a week."

"What did she do here?"

"Filing mostly."

"Is Pete Holloway your husband?"

Tammie laughed. "No. He's my cousin. Why would you say that?"

"I saw your wedding ring and the photos of Pete and the kids. I didn't see another man, so I just assumed."

"Well, you know what they say about assuming, don't you?"

"I do, yes."

"It makes an ass out of you and me."

I leaned back in the loveseat and sank deeper into the cushions. I said, "Dave Massey is the owner of the house on that lease. When he called to complain about the tenants growing pot, what did you do?"

Tammie raised her eyebrows. "I don't recall anything like that happening. You're talking about six years ago here."

"How well did you know Winona Stapely?" I asked.

"Winona? I don't know. Pretty well."

"Only pretty well? She was your cousin's assistant

for twenty years, and it looks like you and your cousin are pretty close. Or am I assuming too much again?"

"No, we're close, and I used to see Winona all the time, but we never really hung out."

"Who would you say was more likely to be growing pot in that house, Winona, or her daughter, Krista?"

"I don't know." Tammie crossed her arms. "This is getting a little silly now."

"I didn't realize that," I said. "But then I don't think fraud is silly."

"Fraud?"

"Fraud, forgery, and looks like money laundering. I don't know how else to explain the discrepancy between those two leases."

"What discrepancy?" she said.

"The landlord's copy has a clause prohibiting more than four tenants. The tenant's copy does not. The tenant's copy also has eight people living in a two-bedroom house, with each of them paying eleven hundred dollars in rent, over four times the going rate for a room in that area at that time. Do you still think this is silly?"

Tammy glared at me in silence for a moment, then said, "You should leave now."

I stood up. "You can keep those copies, by the way. I have more."

On my way out I noticed one of Pete Holloway's old campaign signs from 2014 hanging by the door.

29

Humboldt County Courthouse

THE HUMBOLDT COUNTY BOARD of Supervisors had their offices and their meeting chamber in the Humboldt County Courthouse, which was on the north end of Eureka, between Fourth and Fifth Street, attached to the county jail. The county court, vital records, and the offices of the Sherriff and District Attorney were also in the building.

After leaving Tammie's office, I drove across town, found parking a block away from the courthouse, and entered on the Fifth Street side, where two security guards were herding people through a metal detector. I got in line behind a well-groomed man in a suit, a well-groomed woman in a pantsuit, and an unshaven man in a holey T-shirt. After putting my keys, wallet, phone, and belt in a tray and walking through the metal detector, I found a directory hanging on the wall, which led me to the third floor, where I walked down a hall and turned a corner, looking for a receptionist or Pete Holloway's name on a door. I came across a woman carrying a folder, who stopped when she saw me and said, "Can I help you?"

"Maybe," I said. "I'm here to see Pete Holloway. I have an appointment."

"Okay. Wait here a sec'. I'll get someone for you."

A few minutes later, a woman around my age, maybe younger, came down the hall, wearing black heels, a black skirt, a black coat, and glasses with black frames. She stood in front of me, smiled, and said, "Hi, I'm Andrea Lillard, Supervisor Holloway's assistant. I don't have any appointments for him on my schedule right now. What was your name?"

"Tim Kitchens," I said. "I made the appointment through a mutual friend, so maybe there was some miscommunication. Can you get me in anyway?"

"Well, he's preparing for today's meeting at the moment, but maybe tomorrow, or later this week . . . . May I ask what this is regarding?"

"It's about his missing ex-stepdaughter. It's important."

"Okay, well, if you could just wait here for me, that would be great, and I will be right back. Okay?"

After ten minutes of waiting, of leaning against the wall and nodding at the strangers who walked by, two sheriff's deputies came around the corner from the direction of the elevator.

One of them pointed at me. "Are you Tim Kitchens?" he said.

"Yes."

"Come on, let's go. You can't be here."

"What? Why? I have an appointment."

"No, you don't. You're harassing people. Let's go."

"This is ridiculous," I said. "I'm not harassing anyone. I'm just waiting for an appointment."

"I'm not going to argue with you. Let's go. Do you want to get arrested?"

I went with them to the elevator and rode down to the ground floor. After being escorted outside, I walked down the stairs and around the block, bought coffee and a sticky bun at the cafe on the corner, then got in my car and found parking closer to the courthouse, so I could watch the exit through the windshield. While I waited for Pete Holloway to come out, I Googled him on my phone. An hour of reading articles and skimming through images and comments taught me this:

He was fifty-eight years old and on his third wife. He was a graduate of McKinleyville High School and Texas University, where he had played baseball and majored in business. After getting his Bachelor's, he "pursued several business ventures in Texas" before moving back home to help run Holloway Trucking, the company founded by his dad in 1972. When his dad died in 1994, Pete and his sister became co-owners. In 1998, Pete ran for Fifth District Supervisor and won. He served two terms before bowing out in 2006 "to focus on the family business." He decided to return to politics in 2013 and was re-elected to the Fifth District in 2014. His detractors called him a "spoiled rich kid," who dyed his hair and "pandered to big business." His supporters called him a "community-minded" father of two, who had "real-world experience" and "knew how to make the tough decisions."

In my search, I also learned that the Board of Supervisors was holding a General Plan Update meeting for the public starting at one-thirty.

Pete Holloway must have wanted to get a bite to eat before they started, because he came out of the courthouse a little past noon, followed by his assistant, Andrea.

I hopped out of my car and caught up with them around the block as Pete was using the remote on his keychain to unlock a new white Chevy Tahoe. He was wearing a black suit and smiling. His smile disappeared when he saw me.

"Hey Pete," I said. "You got a minute?"

"No," Andrea said. She hurried toward me and blocked my way.

Pete put his head down, avoiding eye contact with me, and kept walking to his Tahoe.

"I'm not an assassin," I said. "I just have a few questions for you. Come on, let me buy you lunch."

I tried to walk around Andrea, but she side-stepped in front of me, pulled a small black canister from her purse, and sprayed a stream of liquid at my face. I put my hands up to block it, but I was too late. My eyes began to burn. They closed and would not open, even after I wiped them with my shirt. My nose and mouth began to burn as well.

"What the fuck?" I said. "You pepper-sprayed me? Jesus Christ."

Mucus streamed down my chin. I had trouble breathing. I coughed. The burning got worse. I coughed and spit and wiped my face with my shirt. I could not see. I heard Pete and Andrea shut the Tahoe doors and drive off, then I sat down on the concrete and waited for my sight to return. No one came to help me. Twenty, maybe thirty minutes passed before I could open my eyes again. The world was bright and blurry. I walked across the street to a Mexican restaurant and washed my face in their bathroom. I looked in the mirror. My skin was red and blotchy. My eyes were glassy and bloodshot.

When I felt like I had recovered enough, I walked

back to the courthouse. This time I used the Fourth Street entrance. I watched for the two deputies that had thrown me out earlier, but they weren't around. I found the Board of Supervisors meeting chamber. The door was open, so I went inside. The meeting was set to begin in twenty minutes. I took a seat in the back of the public section. I wasn't sure why I was there, or what I was going to do. But I was mad about being pepper-sprayed and wanted revenge. At the least, I was going to embarrass this man.

The chamber was arranged similar to a courtroom, with two tables and a podium in front of a raised bench. Two large pastoral paintings hung on the wall behind the bench, along with the state and federal flags. Video cameras were set up in different spots around the chamber, and microphones were set up on the podium, tables, and bench.

Only two other people were in the room, a man and a woman, sifting through papers at one of the tables. Over the next twenty minutes, five people joined me in the public section, one more sat at the table, and all five district supervisors took their seats at the raised bench. Pete Holloway was on the far left next to a clerk seated a foot lower than him. Pete appeared not to see me.

The Chair was a portly man with a mustache, whose heavy breathing could be heard through his microphone. He asked everyone to stand while he led us in The Pledge of Allegiance.

When that was done and everyone had sat down again, he said, "This is a General Plan Update Meeting. The first item on the agenda is the Housing Element." Then he yielded the floor to the Planning and Building Director, who went into a dry and lengthy PowerPoint presentation on the Housing Element from his seat at the table. When the presentation was finished, the Chair opened the meeting up to public comment.

The first person to walk to the podium was a slight, middle-aged woman with curly black hair and oval glasses. She introduced herself as Helen McBride, an attorney for a group called Housing Equality. She was concerned about "the exemption for solar shading in section HM3," and with multi-family lots that were being developed at minimum density. She also wanted the word "redevelopment" changed to "rejuvenation" in section HM4.

A man in his fifties was second to speak. He wore a salmon blazer with a silver tie and white slacks. He had long bangs and the bulbous red nose of an alcoholic. He expressed his gratitude for the "carrots" provided for developers in HM4 and GP2. "These are excellent carrots," he said. "Those of us with our boots on the ground know what to do with carrots like these." He pointed back in the direction of the attorney for Housing Equality without turning around and said, "And for Pete's sake don't listen to Helen about HM3. She just wants to pin you down on density so she can come back and sue the pants off the county. I thank you for your time. And keep up with the carrots. Thank you."

The next speaker was an older man, in his sixties, bald on top with stringy hair running down to his shoulders. He wore a brown leather vest and camouflage shorts and introduced himself as Crab-Man. He opened with, "Here's a quick little ditty about nine-eleven: Seems to me people aren't asking the right questions. Who made the steel that went into those buildings? That's what I'd like to know, and no one's asked that question yet. And here's another question for you: What is this I hear about an ordinance against the smell of cannabis? What about the smell of barbeques and burning flesh? Some people don't like that. What about that? And can we once and for all abolish the use of the term marijuana? It's racist, offensive, and antiquated. We need to move on as a society, and words are the path forward. They matter." Throughout Crab-Man's time at the podium, the Chair asked him over and over to limit his comments to the items on the agenda, which Crab-Man responded to with variations of, "The last time I checked, this was a democracy. The people are the agenda," or, "I'm a citizen of this country. I'm not one of your sheople you can just herd around."

He was talking about trail and stream setbacks when I felt my phone vibrate in my pocket. I pulled it out and saw that Mitch Runiyon from Hunley, Davis, & Runiyon, LLP was calling. I walked just outside the chamber and answered the phone. After a little small talk, Mitch said, "I was impressed with your interview the other day, and I would like to extend an invitation to meet the rest of the partners."

"Thank you," I said. "I'm happy to hear that. I'm willing to meet anytime." I looked back in the chamber. Crab-Man had sat down and no one else was making a move for the podium. "You mind if I call you right back?" I said. "Something just came up."

"No need. How does lunch at Boulevard sound? One o'clock Friday."

"Sounds perfect. I'm looking forward to it."

As I entered the chamber, the Chair said, "Well, if—" then stopped when he saw me walking up to the podium. "I guess we have one more for the housing element," he said.

Pete Holloway gave me a look like I had just vomited in his lap, then pulled out his phone and began tapping on it.

"My name is Tim Kitchens," I said into the microphone. "I'd like to give you a little scenario that demonstrates the pitfalls I foresee if HM4 is implemented as it stands now. Imagine for a second that a local property management company was managing a house in Shelter Cove, and their books had eight people living there, and these people were paying a total of eighty-eight hundred in rent each month."

"Sir," Pete said. "I would request that you please limit your comments to items on the agenda."

"I am," I said, "if you'd just bear with me a moment. Now imagine that this property management company told the landlord that only one person lived in this house, and they were paying a total of eight-hundred dollars a month instead of eighty-eight hundred. That's a difference of eight thousand. Now, most people would look at that and call it money laundering, and they would most likely be right. And if you're wondering what this has to do with HM4, I'm getting to that. Let's say there is a man who has an assistant who is a tenant of this house, and this man also has a cousin who is the owner and operator of the property management company"

"Sir."

"Let me finish. Would you suspect this man of wrongdoing? Maybe. It's possible. Now let's say this man's former stepdaughter was growing pot in this house—"

"This is absurd."

"Imagine if the landlord found out about it and the stepdaughter went missing shortly after that, and her car was found less than ten miles from this house, abandoned. Would that be suspicious? I think it would be. Now. What if I told you that the assistant in this scenario was Winona Stapely, and the former stepdaughter was July Morrison, and the man was Pete Holloway?"

I pointed at Pete, and he turned to the other supervisors, shrugged, held one palm up, shook his head, and smiled as if to say, "Can you believe this lunatic?"

The Chair said, "I'm going to ask that you direct your comments directly to the housing element, and not attack anyone personally."

"He's gone over his time," Pete said.

"That's a gross misrepresentation of the facts," I said. "I have one minute left. Now let me get back to HM4. In my former line of work, I spent a lot of time around guilty people, and it is my opinion that Supervisor Holloway's behavior today, in my presence, has been consistent with that of a guilty man—"

"Sir—"

"—and because of this, I am now willing to bet— although this is purely speculation and I have no substantial evidence to support it—I am now willing to bet that I am currently in possession of a photograph of Supervisor Holloway's genitals, sent by him to his former stepdaughter, July Morrison, over five years ago."

There was murmuring and snickering throughout the chamber. Pete Holloway did some more smiling, shrugging, and headshaking.

"Okay," the Chair said. "You have to stop now, sir. You're disrupting the process, and frankly, it's bordering on harassment. I don't want this to become a test of wills, but I would ask that you please just leave."

I pointed at Supervisor Holloway again. I must have looked a little crazy with my red face and bloodshot eyes. "You know what I'm talking about, Pete," I said, then turned and walked down the aisle toward the door. Crab-Man, sitting in the public section, began to clap. No one joined him. He stuck out his chin and gave me a look and a nod like I had just done something meaningful and important, then he stood up and followed me out.

"I just want to shake your hand," he said. "What was your name again?"

"Tim Kitchens."

"I'm Crab-Man."

We shook hands.

"I've never seen Holloway squirm like that before," Crab-Man said, shoulders lurching forward as he walked. "I've been coming to these meetings for twenty years. I remember Holloway's first day on the job. He's as crooked as they come, man. It's pay to play with him, always has been. We've had our battles. He knows where I stand."

"How do you know he's crooked?" I asked.

"Because I come to the meetings. You can see for yourself if you want. They got the archives right on the internet. His last term, man, you can see. Some developer wants a property rezoned, it's like boom, it's done. If he's paying, no problem. But if you're a small-time guy, like my friend, it's over for you. My friend bought a plot and wanted to put an apartment building on it, right? But he couldn't pay, and Holloway just nailed him. You can see it online. Holloway's calling for environmental impact reports and shit, and this is just for a small plot. Holloway even claimed he had witnesses who saw a bald eagle on the land. My friend didn't have a chance. He just had to eat it."

"What's your friend's name?"

"Tom Faller. Why?"

"I'd like to talk to him. You know where I could find him?"

Crab-Man stopped walking, put his hands on his hips, cocked his head, and stared at me.

"What?" I said.

"Are you with the FBI?" he said.

I laughed. "No."

"You a reporter?"

"No."

"Then what's your deal?" he said.

"What do you mean?"

"I come to all these meetings, and I've never seen you before. Then all of a sudden you show up and start talking about money laundering and missing girls. That's FBI stuff."

"If I was with the FBI, I wouldn't be taking potshots at a supervisor during the public comments portion of a General Plan Update meeting. That just wouldn't happen." I turned and squared my shoulders to Crab-Man. "Let me lay some of this out for you. I'm an unemployed, disgraced lawyer who just got pepper-sprayed in the parking lot for trying to talk to Holloway before he ate lunch. Now, this might be the pepper spray talking, but I'm starting to think he murdered my friend, that girl I was talking about in there. She went missing five years ago, and they never found her body or her murderer. You know how hard it is to convict someone of murder when there's no body, when there's no body and it's been five years? You need all the evidence you can get. And if there's a chance Tom

Faller has some evidence, then that means I need to talk to Tom Faller. Can you help me out with that, Crab-Man? Can you tell me where I can find your friend?"

Crab-Man smiled. "I knew you were a lawyer," he said. "I always tell people not all lawyers are bad. Look at Ralph Nader."

I raised my eyebrows, and he slapped me on the shoulder.

"I'll be happy to help you, man," he said. "I like your passion. That's what life's about. The last time I talked to Tom he was renovating a house over on Summer Street. That was only a week ago, so he's probably there right now. I can take you to him if you want."

"Sounds good. Let's go."

I followed Crab-Man around the block to a rusty old Volvo station wagon and got inside. Newspapers filled the backseat, a fresh bundle of mint hung from the rearview mirror, and dozens of small crab shells were lacquered to the dash. They had been painted different colors and arranged in patterns, like a mosaic.

"So what's your deal with crabs?" I asked.

"Crabs are my subject," he said. "I'm an artist. Every artist needs a subject. Da Vinci had Mona Lisa, Monet had water lilies, Dali had melting clocks, and I have crabs." He laughed, then reached over my lap, grabbed a newspaper clipping out of the glove box, and handed it to me.

The clipping had a photo of him wearing a crab-shaped helmet and orange jumpsuit, standing at the foot of a dune in front of a tandem bicycle with wide tires, a rudder, a propeller, buoys attached on either side, and a large sculpture of a crab jutting out over the front wheel. A man wearing a lumpy green helmet and a green jumpsuit sat in one of the seats. The caption read: "Crab-Man and the Sea Cucumber on their Crab-Mobile at this year's Kinetic Sculpture Race, waiting for their turn at Dead Man's Drop."

"That was last year," Crab-Man said. "I've been doing the Kinetic Sculpture Race for six years and that's the first time my name showed up in the paper. I never get any press, man. I'm more of an artist's artist, you know? But that's about to change. That new brewery in Arcata just commissioned me to do the label for their IPA. Now Humboldt County's about to see what the Crab-Man can do with a beer label. I'm taking that brewery worldwide, baby."

The house Tom Faller was renovating was five minutes across town in a quiet little neighborhood next to a school, with lots of old, simple homes. Probably mill workers used to live here a hundred years ago, the kind that had posed in crackly, old black and white photographs with the giant redwoods they had just felled.

We parked across the street from the house and walked up to the driveway. Two men were working on the roof of the garage, framing an addition.

Crab-Man said, "Hey Tom."

One of the men looked up, smiled, and gave us the sign to wait a minute. After he finished screwing a board into place, he climbed down the ladder and shook Crab-Man's hand. He was tall and thin with a ponytail. "What's going on?" he said.

"I think I found someone who hates Pete Holloway as much as you," Crab-Man said, and pointed at me. "This is Tim Kitchens."

Tom smiled and wiped the sweat from his forehead with his sleeve. "I don't know if that's possible, but okay," he said.

"He's a lawyer," Crab-Man said. "He just wants to ask you a few questions about what happened."

"Did Holloway finally get caught?" Tom said to me.

"Not yet," I said. "Crab-Man told me that Holloway made it hard for you to build on some property you owned."

"Hard? He made it impossible. He wouldn't let me rezone it. He gummed up the works any way he could: environmental impact reports, fucking bald eagle sightings, just lying whenever he got the chance. And I didn't have money to hire a lawyer, and he knew that."

"Why would he do that?"

"Because I wouldn't pay him. He wanted a bribe and I didn't have the money."

"How do you know that was the reason, specifically?"

"It wasn't hard to figure out. After the first meeting, his assistant, Winona—I still remember her name—she came up to me and gave me an address and said, 'Send it here.' And I said, 'Send what?' And she said, 'Send it here,' and walked off. It wasn't hard to figure out after that. I ended up having to sell that property at a loss since I bought it during a bit of a bubble. The whole thing just about ruined me. I couldn't afford the taxes. That property's still empty to this day."

"Do you remember the address Winona gave you?"

Tom snorted. "No."

"Was it a PO Box?" I asked.

"I don't know, man. I don't remember."

30

Hiller Park

APRIL WOKE ME UP the next morning with a text that said, "Come outside."

I rolled out of bed, threw on a coat and sweatpants, slipped on sandals, and walked out the front door. April was in the driveway, leaning against the hood of her Nissan SUV, dressed for work. When she saw me, her eyes narrowed, and she clenched her jaw.

"Pete called me this morning," she said. "What is wrong with you?"

"I'm not qualified to comment on that," I said.

"You accused Pete of having a sexual relationship with his stepdaughter in front of the whole county. They put those meetings online you know? People watch them. They put them on YouTube, especially when someone makes a spectacle. You disrespected Pete, and worse, you disrespected July."

"Did you watch the video?"

"I don't need to. Pete was like a father to me, Tim, and to July. He would never do anything to hurt us."

"He had his assistant pepper spray me," I said.

"Really?"

"Yeah."

"I wonder why? Could it be because you were throwing one of your tantrums, like when you dumped a bucket of dead fish in a courtroom, or when you were thrown out of a shoe store, or when you got us kicked out of a protest rally?"

"I wasn't throwing a tantrum. I'm just following the facts. Are you going to let me defend myself?"

"No. What's the point?"

"There's a real easy way to see if I'm right, and that's to talk to Pete's second wife. All I have to do is show her that picture on Krista's old phone."

April threw her arms up. "You can't just go around showing people photos of random penises."

"Why not?"

April looked over my shoulder, and I turned around. My dad was standing on the porch. "Hi, April," he said. "What's going on?"

"I'm just yelling at your son," she said. "Sorry to bother you, Mr. Kitchens. I'm done now, anyway. I have to go to work." She walked around the hood, got in her vehicle, and shut the door. As she started the engine, I knocked on the driver-side window, and she opened it a crack.

"I'm not crazy," I said. "Just please watch the video for me. Watch Pete's reaction."

April studied my face for a moment, then backed out of the driveway and drove off.

After breakfast, I looked up the website for Sitting Pretty Dog Training and learned that Pete's ex-wife, Shannon Cope, held training courses Monday through Wednesday at Hiller Park in McKinleyville from two to four.

I spent the rest of the morning and afternoon

researching California tort law, cases Runiyon had tried and appealed, preparing for my meeting with the partners of Hunley, Davis & Runiyon, LLP. Then, at three-thirty, I took a break and drove five minutes across town to catch Shannon Cope at the end of her training course.

Hiller Park was divided into two sections by a parking lot and the Hammond Trail, which ran from the Arcata Bottoms to Clam Beach along an old railroad line. The eastern side of the park had baseball and soccer fields. The western side had picnic tables, a playground, and a wastewater management facility with six ponds, each the size of half a city block or larger.

When I got out of my car, I could smell the sewage. I walked up a narrow dirt path on the western side of the park, past the playground to the top of a small hill, where I looked down on a large grassy field. Over a dozen people were walking dogs across the field, following a woman with an Irish Setter. A small forest was on the other side of the field. The Mad River and the Pacific Ocean were beyond that.

The forest was called Eighteen Acres. My friends and I had played there as kids, built forts, waged war with pine cones and water pistols, found porno magazines in a hollowed-out stump, and argued about whether or not professional wrestling was real. We once swam across the Mad River and built a fire on the beach and pretended like that was our new home. As teenagers, we came to Eighteen Acres to drink and smoke pot.

A little after four, the people in the class began to disperse, taking their dogs into the woods or up the trail toward me and the parking lot. I waited until the woman with the Irish Setter was alone before walking down to meet her. She was a little older than me, in her early forties maybe, with black hair, green eyes, and a full figure. Her cheeks were rosy from the cold wind blowing off the ocean. She wore a Talking Books T-shirt under her open coat. The Talking Books were a big local band when I was eighteen, playing mostly funk and R&B covers from artists like Stevie Wonder, Al Green, and Aretha Franklin.

"Hi," I said when she looked up. "Are you Shannon Cope?"

"Yeah," she said. Her dog sat at her feet, calm but alert. "Are you looking to sign up?"

"Not today." I pointed at her chest. "I remember the Talking Books. They were a great band."

"We still are."

"You're in the band?"

"Yeah. I sing."

"I thought you looked familiar. You have a great voice."

"Thank you."

"You guys still play?" I said.

"All the time."

"I was in a battle of the bands with you guys once."

"Really?" She put her hands on her hips. "When was that?"

"About eleven years ago now. You guys won the whole thing, I remember. You had a horn section. I'd never seen a local band with a horn section before."

She smiled. "What band were you in?"

"We were called Ophelia at that time. All we did was play Ophelia over and over again."

She laughed. "I remember you guys. You did different versions, right? Like you had a metal version, a country version, and you even had a doo-wop version, didn't you?"

"Yeah. I can't believe you remember that."

"You guys were hilarious. I remember your whole band was so drunk you could barely stand, but you played the shit out of Ophelia. I still tease Levi about that sometimes."

"You know Levi?"

"Yeah. I'm like his biggest fan. I go see him whenever he plays. He keeps getting better. That man is a poet."

"Yeah, he's one talented son of a bitch," I said. "He's actually part of the reason I came to see you. I'm Tim Kitchens by the way. I'm trying to help Levi out with some issues he's having."

"Why? What's going on?"

"He's a suspect in a murder case. Did you hear about Krista Stapely?"

"Of course. Just horrible. They think Levi did that?"

"He was one of the last people to see her alive. They were hooking up at the time."

Shannon looked at her feet. "Jesus."

"Yeah. He's innocent of course, but he's in a tight spot. That's why I came to see you. I suspect your ex-husband was involved somehow."

"Pete?" she said.

"Yes. You were still married to him when July disappeared, right?"

"I was, yes. What does that have to do with Krista?"

"I believe they're connected. Do you remember where Pete was that night?"

"Yeah. He was at his cabin in Ruth Lake with Winona and her daughter."

"Krista?"

"No, her younger daughter, Jennifer."

"Was that normal for him to go to the cabin with Winona?"

"Yeah. They were very close. She was like a second mother to him. She was only six years older, but still . . . . Pete's the type of guy that collects mothers. Women just want to take care of him for some reason."

"Did Winona ever help you with your business, like paperwork, or anything like that?"

"Yeah, she helped me with the books sometimes," Shannon said. "Why?"

"Just curious. Do you remember July's boyfriend at the time? He's a professor."

"No."

"He thought there might have been something going on between July and Pete. Did you ever have suspicions like that?"

"Oh God," she said, and let out a sigh. Then she smiled. "This is getting a little heavy."

"I'm sorry," I said. "But it's important."

"No, I know. It's just . . . . . At that time, I didn't think anything. But a few years later, after we got divorced, I kind of looked back, and I noticed some things I might have been blinding myself to."

"What do you mean?"

"I only caught him cheating on me once, but if I'm honest with myself, I think he might have been doing it the whole time, and I think he might have done it with July too."

"What makes you think that?"

"Just little things. She would come over when I wasn't there, and then leave when I got home. Sometimes the bed would look a little different than the way I left it, at least in my mind anyway. And sometimes I would smell her perfume in the bedroom. Just little things like that. They're easy to ignore when you don't want to believe them."

"Did you ever tell the police about your suspicions?"

"No. Why would I?" she said.

"If the police get enough new information on a case, sometimes they reopen it."

"Pete might be an ass, but he would never hurt anyone, let alone July. He doesn't have an ounce of violence in him."

I nodded. "Did Pete ever like to wear women's underwear?"

Shannon laughed. "That's a little personal, don't you think?"

"I'm sorry. It's just that the night July disappeared Krista sent a photo of a man wearing pantyhose to July, but the man's face is out of the frame, so I was hoping you could take a look at it for me."

"Because you think it's Pete?" she said.

"I think it could be."

"How did you get it?"

"Krista left me her old phone when she died."

"This sounds a little crazy."

"That depends on your definition of crazy, I guess," I said. "Do you mind taking a look at the photo?"

"A little, but I'll survive."

When I showed her the picture of Dick Pants on my phone, her eyes got big, and she covered her mouth with one hand.

"Is that him?" I asked.

"I don't know," she said in a voice just above a whisper.

"Your acting like it is."

"I don't know. He liked to wear things like that, and it looks like him, but it's hard to say. It's all pixilated. But it looks like him."

"He liked to wear pantyhose?"

"Yes."

"When you say it looks like him, how sure are you? Seventy percent? Eighty percent?"

"I don't know. Ninety percent maybe. He . . . . It looks like him, I'll just say that."

I took my phone back. "Thank you. This really helps."

After saying goodbye to Shannon and promising to let her know the results of my investigation, I walked across the field to Eighteen Acres, where I followed a dirt path through a small forest of fir and pine. Lichen grew on their trunks and hung from their branches. The ground was littered with pine cones and needles. There were small openings in the underbrush for rabbits and foxes, and a few large ones a man could fit through. I sat on a log at the top of a bluff that rose just fifteen feet above the banks of the Mad River. Exposed roots curved out from the dark soil on the side of the bluff. Black and gray clouds filled the sky. The river was muddy and high, and although the dunes on the far bank hid the ocean, I could smell it on the wind, and I could feel its mist on my face as the fog rolled in.

Blocking the wind with my coat, I lit a joint I had rolled with my mom's weed. I inhaled the thick, fragrant smoke, pulled out my phone, and considered calling April. The thought of talking to her gave me butterflies in my stomach. But then I remembered what she told me: "I like you, and it's only getting worse," which made me think of my failed marriage. Then the butterflies became a pit.

I tried to call Becky instead, but her phone went straight to voicemail. I left a message asking for Jennifer Stapely's phone number.

I walked back to my car as the light faded. The park's caretaker was waiting by the gate when I drove out. On the way home, I stopped at the taco truck on Central Avenue and bought a burrito. While I ate it in my car, with the dome light on, struggling with the little plastic salsa container, my mom called.

"Where are you?" she said.

"At the taco truck on Central. Why?"

"I need you to come home."

"What's going on?"

"Someone broke into the house."

"What?" I spilled the salsa on my leg. "Shit."

"The house is upside down."

"You guys weren't home were you?"

"No. We were out to dinner."

"Okay, I'm on my way."

When I walked into the house, my parents were lifting the Christmas tree off the living room floor. Shattered ornaments and loose needles were around their feet. The couches and chairs had been moved, cushions overturned. The drawers and cabinets of the entertainment center had been emptied onto the floor. The TV was on the floor too, along with broken lamps and picture frames, and all the books from the bookshelf.

"The whole house looks like this," my dad said when the Christmas tree was standing again. "They broke in through the back-door window. I still haven't found anything missing. It's like all they wanted to do was wreck the place. I think those man-babies did it."

"What are man-babies?" I said.

"Those teenagers that run around the neighborhood jumping into people's hedges."

"The man-babies didn't do this," my mom said. She turned to me with pity in her eyes. "Tim, I have to tell you something. Tuna's dead. Someone shot her."

"What?"

"I'm sorry, honey."

"Where is she?"

"She's in the backyard. We didn't want to move her until you got here."

My dad grabbed a flashlight off the kitchen table, and I followed him into the backyard and around to the side of the house.

"She crawled under the boat to die," he said.

He handed me the flashlight, leaned under the boat, and pulled a tarp off Tuna's body. She was on her side. Her mouth was open, and her tongue was hanging out. There was a small hole above her stomach. The fur around it was wet. She had been licking her wound before she died. I turned her over and saw that the bullet had passed through the other side of her stomach, near the back leg.

I spent the next half hour searching the backyard for a slug or a shell casing, but in the dark, I found only Tuna's blood.

When I went back inside, my parents were standing by the foot of the stairs, talking to a sheriff's deputy.

"This man wants to know if we have any enemies," my mom said.

"The fact that nothing was taken tells me this was probably done by someone you know," the deputy said.

"There are three people that could have done this," I said. "Don Tidwell, Jared Tidwell, or Supervisor Pete

Holloway. I'm not sure which one it was, but I'm leaning toward Pete Holloway because he's been acting cagey, and he assaulted me with pepper spray not long ago. I need you to call Detective Westbrook at Eureka PD. He's the lead investigator on the Krista Stapely murder case. Tell him the same person who killed Krista might have just killed Tim Kitchens' dog, maybe even with the same gun. And tell him we need a forensic team over here."

The deputy gave me a confused, almost contemptuous look.

"I'm not joking," I said. "Call Westbrook. He'll know what I'm talking about."

"What was your name again?" the deputy said.

"Tim Kitchens."

"Okay. I'll be back." He left the room.

"What's going on Tim?" my mom said.

"I'm not sure."

"What do you mean you're not sure?" my dad said.

My parents knew a little about my investigation, but not everything, so I spent the next twenty minutes filling them in and answering all their questions. Neither of them was happy with me when I had finished. After apologizing as best I could, I went to my room and began cleaning up the debris. The floor was covered in clothes and papers, and my childhood possessions from the closet.

Now and then I heard my mom lamenting in the living room over some broken object that had meaning to her: an ornament, a vase, a lamp, an old record . . . . Several times my dad expressed regret for not having wall-mounted the TV.

After an hour of work, Detective Westbrook showed up, introduced himself to my parents, then asked to talk with me in private. I took him to my room.

"So it's my understanding that you think what happened here has something to do with Krista's death," he said. "Is that correct?"

"Yes," I said. "Did you get my package?"

"I did."

"Okay, just give me a minute to lay out the facts for you: Krista gives the lease and photo to her friend with instructions to give them to me if anything happens to her. Then someone kills Krista and searches her hotel room and her car. What are they looking for?" I handed Westbrook the Shelter Cove lease, the one with two tenants, and explained how I had found it and why I thought it was evidence of a money-laundering scheme. "I think Pete Holloway is involved," I said.

"I thought this was coming," Westbrook said.

"I confronted Pete with the lease and the photo yesterday, and now, a day later, my house is searched. I don't think that's a coincidence."

"You think Supervisor Holloway murdered Krista, then came over here tonight, climbed your fence, shot your dog, and ransacked your house?"

"I talked to Pete's ex-wife today. She thinks that's him in the photo."

Westbrook smiled. "Look. I heard Supervisor Holloway got in an argument with Krista at her mom's funeral, so I looked into it. The night Krista was murdered, Supervisor Holloway was in Sacramento at a memorial for a former member of the State Assembly."

"He could have hired somebody."

"Come on, Mr. Kitchens. Would he go through all that for a lease and a photograph?"

"Why not, if Krista was blackmailing him? And

maybe she had something else. Maybe that's why my house was searched."

"Okay," he said. "Now it's your turn to listen to some facts. You visited Krista at her house in Ettersburg a few days before she died. You pretended to be her cousin and you got in a fight with her neighbors. Shortly after that, she breaks up with her boyfriend. Then she meets Levi, who is the last person to be seen with her alive. You call her several times the day of her murder, then you and Levi discover her body. Now doesn't that sound a little more suspicious than your scenario? Here's what I think: I think you know something that somebody doesn't want you to know, and that's why your parent's house looks like this. Now. I know you're scared, but I can protect you as long as you tell me the truth."

"Jesus Christ," I said. "You think Levi killed my dog? This is ridiculous."

"I never said Levi killed your dog," he said. "You said that."

"You're right. You got me. Come on."

Westbrook shrugged, then handed me his card. "If you feel like talking to someone just give me a call. I'm here for you."

"That's nice to think about."

"By the way, you're going to want to stay away from Supervisor Holloway. He filed a restraining order against you."

"What?"

"It's going to be approved, too, cuz he's a Supe."

Westbrook turned and walked out of my room.

31

Fortuna

MY MOM PLACED TWO photographs in front of me as I finished a bowl of cereal, one of a thirteen-year-old me hugging my sister at her high school graduation, and one of me and July posing at our prom.

"I found these cleaning up," my mom said. "You look so young."

"I see that," I said.

"The anniversary of your sister's death is coming up."

"I know."

My mom smiled. "Remember when you were little and you peed on her dollhouse."

"I was two, so no."

"It's okay to talk about her Tim."

"I know."

"Your father and I both think you haven't dealt with your grief."

"Are you kidding me?"

"You're obsessive," she said. "It's unhealthy. This new thing you have with finding July's killer, it's not going to bring Melissa back. You can't save everybody,

Tim."

"Are you sure about that? There are only seven billion people in the world."

"Don't be a shit," my dad said. "Your mother's right. You're not acting like a healthy person. The mind is like a house, Tim. If it's full of rot you have to cut it out. Otherwise, it'll spread. Trust me, your mother and I know."

"Understood," I said. "My brain is rotten." I grabbed my cereal bowl and got up from the table. As I walked to the kitchen, my dad stood up and slammed his palm into my chest. I almost fell into the table. Milk went everywhere.

"Listen to me," he said. "Weakness always comes with a price. And there's nothing weaker, nothing more dangerous than a man who doesn't know where his anger comes from. The price for that is always the highest. Do you understand?" My dad's voice cracked, and tears gathered in his eyes. "You're not going to make it like this, son."

I had never seen him even come close to crying. "Okay Dad," I said, stunned.

He walked down the hall and up the stairs, and my mom began cleaning up the milk on the floor.

I put my bowl in the sink, went out back, grabbed a shovel from the shed, and dug a grave for Tuna between the apple trees. After I laid her inside and covered her, I drove to Hiller Park and took another walk in Eighteen Acres. I sat on the bluffs above Mad River and watched the seals beached on the northern side of the mouth, jostling and barking. One of the baby seals wouldn't let the others sleep.

Just before noon, Becky came through for me again by texting me Jennifer Stapely's phone number. After thanking her, I called the number, but the voicemail answered. I left a message. A few minutes later, Jennifer, not having listened to the message, texted me, "Who's this?"

I sent back, "My name is Tim Kitchens. I was a friend of your sister's. I was hoping we could talk. Can we meet somewhere?"

Jennifer: "I don't know you."

Me: "I have something that belonged to your sister that I think you should have."

Jennifer: "What?"

Me: "Not sure. Papers. I thought you would know."

Her reply came a few minutes later: "Meet me at the parade tonight."

Me: "What parade?"

Jennifer: "Truck parade in Fortuna."

Me: "What time?"

Jennifer: "530."

Fortuna was a small town on the banks of the Eel River, just off Highway 101, forty minutes south of McKinleyville. It had a narrow Main Street, lined with old storefronts, some with Western-style facades. Signs for small local shops and restaurants hung above the windows. On the southern end, Main Street turned into Fortuna Boulevard, which was four lanes and lined with shopping centers, parking lots, and fast food.

I drove into town at five fifteen. The sun had set, and the sky was nearly dark. The streetlamps were wrapped in green and red garlands, and the storefronts were lit up with Christmas lights. People, bundled up in coats, scarves, and hats, clogged the sidewalks, standing, or sitting in camping chairs, waiting for the parade.

I found a parking space in a neighborhood four blocks off Main Street and sent a text to Jennifer: "I'm in Fortuna. Where should I meet you?"

She responded ten minutes later: "Movie theater."

I walked down the crowded sidewalk toward the marquee, passing families and groups of friends. Most people were smiling. I heard loud conversations, laughter, and crying children. When I reached the theater, a dozen or so people were standing out front. "Jennifer?" I said as I walked by them. "Jennifer Stapely?"

A woman standing next to two men turned to me, smiled, and said, "Tim?"

"Yeah," I said.

She hugged me, and I smelled alcohol on her breath. She was in her early to mid-twenties, with a skinny neck, full cheeks, big brown eyes, and short, thin black hair. She wore tight blue jeans and a gray hoodie large enough for a man. She kept her hands inside the sleeves.

"So what do you have for me?" she said.

"I'd like to talk in private if you don't mind," I said.

"Sure. We can go to my car."

I followed her around the corner. She was buzzed, but not stumbling or slurring words. She got in the driver-side of a dirty, white Ford Escort with a dented fender and hood, and turned on the dome light. I sat in the passenger seat. The inside of the car smelled like mildew, spent cigarettes, baby powder, old diapers, and vanilla air freshener. The ashtray was overfilled with cigarette butts, and the change in one of the cup holders was covered in a red film. The windshield was foggy, and mushrooms were growing out of the floor mat between my feet.

I heard a small breathing noise and turned around to see a baby in a car seat, wrapped in a blanket.

"That's Frank," Jennifer said. "He's my little man." She grabbed a glass pipe and a bag of bud out of the center console, loaded the pipe, and took a hit. The smoke hung in the air, stagnant, even after I rolled down my window. She offered the pipe to me, and I turned it down.

"So what are these papers you're talking about?" she said. She had a low, nasal voice.

I pulled the Shelter Cove lease out of my pocket and handed it to her. "That's a lease for a house in Shelter Cove. It's signed by your mother."

"Okay?" she said.

"Did you ever go to that house?"

"No. I don't know anything about it. How did you get this?"

"Your sister gave it to me. I think she was trying to help me find out who killed July Morrison. You remember her, right? Krista's friend?"

"I remember." Jennifer took another hit and exhaled. "Were you and my sister fucking?"

"No. We were just friends. Do you know what she and Pete Holloway were arguing about at your mom's funeral?"

"They were arguing? I never heard that."

"Yes, according to Becky."

Jennifer shrugged. "Okay."

"The night July disappeared you were at Ruth Lake with Pete and your mom. Were you with them all night?"

"Why do you ask that?"

"It's important. I think the same person who killed your sister also killed July."

"Are you a cop?"

"No."

"Then why are you asking these weird questions?"

"Because I don't think the police are going to find your sister's killer. All I need is a few answers from you. Please."

Jennifer smiled. "You *were* fucking my sister, weren't you?"

"Were you with Pete and your mom that whole night at Ruth Lake?"

"No. I remember that night. I met my friends and stayed with them."

"Did you or your sister inherit any money from your mom?"

Jennifer laughed. "My mom didn't have any money."

"How about a house?"

"No. She lived rent-free on one of Pete's properties. She spent all her money on clothes and traveling. She traveled the world. My mom lived her life. She didn't care about leaving anything behind."

"Did you know that your sister was growing pot with July?"

"No, but it's not really surprising."

"When was the last time you spoke with your sister?"

"I talked to her on the phone the day she died."

"What did you talk about?"

"Not much. She just wanted to borrow some makeup."

"Do you have any idea who might have killed her?"

"No."

"Do you have any idea why someone searched her hotel room and her car?"

"No. I don't. I wish I did."

"Why are you lying to me?" I said.

"What?" Her head jerked back as if she had just smelled sour milk.

"If you're going to lie to someone, don't get stoned first," I said. "It makes you too self-conscious. I know you and Krista weren't talking about makeup that night. What were you really talking about?"

"Fuck you. I don't have to answer to you. Get out of my car."

"I'm trying to find your sister's killer. Why won't you help me?"

She showed me the whites of her eyes and screamed, "Get out of my car!" Her face turned red, and the vein on her forehead bulged. "Get the fuck out of my car!"

She didn't stop screaming until I was on the sidewalk. Then she rolled up the windows, locked the doors, and got out. "I should have Steve and Dave come beat your ass," she said, walking away. "Don't ever call me again."

I looked at the baby still in the backseat. He was crying. Then I looked back at Jennifer, stomping toward Main Street under the streetlamps. "You're just going to leave Frank here?" I shouted after her. She ignored me.

When she turned the corner, I went into a yard nearby, where the flower beds were bordered with fist-sized river rocks. I took one of the rocks back to Jennifer's car and used it to shatter the passenger-side window. There was no alarm. I opened the door and took out the car seat with the baby inside. He was still crying. I carried him at my side like a tackle box as I walked through a neighborhood in the direction of my car, which was on the other side of Main Street. When I felt like I had put enough distance between me and the theater, I attempted to cross, but by that time the parade had begun. Semi-truck after semi-truck drove by at five miles per hour, honking at the bystanders, with trailers covered in blinking Christmas lights dampened by the fog. They passed like submarines floating underwater. The line stretched as far as I could see. Frank never stopped crying. The people around me began to stare with eyes like trout—suspicious, alert, round, and unblinking. I saw a gap between the trucks, and I jogged across the street, headlights shining in my eyes and shadows moving all about me like seaweed swaying in a swift current.

When I got to my car, I laid Frank in the backseat, removed his diaper, and wiped his butt with some McDonald's napkins I had found in the glove box. The smell was worse than crab bait. After throwing the dirty diaper and napkins in a trash can someone had left in front of their house, I took off my undershirt and wrapped Frank in it as best I could. He was dry and clean, but he continued to cry. I strapped him into the car seat, started the car, turned on the heat, and called Jennifer. I had to call her six times before she answered.

"What?" she said.

"I have Frank," I said, and held the phone out so she could hear her son crying.

"No."

On her end, the sound of the crowd and the trucks in the background faded until all I could hear were her footsteps and heavy breathing. Then she said, "Oh my God. My car. What the fuck did you do? Bring me my son back right now!"

"Yelling's not going to solve this problem for you," I said.

"I'm calling the police."

"That's not a good idea. I have your son. You understand?"

"Oh my God."

"I'll bring him back as long as you do what I say. All I want is for you to answer a few questions for me, and I want you to answer them truthfully this time."

"Okay. Whatever you want. Just bring him back."

"What do you think Krista's killer was looking for in her hotel room?"

"Keys. I'm pretty sure."

"Keys?" I said. "What keys?"

"The keys she found in my mom's safe."

"Can you please elaborate for me?"

"She got them after my mom died. She had Miguel break into the safe and we found those keys and a bunch of papers, and then a few months later she gave me and Miguel the keys and told us to put them in one of those boxes that have newspapers in them. And that was the night she was killed. And that's everything I know. I swear."

"You think someone killed her over those keys?"

"Yes."

"Why?"

"I don't know why. They were important to someone, I guess."

"You don't know who?"

"No."

"Did you tell the police about this?"

"No. Miguel's illegal. If I told them, they'd send him back to Mexico. I can't do that to him."

"Then leave Miguel out of it. This is your sister we're talking about."

"I don't want to get in trouble," she said. "They don't need to know about this to find out who killed my sister. They got CSI shit for that. And they definitely don't need to know about my mom's business."

"What type of keys were they? House keys? Car keys?"

"Car keys."

"Do you still have them?"

"No. We lost them. Krista told us she would call when she wanted us to put the keys in the newspaper box, but then she never called. Me and Miguel got drunk at the Shanty bar waiting, and he wanted to go get cocaine in Manilla, so we put the keys in the box in case she called when we were gone, but when we got back the keys were gone, and Krista wasn't answering her phone."

"What newspaper box did you put them in?" I asked.

"The one across from that restaurant, the Irish one in Old Town."

"Eureka?"

"Yeah," she said.

"Describe the keys."

"They were in a plastic bag, and they were Honda keys with a Puerto Vallarta key chain, and they had some black stuff on them."

"What do you mean black stuff?"

"Like stains."

"Are you sure they were Honda Keys?" I said, almost holding my breath. The keys to July's Honda Accord had disappeared with her that night on Shelter Cove Road.

"Yeah."

Frank had stopped crying. I turned around to check on him. He was smiling and staring at the ceiling as if it was the most fascinating thing in the world.

"Did Pete Holloway know anything about this?" I asked.

"I don't know. He never said anything to me about it."

"Okay. That's about all I have for you. Why don't you meet me at that gas station on the south end of town, the one by the river? Let's say fifteen to twenty minutes."

"Are you bringing my son?" she said.

"Of course."

After hanging up, I drove to the Fortuna Police Department, carried Frank inside, set him on the counter, and told the man behind the glass my version of what had happened: "I found this baby abandoned in a car. One of the windows was broken out, and it smelled like pot, and I didn't see anyone around. I was scared he might freeze to death or get kidnapped or something, so I took him here. I got the license plate number for the car if you want it."

The sergeant made me fill out a statement. I wasn't worried about putting down my real number, because I had called and texted Jennifer with my burner phone. And there was very little chance they would believe her story over mine. She was stoned and drunk, and no one could prove I broke her window or used her baby as leverage to get her to answer questions.

She called me as I was walking through the parking lot.

"Where are you?" she said.

"The Fortuna Police station," I said, and hung up.

32

The Old Creamery Building

LEVI CALLED ME ON Friday, after my second interview with Hunley, Davis, & Runiyon, LLP, as I was driving over the Golden Gate Bridge on my way home.

"That detective came to my house today," he said. "He thinks I killed Krista."

"Did he say that explicitly?" I said.

"Pretty much. He was trying to intimidate me, talking about all this evidence they have against me."

"What evidence?"

"I guess the people in the room next to us said they heard arguing, but I don't see how, unless they think arguing sounds the same as sex. And then he said the hotel cameras got me leaving her room within the time range of when they think she died. It sounded pretty serious. I don't know. What do you think? Is it bad?"

"He could just be fishing," I said.

"I'm starting to freak out here, Tim. I don't know. I'm just . . . . I'm freaking out a little."

"Don't freak out. You're not going to prison for this Levi. I promise you."

My promise was based on a theory I couldn't prove, but Levi didn't need to hear that. The theory was this: Pete, AKA Dick Pants, murdered July; Krista blackmailed Pete with evidence she had found in her mom's safe; then someone involved with Pete murdered Krista to silence her.

On Thursday, before leaving for my interview in San Francisco, I had deposited fifty cents in every newspaper vending machine in Old Town, hoping to find a set of Honda keys with a Puerto Vallarta key chain. I had also rummaged through the lost-and-found boxes of the surrounding businesses. The search had taken all afternoon, but I had nothing to show for it. The keys were gone.

I crossed the Humboldt County line at five-thirty. After driving another hour and a half, I took the second Arcata exit, stopped at a grocery store, and bought a bouquet of Stargazer lilies. The first showing of *A Christmas Carol* was at seven, and I wanted to talk with April afterward.

I reached the Old Creamery Building ten minutes late, but the doors were still open. I bought a ticket—the proceeds of which went to the Women's Herbal Symposium—walked through the lobby and entered the theater. The house lights were off, and the first scene had already begun. I found an open seat in the back row and sat down.

April made her entrance with the rest of the dancing spirits, while the ghost of Jacob Marley sang "Link by Link." She was the only spirit with a black curly wig and beard, and a fake nose. I felt nervous for her, but she seemed to do fine.

Intermission was after the Ghost of Christmas Past made her exit. The house lights came on, and members of the audience left their seats, chatted with one another, went to the bathroom, bought drinks, attended to their phones, and attempted to reason with their children.

While waiting in line for the men's room, I spotted Pete Holloway across the lobby having a conversation with two women. He wore a red-striped dress shirt and black slacks, and he had a glass of white wine in his hand. His aging baby face was flush, and his head wobbled as he talked. I watched him smirk and laugh and drink his wine, knowing there was a possibility he had murdered July and gotten away with it for five years. I wanted to ask him a few questions, but I knew he wouldn't talk to me, so I decided to try a bluff. I left the bathroom line, walked outside, and called Levi.

"What's going on?" he said.

"I need a favor," I said.

"The last time you wanted a favor I ended up a murder suspect."

"I know. Now I'm trying to clear your name. How far are you from the Arcata Playhouse?"

"You're at the play right now? I'm not going there."

"Your ex-girlfriend's busy acting. She's not going to see you. I just need you to park out front and wait for a guy in a red-striped shirt. He's going to get into a white Chevy Tahoe. I want you to follow him and tell me where he goes."

"How is this going to help clear my name?"

"I'll tell you later. How long will it take you to get here?"

Not long after I went back inside, the lights in the lobby turned off and on three times, indicating the end of intermission, and everyone began filing back into the theater. I watched Pete take his seat three rows down from me, across the aisle. Fifteen minutes later, while the Ghost of Christmas Present was in the middle of singing, Levi texted me that he was out front.

Crouching, I tiptoed down the aisle to Pete's row. He was three seats in. I squeezed by the people between us, managing not to step on any feet, and knelt in front of the woman to Pete's right. Her knees pressed against my left shoulder. She and Pete were both looking at me like I had just bitten the head off a chicken. I smiled. The Ghost of Christmas Present was talk-singing through a verse.

"I have July's keys, Pete," I whispered. "The Honda keys with the Puerto Vallarta keychain and the bloodstains all over them. At least, I assume they're bloodstains. Why did Winona keep those in her safe? Was she blackmailing you too? Like mother, like daughter? Or did she kill July?"

Pete didn't say anything. He just stared at me with the same horrified expression on his face.

"You don't have to answer now," I said, and handed him a piece of the program I had ripped off and written my number on. "Call me later. I'm willing to negotiate." I smiled and patted him on the knee, then turned around and went back to my seat.

A few minutes later, when the Ghost of Christmas Present had stopped singing and the audience was clapping, Pete stood up and walked toward the exit. He kept his eyes forward as he passed me.

I texted Levi, "He's coming out."

He texted back, "I'm fried rice. He's ice cream."

After the play ended, the actors trickled into the seating area to be congratulated by friends and family. I found April in front of the stage. She had removed the wig, beard, and nose, and washed off the makeup. Her eyelashes were still wet. When she saw me, she smiled. Her eyes sparkled. I handed her the flowers, and she hugged me.

"Thank you," she said. "I'm glad you're here. I've been wanting to talk to you."

"Did you watch the supervisor's meeting?" I asked.

"I did, but I don't want to talk about that."

"Okay."

"I miss you," she said. "Can you walk me to my house? I need to take a shower."

"Sure," I said. "You have an after-party or something to go to?"

"I do, but I'm not going."

"Why not?"

She smiled. "Come on. Walk me home."

Her house was only six blocks away. The night was cold, and the stars were out. April held my hand, and we walked in silence. When we reached her front door, I noticed the Dodge Dart was missing from the front yard.

"What happened to the car?" I said.

"I finally sent it to the junkyard. There were mice living in it. The neighbors are happy now."

While April was in the shower, Levi called me.

"What's up?" I said.

"He went to the sheriff's station in Eureka," Levi said.

"Really? You saw him go in?"

"Yeah."

"How long was he there?"

"I don't know. I took off. I thought maybe he knew I was following him."

"I doubt that, but that's okay."

"How does this help clear my name?" he said.

"I'm not sure yet." I heard the shower turn off. "I'll call you in the morning."

April came out of the bathroom with a white towel wrapped around her chest. Her hair was wet.

"I want to show you something," she said, and went into her room.

I followed.

"This is my bed," she said, pointing.

"I know," I said. "I've seen it before."

She smiled. "I thought so. I just wanted to make sure." Still smiling, she stepped in front of me and looked up into my eyes. She kissed me and began unbuckling my belt. Her towel slipped open, and I took my shirt off, and we lay down on her bed together.

Later that night, April cooked me dinner: grilled cheese and tomato soup from a can. After eating, we spooned on the couch and watched the local news, which she never missed. During a commercial break, I said, "I was in San Francisco today. That law firm offered me the job. I didn't take it."

"Why not?" April said.

"They wanted me to start right away." I pressed my cheek against her back. "I can't believe how good it feels just to hold you."

April rolled over with the swiftness and terrible grace of a crocodile. She smiled and searched my eyes. "I love you, too," she said, and we kissed.

The next morning, I woke up in April's bed, alone. I could hear her talking in the other room, but I couldn't make out the words. I got up and put on my pants. As I looked for my shirt, the talking stopped, and I noticed April standing in the doorway, smiling.

"Good morning," she said.

"Good morning."

"I just got off the phone with Michael Pryor."

"Who's that?" I asked.

"He works the crime beat. He wanted a statement from me."

"Why?"

"The Tidwells got raided yesterday."

I sat up. "Holy shit."

"Yeah. I guess they found a bunch of marijuana and eight children without Social Security numbers. Two of them were pregnant. They also found what looked like graves, small ones."

"Jesus Christ."

"I know. It's horrible, but I'm so glad Sage is finally out of there. They took all the kids to a shelter. I have to call Child Welfare. There's some eggs in the fridge if you're hungry, and some cereal if you want."

While April talked on the phone, I pulled up *Times-Standard*'s website and read what they had so far:

EIGHT CHILDREN IN PROTECTIVE CUSTODY AFTER SOUTHERN HUMBOLDT POT, ABALONE BUST

Press release from Humboldt County Sheriff's Office:

On Tuesday at approximately 10:00 a.m., responding to an anonymous tip regarding the illegal harvesting of abalone, the Humboldt County Sheriff's Office and Humboldt County Drug Task Force assisted Game Wardens with the California Department of Fish

and Wildlife with a search warrant in the

9000 block of Crooked Prairie Road, Ettersburg. A Fish and Wildlife Warden obtained a Humboldt County Superior Court Search Warrant after learning that the owner of the property, Don Tidwell, 58, filed a total of 19 affidavits for lost abalone report cards between 1999 and 2016, receiving 36 report cards and 852 abalone tags, amounting to 450 more tags than would have legally been issued.

After arriving on the property, investigators located and detained Tidwell. During a search of the house and the property, officers located 292 growing marijuana plants, approximately 12 pounds of untrimmed marijuana bud, thirty pounds of processed marijuana, $252,000 in cash, four handguns, three shotguns, five rifles, two assault rifles, and 12 untagged and unshelled abalone stored in a freezer.

Investigators also located three girls and five boys, ranging from approximately two to 15 years old. Two of the girls were perceived to be pregnant. Due to unsafe living conditions and concerns about their wellbeing, Child Welfare Services took the children into temporary protective custody.

Tidwell was arrested for cultivation and

possession for sales of marijuana, illegal possession of firearms, and five misdemeanor Fish and Wildlife code violations. Tidwell's son, Jared Tidwell, is a person of interest in this investigation and is being sought for questioning by the Sheriff's Office."

After failing to find any useful information in the comments below the article, I sat down on the couch and watched the morning local news. They led with the Tidwell bust, but they had nothing to report beyond the press release.

When April got off the phone, she walked back into the living room. "Child Welfare is going to have the sheriff's office run a check on me and my dad," she said. "Then they're going to interview Sage about us. If everything goes well, I should be able to pick him up later today. Right now, though, I need to go pick up my dad."

"Do you want me to go with you?" I asked.

"No. I want to be alone with him. We need to have a long conversation. He's saying he wants to be the one to take care of Sage now. He says he's going to get clean, so, I don't know, we'll see." April sat in my lap and wrapped her arms around me. "Thank you," she said, and kissed me. "What are you doing today?"

"I have to do this thing with my parents," I said, "but it won't take long."

"Can I call you later?"

"Yeah. Of course."

"Good. I'll call you when I get back into town." She got up and began putting on her shoes.

I walked to the front door and opened it. Before I

left, I said, "You don't happen to remember if July had a keychain on her car keys, do you?"

"Why?" April said, looking up.

"It's a long story. Do you want to hear it?"

"No, not right now. But she did have one: a little palm tree that said Puerto Vallarta—like a tourist thing."

33

College Cove

LATER THAT DAY, WHILE sitting in the back seat of my parent's car on the way to visit the forest where my sister's ashes had been scattered, I got a call from a number I didn't recognize. "Hello?" I answered.

"Tim Kitchens?" a man said.

"Yeah. Who's this?"

"Listen to me. The gun that killed Krista is hidden somewhere in your friend Levi's house. In an hour and a half, the sheriff is going to serve a search warrant there. You can either look for the gun and hope you find it in time, which I guarantee you won't—and you can trust me on that—or you can give the keys to me, and I'll tell you where to find the gun so your friend doesn't get arrested for murder. I'll be on the beach at College Cove in twenty minutes."

"Pete?" I said. There was silence on the other end. "I'm surprised you didn't have your assistant make this call. How do I know you're not lying?"

"You don't," Pete said. "You can wait and see, or you can take my word for it."

"I'm more than twenty minutes from College Cove

right now. Can you meet me somewhere else, like Eureka or Arcata?"

"No. And come alone. Otherwise, there's no deal."

"You have to give me more time."

He didn't respond.

"Pete?" He had hung up. I tried calling the number back, but a generic voicemail answered. "I need to go back home," I said to my parents in the front seat.

"What?" my dad said.

"You have to face your grief, honey," my mom said.

"This has nothing to do with grief," I said. "It's an emergency."

"What happened?"

"The sheriff's about to search Levi's house. He needs my help."

After I answered a few more questions, my dad turned the car around. We got back to the house in ten minutes, and I jumped in my car and took off. College Cove was in Trinidad, fifteen minutes north of my parent's house, off Highway 101. While I drove, I called Levi. I heard voices and a jukebox in the background. He was at a bar. I explained the situation to him and promised I would learn the location of the gun before the sheriff arrived, but he got upset and told me he was leaving town. After a short argument, we came to a compromise: He would go home and wait for my call, and if he hadn't heard from me in half an hour, he could do whatever he wanted.

By the time I got off the phone, I was taking the exit to Trinidad. I drove past the grocery store, gas station, and bait and gift shops, and turned right at the school onto Stagecoach Drive, a narrow, winding road lined with trees. My tires chirped as I sped around the corners. After half a mile, I came to a straightaway and turned left, driving over deep mud puddles into a gravel parking lot surrounded by tall fir, spruce, and alder. There were three cars in the parking lot, but Pete's white Tahoe was not among them. I checked my phone. Twenty-five minutes had passed since my conversation with Pete, which meant roughly an hour until the sheriff arrived at Levi's house.

I stepped out of my car, put on a coat, and jogged down the trail that led out to the bluffs. The trees blocked out the light, and the air was cold enough to sting my nostrils as I breathed in. I passed three young men walking toward the parking lot. They smelled like pot and one of them had blond dreadlocks. I heard them laughing behind me as I turned down the spur trail to College Cove.

The trail was narrow, steep, and slick, buffeted by trees and underbrush, with wooden steps of varying heights notched into the earth between rocks and exposed roots. Halfway down, I had to step aside to make room for a middle-aged couple climbing back to their car, breathing heavily. We exchanged smiles and nods. When I reached the bottom of the trail, fifty-five minutes remained until the police arrived at Levi's house, twenty-five to thirty minutes until Levi stopped waiting for my call and left town.

The beach was bordered by a cluster of large boulders to my left and a rocky bluff on my right that extended straight out to sea two hundred yards. There was a fading red smear on the horizon where the sun had set, and a blanket of white clouds high in the sky. Sea stacks—large, craggy rocks—jutted out of the water here and there, dwarfed by a rocky promontory to the south that was capped with trees. Hidden beyond that was a long stretch of beach below the bluffs of Trinidad.

I saw a man sitting on a boulder fifty yards from me, near the surf. He and I were the only people on the beach. I walked toward him. The waves roared and hissed as they broke and receded. The light was failing, and I couldn't make out the man's face until I was ten yards from him.

"I figured I might see you here," I said, walking closer.

"Yeah?" Lou Da Rocha said. "How's that?"

"Dog training school. That was your alibi for the night July went missing, right? But you weren't actually there. Pete gave that alibi to you. His wife owned the company and his assistant did the books. She could have easily drawn up an invoice with your name on it. I wasn't sure until last night when Pete went running to you after I told him I had the keys. He was so frantic he went and bothered you at work. How did that go?"

"None of that proves anything."

"Maybe. But I have more, and circumstantial evidence paints a pretty vivid picture when all the pieces start fitting together."

"Give me your phone," Lou said.

"Why? You think I'm recording this?"

"Give it to me or I leave. Unlock it too."

I unlocked my phone and handed it to him. While he looked through it for an open app, I said, "Did Pete hire you to kill July, or did you do that on your own? Maybe you never got over her leaving you. Maybe you couldn't stand the idea of her moving to Paris with the man she left you for. So you killed her. But then how did Pete get involved? Was he there with you? Did he help you?"

Lou smirked and shook his head, then put my phone in his pocket.

I said, "Then Krista found out about it and you got tired of her blackmailing you, so you killed her, but you didn't get the keys first, the keys July used to defend herself when you attacked her, the keys she drew blood with, your blood."

"You're running out of time," Lou said. "The sheriff's going to be at your friend's house any minute. Give me the keys."

"I don't have them," I said. "I left them at Levi's house. And I don't think there's time to go back and get them before the sheriff arrives. But I'll tell Levi to get rid of them for you if you tell me where to find the gun."

Lou stood up. "He needs to get those keys out of the house right now. I'm not fucking playing with you."

"Tell me where the gun is."

Lou reached into his coat, pulled out a handgun, and let it dangle at his side. "This is the only gun you need to worry about."

My heart beat faster, my breathing became shallow, and my stomach flipped, giving me the sensation of falling. "Is that why you wanted to meet me on a secluded beach? So you could kill me? People know I'm here, and they know I'm with you or Pete or both. If you kill me, you go to prison the rest of your life."

"Not if they don't find your body."

"I have files on you and Pete, with numerous statements from witnesses. I have evidence that Krista gave me, and I have the keys, but if you kill me, the sheriff will have all of that."

"That's fine. I don't care. You can have your files, you can have the gun, but if the police get those keys,

I'm going to kill you." He tossed my phone to me. "Call your friend."

"Where's the gun?"

"In his backyard. I buried it in the horseshoe pit. Put the phone on speaker."

I called Levi, and he picked up after one ring. "Where is it?" he said.

"In the horseshoe pit."

"Okay."

I hung up and put the phone in my pocket.

"What are you doing?" Lou said. "Call him back."

"There's no reason to," I said. "The keys aren't at his house."

"What?"

"They're in a safe-deposit box. I can get them for you tomorrow."

Lou clenched his jaw and looked up at the sky. "So now they're in a safe-deposit box? Are you sure this time? Because if you're lying to me again, I'm going to kill you whether I get the keys or not, then I'm going to hurt April."

"They're in the safe-deposit box," I said.

"Okay, then. The banks are all closed now, so we'll have to go in the morning. That means you're staying the night in my trunk. Now turn around and put your hands behind your back."

I didn't move.

"Don't make this a test of wills," he said. "Turn around and put your hands behind your back."

As he took a pair of handcuffs out of his pocket, I heard the crack of a rifle, and Lou fell against the rock. I turned toward the sound. Someone was on the trail, ten feet above the beach. I heard another crack. Lou grunted and gasped for air. I ducked behind the rock.

My feet and knees sank into the sand, while the tail end of a wave soaked my shoes and pants. The cold shocked the air from my lungs in one quick exhale.

I crawled around the rock to see if I could reach Lou's gun, but when I poked my head out, the shooter was already on the beach, running toward me. Lou was lying in the sand, not moving, his head a few feet away from me. I couldn't see the gun. Before I could jump out and search for it, the shooter stopped running and took aim. I pulled my head back as another shot split the air.

I had to move, but there were at least twenty yards of open beach on either side of me. I would have to run through the sand to reach any kind of cover, making me an easy target. Instead, I took off my shoes and crawled straight into the surf. I leapt over the first wave and dove under the next. When I popped up again, I was past the breakers and swimming toward a sea stack in the middle of the cove, a hundred yards out. Saltwater sloshed into my mouth and nose. The cold was painful at first, but then my skin went numb. I heard only my breathing and the crashing waves behind me.

The muscles in my arms and legs were burning when I reached the sea stack. It stood ten feet above the waterline, a sheer rock cliff. I swam around to the side opposite the shore. Bobbing in the waves, I found two handholds in the rock, but when I tried to pull myself up, my feet slipped on the algae beneath the surface, and I fell, scraping my hands and elbows. Then a large wave came and lifted me high enough so that I was able to scramble onto the face of the rock. I climbed to the top, shivering in the open air, the scrapes on my hands and elbows stinging with saltwater. The silver light from the half-moon illuminated the high clouds and reflected off the sand and seafoam.

The shooter was walking along the base of the bluff. I could barely make out his silhouette against the dark rocks. He stopped, and I saw a small flash and heard a shot. I ducked, waited a moment, and poked my head up again. As he moved away from the shore, I sidestepped toward it, keeping the sea stack between us. We did this for less than a minute before I lost him in a shadow. I ducked again in case he decided to shoot.

Then I heard a splash.

When I lifted my head and looked out, he was in the water, dark arms and head moving toward me, a forty-yard gap of ocean separating us. I thought about jumping off the rock and swimming back to shore, or to the nearest sea stack over a hundred yards out, but I was exhausted and afraid of being overtaken in the open water, or even being swept out to sea. So I climbed down to the waterline and around the rock until I was facing the bluff and in the path of the shooter. I watched and waited.

He swam to my right, around the rock, and I followed him. When he tried to pull himself up, I was there, and I kicked him in the head. But my balance was off, and there was no power behind the blow. He threw his head back and showed me the whites of his eyes, and I saw that the man trying to kill me was Jared Tidwell.

I found better footing above him, and I stomped down at his head and connected. He screamed like a weightlifter and grabbed at my leg, but I shook his hand loose and brought my heel down on his temple. As my leg extended, I lost my grip and fell on top of him.

Then we were both underwater. I felt his body against my legs, and I kicked frantically until I was free.

When I reached the surface, I swam to the bluff where Jared had jumped into the water, and I crawled onto the rocks. Water dripping from my clothes, I searched for Jared's rifle and found it. I looked for Jared in the ocean, but I didn't see him. After waiting a few minutes, I made my way back to shore, slowly, through the darkness and over the wet rocks, my teeth chattering.

Lou was lying on the beach where I had left him, two bullet holes in his chest. I checked his pulse: nothing. My phone was somewhere in the ocean, so I grabbed Lou's, along with his gun. And while I jogged back up the trail, I called 911 and reported the incident. In the parking lot, I moved my car and shined the headlights on the trailhead. I set the rifle and handgun on the roof while I undressed. My skin was on fire as it regained feeling, and my feet were bleeding from climbing on the jagged sea stack. I threw the guns in the front seat, got in my car naked, and drove home with the heat turned all the way up.

34

Woodley Island

I WAS ARRESTED LATER that night, and my car and wet clothes were taken as evidence. At the station, a deputy sheriff checked for gunshot residue on my hands, arms, face, neck, and clothes. After another deputy interviewed me, Detective Westbrook and Detective Blatt of Eureka PD, who had apparently been coordinating with the sheriff's office on their investigation, took their turn interviewing me. One of their own had been murdered, and they weren't "fucking around." I answered all of their questions truthfully, although I never mentioned the gun that had been hidden in Levi's horseshoe pit. And I offered my version of events, from what I had heard at Stone Lagoon about Don's abuse of Sage, "Dick Pants," and the abalone cards, to July's keys, the phone call from Supervisor Holloway, and what Lou and I had talked about on the beach.

When Westbrook and Blatt were done with me, I was taken to a holding cell, where I slept for a few hours before being woken up and taken back to the interview room. It was ten-thirty in the morning.

Westbrook brought me coffee and donuts. His mood had changed. He was less angry. He told me he thought I was telling the truth. Evidence supporting my story was beginning to pile up: Jared's body had washed up on the beach at College Cove, and he appeared to have drowned; bullets seeming to match the murder weapon had been recovered from Jared's truck; my complaint against Jared and Don Tidwell for assaulting me and threatening to take my life had been found; Warden Tomlin had confirmed my part in the investigation of Don Tidwell's abalone poaching; and two of Jared's acquaintances had revealed conversations with him in which he blamed me for the raid on his property and the arrest of his father, claiming I had been behind the anonymous tip mentioned in the sheriff's press release. When I heard that, I realized Jared could have been following me for some time, waiting for the best opportunity to get his revenge. If I had gone to visit my sister's ashes with my parents as planned, he might have killed the three of us.

Around four, the DA decided not to pursue charges against me, and I was released. I called April from the Courthouse Market across the street from the jail, and she pulled up fifteen minutes later. "Are you okay?" she said when I got in the car. She hugged me. "You're in the news."

"I figured."

"What happened? They're saying you killed Lou?"

"I was there but I didn't do it. Jared killed him. I think he thought it was me. It was dusk. Or he just didn't want any witnesses. He tried to kill me after Lou, but he drowned before he could. They found his body this morning. That didn't make the news yet?"

"No. Why was Jared there? Why were any of you

there? What were you doing at College Cove with those guys?"

"It's a long story."

"That I'm assuming has something to do with my sister. Did you find out who killed her?"

"I think so, but I want to be sure. There's one more thing I need to know. Do you mind if we stop by Woodley Island?"

"Why?" she said.

"I heard Pete goes to the restaurant there for happy hour on weekdays."

"You want to talk to Pete right now?"

"I just want to ask him a few questions. I know he was involved in your sister's death. I just don't know how much. If you don't want to take me, I understand."

She started the car. "I'll take you," she said.

We took the Samoa Bridge over the eastern channel of Humboldt Bay, turned off at Woodley Island, passed the National Weather Service building, and parked in front of the restaurant. As we walked inside, I smelled hamburgers and fish. Buoys, nets, gaffs, and pictures of old fishing boats hung on the walls. Large windows provided a view of the Woodley Island Marina, Old Town across a narrow channel, and the moth-balled pulp mill on the North Spit toward the mouth of the bay. We found Pete at the L-shaped bar, sitting by the doors to the patio, drinking a dark beer. We stood behind him.

"Hey, Pete," I said.

He turned around, looked at me and April, and made a face like he had just eaten something sour. Then he smiled at April. "What's going on, sweetheart?"

"Tim wants to ask you a question," she said. "I

would like you to answer it."

"I hope you're not listening to this guy," he said, pointing at me. "He's a kook and a fraud."

"The sheriff's department doesn't think so," I said. "They're searching Lou's house right now. When they're done, they'll have the gun that killed Krista. Trust me on that." I knew this because I had asked Levi to hide the gun behind the woodpile in Lou's backyard. "And I'm guessing they'll also have July's burner phone, which I'm guessing has enough on it to ruin you, otherwise we wouldn't be talking right now."

"You are a sad man," Pete said.

"That's neither here nor there," I said. "You can't smirk your way out of this one, boss. Before the sheriff gets around to you, they're going to get statements from your ex-wife, your cousin, Krista's little sister, and maybe even Crab-Man's contractor friend, Tom Faller—anyone they can find. They're going to know about the bribes, the money laundering, July's keys in your assistant's safe, your nude picture on Krista's phone, and they'll probably find communications between you and Lou. They already have witnesses that saw you talking with him at the sheriff's office the night before he died. And once it gets out that you're being investigated, all the enemies you've made over the years are going to smell blood, and they're all going to come forward. They always do. They're going to throw the book at you. When it's all done, you'll go to prison for extortion and money laundering at the least, and maybe even first-degree murder for Krista. But what I'm not sure about is July. Was it murder or accessory after the fact? Was your assistant blackmailing you?"

Pete's hands had begun to shake. "This is ridiculous," he said, almost whispering.

"Answer him," April said.

Pete looked down at his lap and squeezed his thighs.

"Answer him, Pete. You owe that to me."

He moved his gaze to April's shoes. "Winona would never blackmail me," he said. "She had the keys in her safe because I trusted her with my life."

"Then it was Lou who murdered July and was blackmailing you," I said. "And you were an accessory after the fact. How did you find the keys?"

"I was driving back, and I saw her car. The keys were on the ground."

"But why did you take them? Why didn't you go to the police?"

"I tried to call," he said, "but I had no service. Then I saw the keys had blood on them, and I thought a wild animal might run off with them. I didn't know. I was scared. I wasn't thinking right. So I took them. Then when I got back into service, I got a call from July's phone, and I answered, thinking it was her . . . but it wasn't."

"So you chose to save your reputation over reporting July's murderer," I said.

"Where's my sister?" April said, raising her voice. "Where is she?"

"I'm sorry," he said. "I don't know. I loved your sister. I love you too."

"Where's her body? Where did you put her?"

The other people at the bar looked up from their drinks and stared.

"We should go, April," I said. "Come on. I'll explain it in the car."

April turned, threw the patio doors open, climbed over the railing, and walked along the docks toward the south end of the island. I followed and caught up with her past an old lighthouse, near a large bronze statue of a fisherman. The sun was setting.

"Where are you going?" I said.

"I don't feel like driving right now," she said.

"Okay."

She stopped walking, folded her arms over her chest, and looked at me. A few hairs had strayed from her ponytail, and the wind was whipping them around.

"*I'll explain it in the car?*" she said. "Don't patronize me."

"I didn't mean to. I just didn't want you to make a scene."

"You didn't want me to make a scene? You? You're the king of making scenes. That man was like a father to me."

"I'm sorry," I said.

"If Lou killed my sister, then why was he blackmailing Pete?" she said.

"They were blackmailing each other. That's the only explanation that makes sense. If Winona wasn't blackmailing Pete, there's only one reason he would hold onto July's keys for five years: Lou had something on him."

"What did he have?" April said.

"I'm only guessing, but I think it was July's burner phone. July worked for Pete and his cousin, Tammie Campbell. She helped them launder the bribes Pete was getting from developers who wanted their rezoning bids to go smoothly through the board of supervisors. The bribes went to her PO Box, and Pete trusted her, not only because she was like a daughter to him, but because they were sleeping together. Pete's ex-wife pretty much confirmed that for me. That was his picture on Krista's phone.

"He was 'Dick Pants.' He was at the property in Shelter Cove the night July disappeared. The landlord found out about the pot Krista and July were growing, and complained to Pete's cousin. Since that was one of the properties he was using to launder the bribes, Pete was angry that any kind of attention was being brought to it, and he wanted the plants out of there. That's why July was on Shelter Cove Road that night. She was on her way to get rid of the plants. Maybe it was her last harvest before moving to France. I don't know."

"How did Pete get her keys?" April asked.

"When July found out Pete was at the house, she pulled over to wait for him to leave. It's in the texts—at least, how I interpret them. That's when Lou got to her. He had been following her. He was the one leaving threatening notes on her car and ordering pizzas in her name. He still resented her leaving him. He was with her while she was pregnant with Jared's baby and he was there for Sage's birth. Then he transferred to Pelican Bay for six months, and July up and leaves him for the professor. So when Lou transfers back to Humboldt County Jail, I'm guessing he's still upset about that. He thought he had a family. He attacks her on the side of the road, and she hits him with her keys and makes him bleed. Then he kills her and drives off with her body, but he forgets the keys.

"That's where Pete comes in. He's driving back from Shelter Cove at that time, and when he sees July's car on the side of the road, he pulls over and looks for her. At the same time, Lou is driving back to the scene because he realizes he forgot the keys. When he sees Pete snooping around July's car, he doesn't know what to do, so he waits. When Pete leaves, I imagine Lou searches for the keys and can't find them. At that point, he figures Pete has them, so he follows him back to Redway and calls him from July's burner phone. Lou knows how crooked Pete is because he was July's boyfriend for a year, and he was a stalker. He saw where she went and what she did. He knows her burner phone has stuff on it that Pete doesn't want getting out.

"Maybe he doesn't know everything, but he's desperate, and he calls Pete with her phone and threatens to expose him, to ruin his career, and it works. Pete balks. He doesn't call the police. He runs to Winona, and Winona puts the keys in her safe and convinces Krista not to say anything about July and the house in Shelter Cove. Otherwise, they all go to jail. Winona even helps Lou with his alibi. The relationship is based on blackmail and the threat of mutual destruction, and they all stay quiet for five years.

"But then Winona dies and Krista finds the keys in her mom's safe, and she realizes her mom didn't tell her everything, and she suspects Pete of murdering July. That's when she gets in on the blackmail. But she pushes her luck, and she scares Pete too much. Maybe she tells him about my investigation. I don't know, but Pete tells Lou about her. The keys have Lou's blood on them, and they know if Krista goes to the police, they're both going to prison. So Lou tries to get the keys, and when he can't, he kills Krista."

April pointed back to the restaurant. "Why isn't he in jail? Why hasn't he been arrested yet?"

"He will. There's enough evidence. They'll get him for something. Who knows? He might even confess if they put enough pressure on him. He doesn't seem to have much fortitude. Also, I did some thinking in jail. I have something special planned for him. You'll see."

35

Shelter Cove

WE SAT OR STOOD in Evelyn Massey's nautical-themed living room—April, her dad, Rodney, his girlfriend, Cricket, and myself—watching the Community Access Channel, waiting for the Board of Supervisors meeting to start. Each of us held half a stale cookie, except for Rodney, who had already eaten four and apparently found no fault in them. Evelyn kept feeding them to him, and he kept complimenting her, which, to my eye, made Cricket jealous. Rodney was also wearing a hat that had belonged to Evelyn's dead husband—one of three Evelyn had given him.

Evelyn was in the kitchen making another pot of coffee. Sage was outside, playing with the cadaver dogs and, I hoped, staying out of the way of the forensic team. They were investigating unearthed remains in an isolated, wooded corner of Evelyn's property that, by all indications so far—location of the body, state of decomposition, jewelry—belonged to July. Lou had probably buried her there for extra leverage in blackmailing Pete.

Though Rodney had been crying with April until

recently, his chest was puffed out a little, and he looked relaxed and proud as if he had just given his daughter's hand in marriage to a man he respected. I was happy for him. Evelyn had been putting good whiskey in his coffee and providing him with all-you-can-eat cookies, and he was about to see an accomplice to his daughter's murder be embarrassed in public.

I had gotten the idea from watching April's *A Christmas Carol* musical. I was about to be Pete's Ghost of Christmas Past, showing him those he had wronged and the evils he had wrought. With the help of Crab-Man, I had found nine more victims of Pete's extortion scheme, and convinced three of them—the ones that had reason to hate Pete the most—to speak on July's behalf at today's Supervisors meeting.

I had six speakers in all. They each had the same prepared statement, written by me, strategically without pronouns, laying out Pete's involvement in July's death. If one speaker got cut off, the next speaker was to pick up the statement where the last had left off. That was the plan. I told myself the goal was to prime a potential jury pool in our favor, but, if I was being honest, that was just a rationalization. My true goal was to publicly humiliate Pete. Petty, I know, but I was petty, and if anyone deserved to be humiliated it was Pete.

First lined up to speak was Crab-Man, next was the three newcomers, followed by Tom Faller, Crab-Man's contractor friend, and finally Heidi, the dolphin lady. I had apologized to her, and she had forgiven me, and by the end of our conversation, she had even thanked me for helping her "take back her voice." I wasn't sure what she meant by that, but I kept my mouth shut this time.

As April and I and the rest of the group watched,

the Board of Supervisors conducted their meeting, which took seemingly forever, then they opened it up for public comment. Crab-Man, in his brown leather vest, delivered a healthy portion of my prepared statement before being shouted down: "Documentation and investigations to date indicate that Pete Holloway was an accessory after the fact in the murder of July Morrison . . . ."

The next three speakers managed a couple of sentences between them: "Pete Holloway allegedly knew who had murdered July Morrison, but . . . Pete Holloway was likely motivated to keep the identity of July Morrison's murderer a secret in order to protect Pete Holloway's reputation . . . . Multiple local citizens have executed sworn affidavits alleging that, as Supervisor, Pete Holloway habitually solicited money in exchange for approval of rezoning requests . . . ."

There was a lot of murmuring from the crowd, and angry scolding from the Board members. Then the Board Chair called for a break, and I was afraid they would postpone the meeting, but after five minutes, they came back.

Tom Faller got through this much: "Documentation supports the allegations that Pete Holloway laundered the solicited money through his cousin's property management company . . . ."

Heidi did the best out of all of them. She made it to the end, enduring boos from the crowd, who had come to listen to a meeting on the General Plan Update. She even delivered an extra message I had given to her over the phone just a few hours prior: ". . . Five-year-old human remains were found on a property once managed by the company that allegedly laundered money for Pete Holloway."

I could have kissed whoever was in charge of the cameras at that moment, because after Heidi recited her last line, the director went straight to the camera pointing at Pete, and I saw Pete's face change. I saw a man who had charmed his way through life and was just now, at the age of a grandfather, being truly punished for the first time.

36

Headwaters

SAGE SAT ACROSS THE kitchen table from me, wearing batting gloves and sipping orange juice from a glass, while April leaned against the counter beside a steaming waffle iron. The table was set, and the air smelled like vanilla. July's brown vinyl suitcase sat at my feet. Professor Lowell had found it in his storage unit the day before and given it to me on his way out of town for Christmas break.

"Do you want to open it?" I asked.

"After breakfast," April said.

As the waffles cooked, I tried to have a conversation with Sage. He answered my questions about football by looking down at the floor and mumbling short answers. But when I brought up school, his chin lifted, his eyes lit up, and he talked for two minutes straight about the clothes and supplies Aunt April had bought for him, and how cool it was going to be to have a locker. He had seen kids using them on TV and had always wanted one. He already knew what he was going to keep in his, and he wanted to show me. He left the room and came back with a bag, which he emptied onto the table: stickers, comic books, a Spider-Man action figure, a case of special drawing pens, and a toy snake that popped out of a can.

Action figures and toy snakes. I didn't have to be a psychologist to recognize Sage was responding to his trauma with regression. Seeing the excitement on his face, all I could think about was how cruel kids can be. The details of what went on in his home out in Ettersburg were already starting to leak out. "Incest Cult" was the term being used in the papers. The names of the children had not been released, but that meant almost nothing in a small community like Humboldt County. I suggested April should continue homeschooling Sage for at least another year, but she was having trouble saying no to him. The only time he smiled was when he talked about going to school.

After we finished eating, I set July's suitcase on the table. As April opened it, the smell of July's perfume wafted into the air. Her clothes were folded and packed as if she were leaving for France tomorrow. Two black nylon bags lay on top of the clothes, one for her makeup, and one for her toothbrush and other toiletries. Inside one of the pockets, in the lining of the suitcase, April found an envelope with a Eureka address written on it in July's handwriting.

"This is my old address," April said. With a shocked, almost blank look in her eyes, she opened the envelope. Printed on the piece of paper inside was a row of four little square images with a plus sign between each. From left to right, the images were of a beach, a bar, an American Express card, and a wedding ceremony. Underneath them, July had written, "AI-H-B CA-AD-E AA-I-GEH-CF-C"

"Does that mean anything to you?" I asked.

"It's a treasure hunt," she said, turning to me and smiling. "This is what I was telling you about. She did this for all my birthdays. She was probably going to send this to me when she got to France. My birthday was a week after she was supposed to leave, and we were both really sad about it, I remember. I was turning eighteen."

"So it's like a riddle?"

"Yeah. And a code. She always did it like this. I had to solve the riddle so I could break the code, then I would know where my present was." She pointed to the image of the bar. "That's a picture of Central Station in McKinleyville. I have to write this out. I could never get these off the top of my head." She left the kitchen and came back with a pen and notepad, and wrote down words associated with each image:

Image one: "Beach, Sand, Waves, Water, Coast, Shore, Swimming, Summer."

Image two: "Central Station, Alcohol, Party, Beer, Dad."

Image three: "American Express, Credit, Card, Don't leave home without it, Maxed out, Shopping, Buying, Consumerism, Capitalism, Retail."

Image four: "Wedding, Marriage, Ceremony, Priest, Party, Reception, Vows, Till death do you part, Wedding dress, Ring, Diamond, Tuxedo, Ring bearer, Flower girl, Bouquet, Corsage, Garter belt, Wedding night."

April stared at what she had written and mouthed the words to herself, while Sage and I took guesses out loud. Some of our guesses made us laugh, and we eventually incorporated the words farts or farting into all of them. After five minutes of this, April said, "Coast Central Credit Union."

"Really?" I said and looked at the images again. "Yeah. Wow."

"We shared an account there," April said. "That's where they found the Men's Health Magazine, in our safe-deposit box." April walked down the hall, disappeared into her bedroom, and came out a moment later holding the Men's Health Magazine she had kept for the last five years. "The police thought she was mas—" She looked at Sage and stopped herself. "It was actually my treasure map." She opened the magazine on the table. "The code was always the same. The letters represent their place in the alphabet: 'A' is one, 'B' is two, and so on. Then those numbers correspond to the magazine's page numbers, lines, and the words in the line, and you always take the first letter of the word." She flipped through the magazine, writing down a letter now and then. After four letters, she stood up straight. "Falk," she said.

"Falk?" I said.

"Yeah. The ghost town at Headwaters. My mom lived there until she was ten." April was staring into the middle distance.

"That's a pretty big area," I said. "How are you supposed to find a present there? And it's been five years. It's probably gone by now."

"No, it's still there. We're going to need a shovel though."

The Headwaters Forest Reserve was just south of Eureka at the end of Elk River Road. We drove there in my car, Sage sitting in the backseat with the shovel in his lap. The rain over the last few days had overfilled the banks of Elk River, and many of the cow fields and barns on the western side of the road were inundated with a foot or two of brown water. The sky was dark gray, but the rain had ceased by the time we reached the parking lot at the trailhead. Ferns, alders, and young pines with thin trunks lined the trail. Most of the redwoods had been logged, but a stand of the giant old growths still remained five miles in. As we walked, drops of water cascaded from leaf to leaf, making small patting sounds. The rich smell of damp soil and decomposing leaves and needles filled the air. The south fork of Elk River ran along the trail to our right. It was no bigger than a creek, but it was full and moving fast. Alders covered in moss and lichen formed arches over it.

Every fifty yards or so, we came across a plaque with old photographs of Falk, and a few words detailing its history. The mill town had been founded in 1884, abandoned after the depression, and demolished in 1979. The forest had reclaimed the site, but there were still signs of the former residents: small apple and cherry orchards, railroad ties, a dilapidated stagecoach bridge, and square meadows where houses once stood.

April put an arm around Sage and pointed to a concrete slab surrounded by small trees just off the trail. "That's where your grandmother used to live when she was a girl," April said. "Her father was the caretaker here. When people came here to party or hunt for old bottles, it was his job to chase them away. He kept a shotgun loaded with rock salt, and he would shoot them with it."

"Did it kill them?"

"No, but it made them not want to come back anymore."

When we reached an old barn that served as an education center for school children, April led me and Sage off the trail to our left, high-stepping through wet grass and underbrush. My shoes and socks and the bottom of my pants became soaked. Twenty yards behind the barn, we walked out from under the canopy into one of the square meadows.

"This is it," April said. She took the shovel from Sage and began pacing back and forth over a small area five yards from the tree line. With each step, she stabbed the shovel into the ground, and on her fourth pass, I heard it hit something hard. "Here," she said, kneeling.

Sage and I went to her and watched as she peeled back a chunk of sod, revealing two old bricks mortared together lengthwise.

"This is what's left of an old cistern," she said, and stood up. Using the shovel, she found the edges of the cistern, then began digging a hole in the middle. When she was done, the hole was about six inches deep and eighteen inches in circumference. She reached inside and tugged at what looked like a cookie sheet that had rusted through. I squatted over the hole and cleared away dirt with my hands until she was able to get the sheet free. Underneath was a red plastic lunchbox resting against the mortared wall of the cistern.

"Oh my God," April said. "Sage. Look."

Sage got on his knees beside her.

"Your grandmother used to hide little trinkets here when she was a girl. Then when she got older, she would hide presents here for your mom and me. She was fun. Your mom took after her."

April picked up the lunchbox, set it on the flattened grass, and opened it. A vacuum-sealed brick of cash was inside. I handed April my pocketknife and she broke the seal and removed the plastic. On top of the cash was an envelope containing a ruby ring and a letter written in July's handwriting. April read it out loud:

"Happy birthday, sister. I'm really sorry I couldn't be there to celebrate with you. How does it feel to be an adult? Better yet, how does it feel to have twenty-five thousand dollars in your hands? Pretty good, huh? I know you got scholarships and financial aid, but I figured you might need a little spending money, especially if you change your mind about going to Humboldt State. I know we already talked about this, but I just want to say one thing: please please please leave that crap county and go to UCLA. I want to visit you on Venice Beach when I get back. Okay, that's the last thing I'm going to say about it.

Whatever you decide to do, don't put this money in the bank. I know you like to follow the rules, but there's an entirely different set of rules you have to follow when it comes to spending this money, so call me. I don't want to see my little sister go to jail for tax fraud because of me. Anyway, I hope you have a great birthday. I want you to be happy. You're the kindest, prettiest, smartest person I know, and I hope you get everything you want out of life. I love you.

Love,
Juju.

P.S. I'm not giving you Mom's ring forever. It's my turn to wear it when I get back.

P.S.S. And don't get pregnant while I'm gone."

Tears were sliding down April's cheeks when she finished reading, and she was struggling not to sob. She took off one of her necklaces—a plain, silver chain—and slipped it through the ruby ring. "I know you're a boy," she said to Sage, "but you should have this. It belonged to your mother."

April leaned in close to Sage and wrapped the chain around his neck. As she struggled with the clasp, Sage kissed her on the lips.

Acknowledgments

Thank you to the first readers: Aby, Jackie, Marty, Mom, Tash. Your time and thoughts are appreciated. Anything wrong or unsavory found in this book is the fault of the author.